The Crystal Telepath

The Worlds Apart Series: Book Two

Evelyn Lederman

ISBN-13:978-0692327623
ISBN-10: 0692327622

All characters and events in this book are fictitious. Any resemblance to actual persons living or dead is strictly coincidental.

Cover Design by Fiona Jayde Media
Editing by Tina's Editing Services

Dedicated to my good friend Suzanne Browne.

Acknowledgements:

~

To Katherine and Jackie, Two amazing friends who saw me through my mother's illness and death.

To my editor, Tina Winograd. For the 'that' and commas that populate my writing. Special thanks to two of my beta readers, Alice and Katherine, who made Tina's life a little easier.

To Fiona, my cover artist. Another incredible cover! I give her my vision and she brings it to life. Fiona out did her work on 'The Chameleon Soul Mate.' I did not think it was possible.

Chapter 1

〜

Sedona, Arizona

She exited the car, so weak she could barely close the door. The remnants of the second migraine this week had left her feeling lethargic. Shirl Tomlinson knew she had to power through, regardless of how dreadful she was feeling. Her best friend, Alexandra Mann, had been missing for almost a week. As she walked to the front of the Sedona Police Department headquarters, she was oblivious to the beauty of the surrounding area. Several people exiting the building made way for Shirl as she entered. She barely noticed their presence or the way the men perused her body. She was too sick to care.

For a relatively small town, the place was extremely busy. Barely able to stand, she staggered toward the front desk. She had to dodge a number of officers; otherwise, she would have ended up flat on her face on the marble floor. The man who stood behind the counter saw her distress and made his way around the restricted area to aid her. The artificial light was so bright, she had to squint her eyes as she watched him approach.

"Miss Tomlinson, are you all right?" the concerned officer asked. Shirl wished she could remember the young officer's name. He was wearing a name badge, but her vision was blurry and she could not make out the letters. She just wanted to crawl into the corner and fall into a deep, painless sleep.

"I am recovering from a migraine and I am not feeling quite right," she said. One severe headache after another had tapped her strength. She did not know how much more she was going to be able to take. Having only minimal health insurance coverage, her options were limited in her quest to find what was wrong with her. Every doctor she saw scratched their heads, baffled by the escalation at the severity and frequency of the headaches she had been suffering the past two years.

"I'll get Commander Lewis. He will give you an update on our efforts to find your friend." The officer took a couple of steps and then asked over his shoulder, "Can I get you any water?"

Shirl shook her head. She had taken medication before she left the hotel room. Everyone in the Sedona Police Department knew her by now. She arrived on Monday, as soon as she was able to drive. Alex had been missing since last Friday. For three full days, the police station had been her home away from home.

She sat on the bench, clasping the crystals that hung around her neck. As each day ended with no sign of Alex, Shirl got more frantic, fearing she would never see her friend again. What would she do without Alex in her life? They had grown up together in a Phoenix orphanage. Whenever anything went wrong, she always ran to Alex for help. Although Alex was two years younger, Alex was always the responsible one.

Commander Lewis appeared and sat next to Shirl. He was a good looking man, probably in his late thirties. The man was also tall. Generally she had to look up at him when they talked, she liked that. For some odd reason, she did not trust men she had to look down upon. She knew that was stupid, but that was how she felt.

Lewis was the second highest ranking police officer in the department, under the chief of police. Shirl could see from the expression on his face, he did not have good news to share. At least they hadn't found a body. The last two nights Shirl had woken in a cold sweat, dreaming she'd been taken to the morgue to identify Alex's corpse.

"I don't know what to tell you, Miss Tomlinson. There have been no sightings of your friend. We know she checked into her hotel Friday afternoon and was not seen again. Her car was found in a parking lot near Boynton Canyon. We believe she went hiking, but there are no signs of foul play. We have had men up and down that canyon looking for Alexandra. There was a part of the trail that looked like someone was dragged for ten feet or so, but there is no evidence she fell. Why don't you head home? I'll call you if we discover anything."

Shirl felt tears falling down her cheeks and reached into her purse for a tissue. "I can't leave here without Alex or knowing what happened to her."

People did not just disappear off the face of the Earth. Sedona seemed an unlikely place for human trafficking. A new age cult, perhaps, but Alex wasn't the type.

"Can I at least take you to dinner? You look terrible." Shirl had to smile at Commander Lewis's comment. Men usually fawned over her. It was nice to have a man be honest with her about her appearance. He was a no nonsense guy, saying what was on his mind.

She didn't feel threatened by him. Commander Lewis was the type of man to drag his wife along, eliminating any type of impropriety. It would be nice to get her mind off Alex, even for one meal. "That would be nice. I can't remember the last time I ate." She had a couple of power bars in her car, but hadn't been able to stomach the idea of eating them.

"Why don't I pick you up tonight in your hotel lobby after I get off, around seven." The seasoned police officer knew this meet-up location would be non-threatening compared to meeting her at her hotel room. "My wife Carol will meet us at the restaurant." Yup, she called that one right!

"I guess at this point, I should at least ask your first name," Shirl said. "It would be weird calling your wife Carol while calling you Commander Lewis."

"Frank, my first name is Frank."

Commander Lewis patted her hand and returned to work. She watched as he crossed into the restricted area behind the front desk. A large clock displayed three o'clock. She had four hours to kill before he would pick her up. There was no sense staying on the hard bench. She could get an update at dinner tonight. Besides, they had her cell phone number if they found Alex in the meantime.

Shirl walked to her car and sat behind the wheel for a while, not sure where she wanted to go. The medication had kicked in and she felt a little better.

She started toward Boynton Canyon. Shirl rarely went hiking with Alex. She didn't like the dust that covered her on the few occasions she went. Alex didn't make a big deal out of having to go alone.

Generally their friend Candy was along and she would hike with Alex. Candy had grown up in the orphanage with them. It was hard not calling her to join Shirl in Sedona while she waited for news of Alex. Candy was a high school coach and her team had just returned from a tournament. She hadn't even told Candy that Alex was missing. Shirl didn't want to worry her friend in case Alex reappeared. That possibility continued to slip away.

When she arrived, the parking lot was relatively empty. Alex's disappearance had been all over the local newspapers. People were shying away from this particular trail, afraid a wild animal had attacked her friend. There was no evidence to support the claim, but that did not stop the rumor mill from spreading that story.

Boynton Canyon was beautiful with its deep red rocks. Shirl had always been fascinated by this place. It was one of the four vortexes Sedona was famous for. The energy emitted by the vortexes always renewed her.

These sites were believed to be multiple dimensional pathways emitting spiraling spiritual energy. Shirl soaked up any article on the subject as well as anything dealing with mystical powers.

One of the few items she had from her birth mother was an amethyst crystal that started her fascination with crystals and healing stones. She wore four to five crystals a day, depending on her mood. Her mother's amethyst was the only crystal she wore constantly. It seemed to balance her in some odd way. Shirl felt less alone, like having family close by. She knew it was stupid, but maybe one day it would lead her to some discovery of who she was meant to be.

Curiosity about the section of the trail with the drag mark Commander Lewis mentioned got the better of Shirl. Grabbing a power bar, she started toward the trailhead. She'd walk the path Alex had taken when she disappeared. If she got too dusty, she'd take a shower before Frank picked her up for dinner.

She walked slowly, conserving what strength she had. Between nibbling on the nutrition bar, the medication, and the vortex's energy, she felt vitality coursing through her body. As she walked the trail, she held onto her crystals, trying to channel Alex. She was not expecting anything to happen, then her mother's amethyst started to glow.

Shirl held the crystal in front of her and stared at it in wonder. As much as she knew about crystals, she had never read anything about them glowing. She felt a slight pull and stopped.

The air ahead shimmered and she felt the continued emission of energy. Slowly, she approached the anomaly. She could see the trail on the other side of the air displacement.

Shirl looked down and noticed the dirt and foliage along the path looked as if something had been dragged along it. It ended right in front of what she could only think was an event horizon. Alex must have been pulled through the point of no return. The gravitational pull would have been so great, Alex would not have been able to escape from it.

Taking a deep breath, Shirl walked into the unknown.

Inside a black void, she felt as if falling. Twisting and turning, she had no control. Deafening, high-pitched sound pierced her ears. Her crystal glowed brighter.

Terror taking hold, she attempted to grab her crystal necklace. After her second attempt at regaining use of her flailing arms, she secured the amethyst in her hand.

Just short of all-out panic, she started to think about home. It worked for Dorothy in Oz, allowing her and Toto to return to Kansas.

She crashed against the ground, out of the portal's grasp. Shirl slowly climbed to her feet and realized she was no longer in Sedona. It must have been a portal to another dimension. That could be the only explanation why she was no longer on the trail surrounded by red rocks and dirt.

She stood on a mountain path, overlooking a city built of pale stone. The community was abloom with purple flowering trees and plants. The violet sky must be a result of the colored pollen emitted.

Shirl was surprised her mind was reacting rationally, although she was still a little dazed. Her normal reaction would have been to panic. Instead, she took in her surroundings and making scientific assumptions. She could not remember the last time she had thought so clearly. There was no pain or pressure impacting her brain.

Alexandra was somewhere in this city, she was certain of it. Shirl was not sure how she was going to find her or what type of people she would encounter. But she had to start looking.

She started down the mountain pass, paying close attention to her steps. The trail was steeper than the one in Boynton Canyon. Her sandals were comfortable, but not equipped to traverse the rocky path. She was also a little wobbly from the rough ride within the portal and had eaten no food to speak of for days.

Sweat trickled down her neck. She brushed at the liquid and her hand came back covered in blood. Shirl felt the same trickle on the other side of her neck. She was bleeding from both ears.

Another step. Bright red streamed from her nose. Her shirt collar was soaked with blood. A strong wave of nausea washed over her. She grabbed a tree branch along the trail.

Leaning on the tree did not abate the nausea. She fell to her knees and retched along the side of the trail. With little food and nothing to drink, it was closer to dry heaves.

Voices and footsteps were coming closer. Eyes popping open, she glanced through a red haze. Not only was she bleeding from her ears and nose, blood vessels must have broken in her eyes.

Shirl could hear the two men address her, but could not comprehend what they said. Her ears were buzzing and she could barely concentrate through the nausea that still overwhelmed her. One of the men knelt next to her as she felt herself fall into unconsciousness.

Chapter 2

~

The Troyk Universe

Starc Lours woke and noticed the woman he had spent the night with was no longer there. He was grateful she had the sense to leave before he got up. He never knew what to say to women after having meaningless sex with them. Fortunately, he found himself in that particular situation on rare occasions now. Since his breakup with Elzbeth, he did not want anything to do with women. He needed to stop going to bars at night and having too much to drink. It never ended well.

He was not in his own apartment, but the safe house his brother and their friends used when they could not get immediately to the mountain portal. They were members of a covert operation dedicated to overthrowing the government. The mind control telepathic government had been in control for twenty-five years. His group's role was to get dissidents that came to the attention of officials through the portal to another universe. From time to time he used the house for the occasional night of release with a nameless and now faceless woman.

"I do not know how, but Shirl came through the portal. There was an alarm that a gateway was opened and something came through. Two guards were dispatched and found her unconscious. She is being detained at The Palace. I saw them carrying her in a couple of minutes ago," Darden, shared through the closed telepathic channel he shared with his brother and their friends. Sensitive information was never communicated through communal channels that everyone could link into. Various communal channels existed that Troyk citizens could enter simultaneously. Familial channels between people who shared the same blood were also used, but to a lesser

extent. Since Darden was his twin, they shared a unique closed channel that developed when they were in their mother's womb.

Shirl was the best friend that Alex kept talking about. Six days ago, Alex had fallen out of the portal from a parallel universe they called Ginkgo Terra. She was the soul mate of his friend Tarsea Childers.

Starc knew his covert anti-government group would be called to Tarsea's parents' home, where Tarsea and Alex currently lived. He imagined the two of them were frantically brainstorming how to rescue her friend. They were either talking out loud or using the fabled telepathic soul mate link only two destined lovers shared.

Everyone was amazed when Tarsea and Alex proved to be soul mates. Only Tarsea's parents were not overwhelmed with the fact that soul mates existed outside of stories. It turned out the Childers were soul mates that had kept their special connection a secret from everyone, including their children. Stories about soul mates were steeped with special telepathic powers the partners would start to possess once they made love. For their own safety, they kept their relationship to themselves. Now Alex and Tarsea followed suit. Starc knew he would never have that special bond with a woman.

He made his way to the shower, just as the summons from Tarsea was communicated. *"I need everyone to meet at my parents' house. Darden, stay at The Palace and keep an eye on where Shirl is being held."*

The Palace was the seat of the Troyk government, as well as the home of the Prime Ruler Jeryl Jarlyn. It was a standing order that anyone who came through the portal would be brought to The Palace to be interrogated.

He quickly dressed and started walking to meet up with his friends to discuss their latest crisis. It seemed since Alex came through the portal, it was one emergency after another. He actually did not mind. It kept his thoughts off Elzbeth, what he lost, who was responsible, and why.

Alexandra Mann paced, waiting for everyone to arrive. The common room was enormous, giving Alex plenty of space to work off her frustrations. All entertaining in Troyk homes was conducted in a single, multi-purpose great room. The rest of the house had small and intimate living spaces, like the one she shared with her soul mate.

Her head continued to pound from the concussion, she received last night at the hands of Raine Narmouth. The man was fixated on Alex. For the life of her, she could not imagine why Raine had singled her out. Alex tended to fade into the background, becoming perfectly forgettable. She was fighting nausea from both her head injury and being worried sick about her best friend.

Shirl was at the mercy of Jeryl Jarlyn and Alex felt helpless. She was grateful she had her soul mate Tarsea as well as their friends and family who would move heaven and Earth to rescue Shirl. Alex thought she needed to change that "Earth" expression now that she was in the Troyk Universe.

It had been just under a week since she had been sucked into the portal and ended up in this parallel world. She had never spiritually connected with a man until she laid eyes on Tarsea. Was it really only a few days ago when Alex laughed in his face when he told her they were soul mates?

If not for the opening of the soul mate telepathic pathway upon their first touch and the cranial hormone excretion when they made love the first time, she would not have been convinced. She was still weirded out by that experience. Not the sex, but the brain excretion.

Tarsea came from behind, pulled back her light auburn hair and kissed her neck. God, she could not get enough of this man. "As I told you this morning, we will rescue Shirl. Your cousin is in charge of Troyk intelligence, after all."

With those words, Solfa Theffar entered the room. Alex hugged her cousin and they sat on the nearby couch. Solfa was stunning. Today she wore her rich chestnut hair loose, cascading down her back. Alex was relieved they were related. Solfa's penetrating stares originally scared her to death. Jeryl Jarlyn did well selecting her to run his intelligence division.

Alex imagined her cousin could get anyone to confess to any wrong doing. Solfa was not a mind control telepath. However, when her eyes bore into you, it felt like she knew all your deep, dark secrets.

What Jarlyn did not know was that Solfa had quietly been helping the resistance that wanted to overthrow his mind-controlling government.

"What do you know so far?" Alex addressed her cousin. Due to the head injury she received last night, she spoke to her cousin out loud instead of through the familial link. The last thing Alex wanted was another nose bleed. They occurred when she overtaxed her brain using telepathy.

"Shirl had several crystals around her neck. One of them has been identified as having belonged to Jenka Thork. They knew that Jenka was the crystal telepath who navigated the portal for Benko when they escaped. It was not hard to determine that Shirl was the baby Jenka carried through the portal. Jarlyn has moved her to the special quarters on the fourth floor of The Palace. He has been waiting for years to have someone occupy those rooms."

Jarlyn's son Benko had failed to overthrow his father's government twenty-two years ago and fled through the portal with a number of his followers. Jarlyn was obsessed with finding his son, his followers, and their children. Tarsea and his friends were able to get to Alex before governmental officials found out about her. When she finally met with Jarlyn, Alex represented herself as a cousin of the people who had gone through the portal with Benko. She was known as Alexia in this world. To reduce confusion, she was referred to as either Alex or Alexia both in private and public telepathic or oral conversations.

"He had special rooms set up for us? Why?" As Alex asked the question, Tarsea's mother Leenea came in with the herbal beverage that reduced the static in her brain caused by the communal pathways. "Thank you, Leenea."

In the short time Alex had known Leenea, she had become a mother to her. As of late, she lectured Alex on one topic or another, as mothers tended to do. Tarsea would sit back and enjoy the sight of his mother explaining the proper way to do things to his soul mate. He would telepathically tell her through their channel, *"Better you, than me."*

Leenea kissed Alex on the cheek, then headed toward the door. "You sit and rest, Alexia. We want to make sure your brain mends. Stay out of the communal channels as much as possible."

Solfa had not forgotten Alex's question. "Jeryl Jarlyn has been waiting for Benko's return for years. The quarters are quite luxurious. I do not think he is going to hurt Shirl. She will no doubt be questioned about Benko's whereabouts when she regains consciousness."

Solfa's family had been deeply impacted when Alex's mother left the Troyk universe with Benko. Her cousin grew up hating the mind control faction. Solfa felt she could make a greater impact for change working within Jarlyn's administration.

"She does not know anything about Benko," Alex replied. "I had not heard about the man until I came here. It was news to me that he had been watching over us our whole lives." Earth's atmosphere was toxic to the adult telepathic brain. All of Benko's followers died of brain embolisms by the time they reached twenty-five. He alone survived, perhaps because he was a mind control telepath or had a natural immunity. Benko kept them in an orphanage so they could grow up together. If anything happened to him, Benko at least knew the girls were safe.

"Then it will be a quick interview. Jarlyn will ascertain the girl knows nothing. I just need to convince him to turn her over to the Childers for care in the short term." Solfa frowned. Alex knew her cousin was concerned whether she would be able to get Shirl out of The Palace. The knot that had been developing in Alex's stomach doubled in size.

Starc entered the room as Solfa finished her last statement. Alex was fond of him. All of Tarsea's friends had become like brothers to her. Starc had been there last night after Narmouth attacked her. She knew there was bad blood between Starc and her attacker. Starc would not confide in her about what caused the rift, but she knew it had to be related to a woman.

The whole discussion that just occurred had been communicated through the warrior link, as well as conducted orally. Starc would have heard everything they just said prior to him entering the room. The warrior link was a closed telepathic channel that existed between the true ruler of the Troyk universe and his most trusted advisors. It had originally opened between Benko and Darden, but grew almost daily. Something was definitely on the horizon.

"I am supposed to report to work in an hour," Starc said. He was a Crystal Telepath Guard, commonly known as the CT Guard. They were responsible for guarding the portal and protecting crystal telepathic individuals as they entered hostile parallel worlds. Starc could have been one of the men who had found Shirl, had he been on duty.

Alex knew that Starc was taciturn, he used words sparingly. She needed more information about what was happening to her friend. "Do you think you will be asked to guard Shirl?"

Starc shook his head, "The Palace Guard. Darden has managed to get on the fourth floor, talking with one of his friends who works in that capacity."

Tarsea wrapped his arms around Alex. "We have to see what transpires over the next several hours. After the interview, we will have you try to communicate with her. I would imagine a telepathic communal link opened between you girls in the orphanage, but you did not know how to use it. If such a link was established, you should be able to talk with her securely before the communal link broadens and others start entering. It is best she is as ignorant as possible when she is interviewed."

Alex could not fault Tarsea's recommendation. She would have loved to talk to her friend as soon as she woke and reassure her that everything would be all right. Alex leveraged the soul mate channel, *"I love you, Tarsea. I have every confidence, we'll get Shirl out of The Palace and here, safe with us."*

She took another sip of the herbal beverage and prayed her words became a reality. Heaven only knew what was happening to Shirl within The Palace.

Chapter 3

～

"Shirl, you can wake up now." An unfamiliar voice cut through the confusion and static, making it difficult for her to wake. Deep sleep eliminated the pain of migraines. Why was this woman trying to release her from what little peace she had?

Reluctantly she opened her eyes. She did not recognize the room she was in or the strikingly beautiful woman sitting next to her. The room was elegant with its rich wood furniture. Fresh purple flowers graced a number of crystal vases.

Grogginess still held her within its grasp. Had her mind been functioning, there would have been a myriad of questions to ask. Shirl only knew that she was comfortable in the bed and did not want to be disturbed. She imagined what it was like to be a chrysalis, until forced to leave its cocoon as a butterfly.

"My name is Solfa. Do you know where you are?" The woman now had a name, but Shirl did not feel comfortable sharing where she thought she was. People tended to only believe what was right in front of them. The idea of parallel worlds would probably get her placed in a padded cell, or did these people know about the portal she entered this universe through? Silence would be the best policy at this point.

Wait, the woman called her Shirl! "How do you know my name?"

"How, indeed," was all Solfa said. Shirl noted for the first time the way she was staring at her. There was an intensity that made her nervous. The woman apparently wanted something from Shirl. She did not know what to make of the brief words the woman shared with her. Providing as little information about herself and where she came from still seemed prudent. The more Solfa looked at her, the more uncomfortable Shirl became.

Shirl looked away, escaping her relentless stare. She examined the room, trying to calm her frayed nerves. The flowers were beautiful. Her mind wandered back to the mountain trail where she looked down on a city shrouded with violet pollen. She then remembered seeing the red stains on her hands.

Panic consumed her. "There was so much blood!" she cried, rising in the bed and examining herself.

Soft but firm hands pushed her back onto the mattress. "You entered the portal with no understanding of how to navigate. By some miracle you ended up here, instead of some God forsaken universe. Bleeding through every orifice near your brain is a common symptom of severe portal sickness. You have received a blood transfusion and you will be fine." Shirl barely heard what had been communicated about her health. The woman spoke so casually of travel between parallel dimensions. It was clear Solfa knew where she came from, not necessarily from Earth specifically. The idea that there was a way to control where you went within a portal intrigued her. But she was not comfortable enough with this woman to redirect the discussion.

"Where am I?" Shirl imagined most people would question the whole parallel world premise. However, she was a believer in String Theory so she had an idea that she might be going somewhere else when she entered the event horizon. The only question was where did she end up?

"You are in the Troyk universe. The Aster Province to be exact. We were able to determine who you were from your mother's crystal. Like her, you are a crystal telepath."

"A crystal telepath?" For the first time since waking, Shirl went to grab for the crystals she always wore around her neck. To her relief, they were still there.

"Our people are telepathic. A rare talent among us is to control the energy of the portal through crystals. Even rarer is having a female with that ability. Crystal telepathic people can navigate from world to world. Every crystal used for such a purpose leaves a signature behind. The amethyst you wear shows that your mother used it several times and you had only used it once."

Shirl held the crystals tighter, until their edges dug into her hand. There had always been a connection between her and the amethyst. She never knew why. It had always seemed more than just sentimental feelings for a mother she hardly remembered. With the crystal, she had the power to travel to other worlds. She had been a rabid *Star Trek* fan. Now she could boldly go wherever she wanted.

"Can I learn to navigate the portal?" She barely contained her enthusiasm. Her reservations concerning this woman were dismissed, replaced by excitement to learn about the ability she possessed.

"In all due time. You will learn everything there is to know about your gift. How about you get dressed? There is someone I would like to introduce you to. He has been waiting a long time to meet you."

Shirl had no idea who knew of her existence in this universe. Frankly, she was so consumed about learning what it meant to be a crystal telepath, she did not give that person a second thought.

Solfa pulled out clothes from a dresser. "This is standard Troyk fashion. We wear a tunic and leggings. You will find them very comfortable. There is also a beverage on the nightstand I would like you to drink. It is full of herbs that will reduce the static in your head."

Shirl was not going to ask how Solfa knew about the static. Compared to the migraines, what she was currently experiencing was not worth mentioning. She picked up the mug and started to sip the tea. Almost immediately her brain was clear of any pain or pressure.

"This stuff is amazing!" Shirl said. "The herbs eliminated what little pain I was feeling." It had been so long since she had not suffer from a headache or the aftermath of one. Considering she had just needed a transfusion, she felt great.

"I am glad. There is a bathroom behind that door to your right. You will find make-up to cover the residual evidence of the portal sickness you experienced. The discoloration caused by the broken blood vessels will fade in a matter of days. Do not be alarmed by your appearance. I will come back in twenty minutes and we can meet Jeryl. That will give you time to shower and dress." With those words, Solfa left the room.

Shirl had no idea who Jeryl was, but a shower sounded wonderful. She was not going to look at her face until after she bathed. In her excitement about being able to travel between universes, she had forgotten about her quest to find Alex. What were the odds that she would have exited the portal in this world? There were potentially infinite parallel worlds that existed. How was she ever going to find her friend?

The minutes Solfa had given Shirl flew by. Shirl was shocked at how black and blue her face was, but the make-up Solfa provided hid most of the damage. There was still some blood in her eyes, but there was nothing she could do about that. She dressed in the clothing that had been given to her, a yellow tunic with cream leggings. The outfit flattered her figure and blond hair.

Solfa was punctual, knocking on the door to her room. Shirl glanced at the clock, it showed that twenty minutes had elapsed. How similar this world was to her own. They spoke English, appeared to measure time in the same manner, and lived very much like they did on Earth.

Shirl and Solfa walked along a hallway with various crystal figurines placed on small elegant stands. The wall paintings were various landscapes of worlds Shirl had never seen, and could not wait to explore. She wondered if the man she was meeting was a crystal telepath.

They stopped in front of a door. Solfa leaned over and quietly spoke to Shirl. "There is something you should know about Jeryl. He is our Prime Ruler, but he is also a mind control telepath. I imagine he will ask you some questions. You will feel a slight tension in your brain. That will be Jeryl determining whether or not you are telling him the truth."

"Why would I lie?" Shirl was confused why the ruler of this world wanted to meet her. It was also disturbing that he would expect her to lie to him. She did not know what a mind control telepath was, but it did not sound good. Uncertainty replaced her earlier excitement about portal travel. This was a strange world, she had no friends and no one to protect her.

Solfa smiled and placed her hand on Shirl's shoulder. "Do not worry. You do not have the knowledge he is looking for. Just answer his questions and you will be fine." Her companion opened the door and walked into a spacious room. Shirl followed, not having an option. Solfa's words did little to relieve her anxiety.

If the crystals in the hallway grabbed Shirl's attention, the abundance in this room took her breath away. She could spend hours here with her books on crystals and healing stones, identifying all the varieties exhibited. A piece of blue apatite held her attention. Her earlier discomfort forgotten, her fascination related to crystals overtook her thought processes.

She scuttled to the crystal and looked at it in awe. "This is the most beautiful piece of blue apatite I have ever seen. I have a small piece at home I use to cleanse my aura."

A gray-haired gentleman walked up to her and touched the stone. "It increases my personal power, helping me to achieve my goals. I have my gatherers scour different worlds for crystals such as this. My name is Jeryl Jarlyn and it is a pleasure to meet you."

He took her hand and held it for a moment. An instant of disappointment crossed his face. Had she not been attuned to the man, she would have missed the look. He quickly recovered and placed her hand on the crystal. Shirl examined it as she addressed the man. "Thank you for receiving me. Blue apatite is also supposed to bring clarity and expand your insight. It is reassuring that a ruler of a world would value such a stone."

"Yes, I utilize the power crystals provide. Through them, people like you can travel from world to world. I have always regretted not being born with crystal telepathic abilities. You are very special. Please come and have a seat."

Shirl reluctantly released the crystal and followed. As they made their way to the main sitting area in the room, he showed her various crystals in his collection. Some she had never heard of before. She was excited there were crystals from other worlds that did not exist on Earth.

"You mentioned gatherers before. What are they?" Shirl felt like a sponge. There was so much knowledge to absorb and this man seemed to be willing to share what he knew with her.

"Gatherers are my crystal telepathic team who travel to different worlds and bring back various items of interest. I would like you to join them. We can teach you how to use your talents. But before we talk about that, I have a couple of questions to ask you."

Shirl could barely conceal her excitement. "Ask away," she responded. The sooner they covered the questions he had, the sooner she could find out about traveling to parallel worlds.

"Where is my son?"

"Excuse me, your son?" Shirl did not want to disappoint this man, in fear that he would renege on her invitation to join the gatherers. Why would he imagine she would know his son?

"His name is Benko Jarlyn and he left this world with your mother some twenty-two years ago."

Shirl quickly did the math. She was a year old when her mother left this world. That would mean she was actually born in the Troyk universe. No wonder when she thought of home in the portal the crystal took her here, rather than back to Sedona.

"I am sorry, sir. I never met a Benko Jarlyn. I grew up in an orphanage. My parents died when I was two years old. I barely remember them, let alone any of their friends." Shirl could feel a pull on her brain. It must have been Jeryl Jarlyn trying to determine if she was lying. She was glad that Solfa had warned her about the mind control power the Prime Ruler possessed. There was no pain, but the added pressure would have concerned her had she not been made aware of what was causing it.

"Do you know what killed your parents?" Jarlyn seemed to be satisfied with her answer. She wondered what other skills a mind control telepath had beyond knowing if someone was lying.

"I understand they both died of brain embolisms. It always struck me as strange they died of the same cause. Now that I know they were not originally from Earth and they had telepathic abilities, I guess it makes sense. There must have been something about Earth that adversely impacted their brains. I am sorry, sir. It is possible your son met the same fate."

Before Jeryl Jarlyn was able to respond to her, another thought came to her. "Oh my God! That must be the reason I had been getting so many severe migraines. I was dying like they did!" She started to panic again. What happens if the effect caused by living on Earth could not be reversed? Shirl felt blood rushing from her nose, which added to her now frenzied panic.

Solfa grabbed tissues and sat next to Shirl. "Jeryl, you need to stop the mind control focus on her brain. She has not fully recovered from the portal sickness she experienced coming here." The woman put an arm around her. "Shirl, you need to relax. The pressure on your brain will cease."

Shirl could feel the pull reduce and finally end. She was still shaking and could not stop. Alex was the only one who could calm her when she had one of her panic attacks. The fact she was also bleeding from her ears only added to her panic. Solfa continued to address her with a calming voice.

The Prime Ruler sprang up from his chair when she started bleeding. He paced as Solfa tried to get Shirl under control. "You need to care for this girl,

Solfa," Jeryl said. Shirl did not know how she felt about this woman caring for her. She had been very nice to her so far, but she did not seem the nurturing type. "Better yet, we can turn her over to her brother."

"Absolutely not!" was Solfa's reaction to Jarlyn's suggestion. Shirl had not missed that Jarlyn said she had a brother. "Cianan Thork is an embittered son of a bitch. He is a powerful crystal telepath, but I do not feel comfortable giving Shirlyn over to his care. She still needs to heal from her first ordeal within the portal."

"Fine, he can teach her to navigate the portal. Who do you suggest we board her with?" Obviously the Prime Ruler no longer wanted her staying with him. He seemed distressed by all the blood. His whole demeanor changed once she started bleeding.

"I recommend we have her stay with the Childers," Solfa said. "They took wonderful care of my cousin after her fall. We also know they are as loyal as they come. Tarsea's intelligence was instrumental in tracking down who was responsible for your attempted assassination. I would also like Starc Lours to be assigned as her Crystal Telepath Guard. She is new to all of this and I would feel better if she had someone with her to protect her as she enters new worlds."

"Agreed," the Prime Ruler concurred. "I want you to interview Darden Lours about what he may know about Benko. He has been the only gatherer going to Ginkgo Terra for some time. I cannot accept that my son is dead." There was a determination in the Prime Ruler's voice that Shirl could not miss. With attention no longer focused on her, Shirl began to relax.

"I will take care of it," Solfa responded. "In addition, I will set up a meeting between Shirlyn and her brother. He can teach her what she needs to know. However, I want her situated at the Childers's household immediately."

Shirlyn must have been the name she been born with, Shirl imagined. She was going to be turned over to a couple she did not know. Her nerves once again got the best of her. Even the magnificent gems in this room could not comfort Shirl. As always, she reached for the crystals around her neck to give her strength.

Chapter 4

Shirl walked beside Solfa as they headed to the Childers's household. She had no idea who these people were, but she was glad to be outside and breathing fresh air. There were no cars. Everyone walked. Her shoes were covered with purple petals from remnants of blooms from trees and flowers carried by the slight breeze. She took a deep breath, the air was sweet with the scent of lilacs. There was a tranquility about this place. She never really noticed the noise automobiles made and the stress associated with getting around by foot when vehicles were present.

"You called me Shirlyn," Shirl broke the silence that existed between the women since leaving The Palace. "Was that the name I was born with? I know from what Jeryl Jarlyn said that I must have been born in this world." Having been an orphan most of her life, she always felt her sense of identity was incomplete. Who had she been named after? Was she like her mother or more like her father? Shirl was finally going to get some answers.

"From what we have been able to determine, you and another child were carried through the portal when your parents left this world. Jarlyn has been looking for his son ever since. The gatherers he spoke of do more than just pick items up in different worlds. They look for people who escaped from this world and return them home. There is quite a reward out on Benko, his followers, and any children they may have had." It may have been Shirl's imagination, but Solfa's tone had changed now they were no longer in the Prime Ruler's presence. She made gatherers sound more like bounty hunters, than explorers. Shirl's thoughts were interrupted by Solfa saying, "We are here."

A middle aged woman opened the door to a house as they approached. "Please, come in. My name is Leenea Childers." Shirl immediately liked the woman. There was something about her that brought about calm and a feeling of home. She did not shy away from the older woman putting her arm around her waist and walking her across the threshold of her home.

As Leenea closed the door, Shirl caught the movement of a figure from the corner of her eye. She turned toward the person and was momentarily shocked to see Alex. Her friend ran into her arms. By some miracle, Alex had found her.

"Thank God! You are safe. When Darden communicated yesterday that you had somehow come through the portal and were a captive at The Palace, I did not know what to do. Solfa said you slept for twenty hours before gaining consciousness. I've been frantic!" She had no idea who Darden was, although Jeryl Jarlyn had mentioned him before they left The Palace. Shirl needed to escape the daze she was still in and address her friend.

"Alex, I went to Sedona to look for you. You worried me half to death." She took a look at her friend and was amazed how radiant Alex looked. Her friend was in an emerald green tunic that looked great with her light auburn hair and coloring. "Who is clothes shopping for you?" She could not help herself. It had always been a joke between them that Alex could not shop for herself. Things were so topsy-turvy, it was the first thing that came into her brain. All other questions related to Alex and the Troyk universe seemed too heavy to get into now.

"My aunt and Solfa's mother," Alex replied. "I have so much to tell you. But I want you to meet my soul mate, Tarsea."

Alex dragged her into the living room where a number of men sat conversing. They turned when Shirl and Alex entered the room and a black haired man stood and approached. He was probably five-foot-ten inches tall and built like a linebacker. There was an old bruise on his cheek. What caught her attention were his incredible greenish brown eyes. She'd never seen hazel eyes quite that color before. They brought a softness to a man well chiseled and otherwise intimidating.

"It is nice to finally meet you, Shirl," the man who must be Tarsea said. "Alex has done nothing but talk about you the short time I have known her. Let me introduce everyone to you. This is my father, Zane Childers. Darden is next to him. My brother Tolfer is in the kitchen preparing dinner. My parents are dreadful cooks, so we were relieved when Tolfer showed up this afternoon." He had a mischievous smile when he made the last statement. Alex had never fit with any of the men she had dated before. Even though she just met Tarsea, Shirl knew he fit perfectly with her best friend.

Shirl nodded to the men, but was reluctant to leave the security of Alex's arm around her waist. Although Alex was a little woman, she had an inner strength Shirl always envied. Tarsea must have sensed Shirl's need to stay beside her friend. He returned to the couch, sitting next to his father.

"We have trouble," Solfa said as she entered the room and sat next to Darden. "Jarlyn wants me to interview you regarding the whereabouts of his son."

Shirl examined the man Jeryl Jarlyn had mentioned. He looked like he belonged in Malibu, not the Troyk universe. Darden was tall, tan, and had sun-bleached hair. Where Tarsea was built like a tank, Darden had a slighter frame.

Darden rubbed his forehead and replied, "We knew this was going to happen as soon as they captured Shirl. There was no way he was not going to find out what world she had just left."

Shirl felt guilty when she considered the conversation she had with Jeryl Jarlyn and described where she was from. Obviously from her description she had placed this man in danger.

"That does it," Alex responded, as she guided them both to the couch. "You need to head to Ginkgo Terra and have sex with Cassie."

"What?" Shirl was shocked by Alex's response. Her friend was not quite a prude, but she certainly had not dated a lot. She also could not figure out how having sex with someone would help Darden. Shirl turned and presented Alex with a questioning look. They had always been able to communicate somehow without words.

"When soul mates make love for the first time," Alex shared with her, "a hormone that brings about the next evolutionary stage of their telepathic powers is generated. One of those enhancements is the ability to negate mind control and telepathic powers. Mind control telepaths cannot determine if someone is lying to them. Darden is soul mates with Benko Jarlyn's daughter Cassie."

Shirl could feel the discomfort that enveloped the room with Alex's last words. "You are giving out too much information, Alex," Tarsea chided her. Leenea came in and handed them both a steaming mug.

"Tarsea, she's one of us now," Alex said to her soul mate. "Shirl, this beverage is wonderful. It will also help you manage the multiple communal pathways that will keep nagging at you. I would be happy to teach you all about it. However, Tolfer is the master teacher when it comes to managing the different telepathic channels. He has helped me so much, plus he is an outstanding cook!"

She barely recognized the effervescent Alex next to her. This world had done wonders for her friend. Alex was always uncomfortable around people. Yet she seemed so at home with the people in this room. There was a real sense of belonging that existed.

Shirl took a sip of the beverage handed to her. The aroma was the same as the one Solfa had her drink at The Palace. She took a tentative sip, then sighed with relief. It was the same mixture of herbs. As before, what static her brain was experiencing was numbed by the brew.

"Everything my new sister says is true," a curly black haired man said, as he walked into the room. "It is nice to meet you, I am Tolfer. Dinner will be served as soon as Starc and Koel arrive. They wanted to meet you. Alex has been sharing stories about you and Candy, I feel like I know you both." Tolfer had a warm, open manner. Shirl liked him as she had immediately felt comfortable with his mother earlier. He appeared to be a little younger than she was, closer to Alex's age. She once again brought her attention back to her friend.

"How did you get here, Alex?" Shirl still could not believe their luck in both ending up in this universe and being able to connect so quickly.

"Darden is a crystal telepath who had been coming to Ginkgo Terra, what we call Earth. He met Benko Jarlyn several years back. Do you know Benko has been keeping tabs on us all these years? You, Candy, and I are descendants of refugees from this world. Darden and Benko were working together to get us all here. You were supposed to be the first one they brought over, due to your headaches. I accidentally got sucked into an event horizon Darden had opened when I was hiking. You can imagine my surprise to find out our parents were from this parallel dimension. I have met my mother's twin sister and Solfa is actually my second cousin, or something like that." Alex spoke so quickly, Shirl almost expected her to turn blue from lack of oxygen.

Shirl looked at Darden through different eyes now, knowing he was a crystal telepath. "I am a crystal telepath, too. My mother's amethyst opened the portal, but I have no idea how I ended up here. Can you teach me how to use my crystals to navigate the portals? Solfa said I have a crystal telepathic brother, but wanted to keep him away from me for the time being." Shirl was in no hurry to meet her brother. Especially now that she had found Alex, her true family.

Darden nodded his head, "Yes, I know your brother. Cianan Thork never recovered from his parents deserting him when they left with Benko Jarlyn. I am sure they had their reasons for only taking you, but Cianan is not so forgiving. You have cousins in the next province, I was originally going to place you with them. Everything changed when Alex came hurdling through the portal. She is not going to tolerate me putting you anywhere that is not in close proximity to her. Besides, Jeryl Jarlyn knows of your existence. He will no doubt want you in Aster Province."

"In the meantime," Solfa interjected, "we still have the issue of Jeryl Jarlyn knowing Shirl is from Ginkgo Terra. He is not going to let go of the fact that Benko may still be alive in that parallel dimension. We have also shared this information with Shirl, who he may want to talk to again."

"He is not known as Benko Jarlyn in that world," Darden replied. "I can honestly state I never met a Benko Jarlyn in the Ginkgo Terra universe. The fact that Jeryl released Shirl from The Palace, it is unlikely he will interview her again in regards to his son."

"Half-truths will get you through an interview with a mind control telepath," Solfa responded, "assuming the questions are conveniently worded. You are probably right about Jarlyn's further interest in Shirl, outside of her crystal telepathic abilities. However, I am concerned he will send more gatherers to Ginkgo Terra and find Benko."

"That world is known for the headaches it creates," Darden responded. "Gatherers complained about them for years. Shirl's severe migraines have hopefully proved to Jarlyn what an extended stay on that world produces. He knows her parents are dead and in all likelihood, so is his son. Cassie collects bags of herbs so I do not waste any time in that world doing anything but spending time with her. The sheer volume of herbs I bring back should explain the length of time I spend there before the headaches drive me home."

For the first time, Shirl internalized that the headaches she suffered were now in her past. It appeared that Darden's trips to Earth and the headaches he suffered were no longer issues once he returned to the Troyk universe. Darden appeared to be in his mid to late twenties, yet he survived visits to Earth on a regular basis. She had thought she only had a short time to live, but now a whole new world opened to her. Her possibilities in this new world were endless. Once she learned how to navigate the portal, she could go wherever she desired.

Two tall men entered the room, although Shirl only really noticed one. He was well over six-feet tall and had broad shoulders. She figured underneath the tunic he wore, he had a six pack, probably a twelve pack. He had wavy strawberry blond hair and the darkest blue eyes she had ever seen. She could get lost in those eyes. Right above his left eye was a two-inch scar. Shirl generally did not notice things like that, but his scar for some reason made him appear sexy. Her body started to warm, as it had never done before. For some reason, all she wanted was to touch him.

"It is about time," Tarsea snarled. "I am starving. Tolfer was waiting for the two of you before he served dinner. This is Alex's best friend Shirl. Shirl, these two gentlemen are Starc and Koel. Starc is in the black tunic and is Darden's twin. Koel is their cousin. Can we eat now?"

Shirl watched as Tarsea walked up to Alex and grabbed her upper arm, lifting her off the couch. He gave her a passionate kiss and dragged her to the large dining table that dominated the second half of the room. There was a kind of caveman sexiness about Tarsea. She was so happy for her friend. For an instant, she saw Starc doing the same thing to her in her mind. She shook off that thought. Shirl figured her brain was food deprived; she was imagining all sorts of crazy things.

"Let us eat," Solfa said, as she waited for Shirl to rise and join her. "Starc, I have asked that you be assigned to Shirl as her Crystal Telepath Guard." The man who grabbed her attention was to be her personal guard. Things in the Troyk universe were certainly looking up. She also liked that Starc's look kept to her face, rather than gazing up and down her body.

Shirl saw Starc smile at Solfa's words. A smile that would light the city of Phoenix, it was so bright. She had absolutely no issues spending time with this man. Maybe her daydream would become a reality. For the first time in her life, her panties became wet.

Starc looked at the woman he was slated to watch over. She was tall, just a few inches shorter than he was. He liked that he could look into her eyes without having to lower his gaze any significant amount. The trauma she experienced entering the portal was evident all over her face. The make-up she must have put on earlier was wearing off.

Small black bruises were around her nose and eyes from broken blood vessels. Her eyes were still bloodshot from the hemorrhaging and her skin was pale due to blood loss. He was sure they gave her transfusions that would eventually bring back color to her cheeks.

Starc could not take his eyes off her face. A sudden feeling of protectiveness he had never felt consumed him. He knew he would protect this woman with his life. True, it was his job, but he knew deep inside, there was something more. He just could not figure out what their connection was.

There was nothing sexual regarding how he felt about Shirl, any feelings he once had related to sex were destroyed by Elzbeth Southam's betrayal. Rationally, he knew it had not been her fault, but there was never anything logical when it came to matters of the heart. He walked up to the woman and placed his hand on the small of her back. He caressed the soft material of her tunic. Together they moved toward the dining table where Tolfer was delivering the dishes he prepared.

"Sit here, Shirl," Alex said, indicating to the chair next to hers. Starc accompanied Shirl to the seat her friend had reserved and took a chair on the other side of Tarsea. "The purple stuff is keen. It is a grain only grown in the Troyk universe and it's yummy. I don't know why, but food tastes better here." Starc could not help but smile. Alex loved to eat and never seemed to gain an ounce. He imagined it had something to do with her soul mate's constant attentions. They always seemed to be escaping to Tarsea's bedroom.

"What more can you tell me about my brother?" Shirl inquired. Starc knew her brother. They had never been on assignment together and only had conversations in passing. Darden was more acquainted with Cianan Thork.

"I cannot say he is a friend," Darden replied. "He is bitter and unpleasant. I honestly do not know how he is going to react to you. Your presence has only recently been recognized by the communal pathways. As soon as your name is revealed, he will know of your existence. I will help keep an eye on you, as will Starc, since he is your personal guard."

Starc could see the hurt in Shirl's eyes as Darden spoke. The woman had grown up without a family. Now she discovered she had a brother, who would be less than thrilled to meet her. Family could sometimes drive you crazy, but Starc always knew his had his back. There was nothing he could do that would stop them from loving him. He only wished he could find a woman he could feel the same way about.

Shirl peered at him. "How does the whole guard thing work?" Her question startled Starc out of the thoughts distracting him from the conversation.

"I will follow you through the portal wherever you go. Some crystal telepathic gatherers work alone, like Darden. Others like to have a guard with them for protection. When we are not guarding an individual, we guard the portal. If the portal opens and something comes through, we go out and investigate. It was Raine Narmouth and Kelog Potts, who found you on the mountain trail."

Alex stood, outraged by the news. The chair, dragging against the wooden floor, grabbed Starc's attention. His mind kept shifting to thoughts of Shirl. "They let that snake Narmouth go after he stabbed Tarsea the other night," Alex cried. "How is that possible?"

Most of the men present had found Alex after Narmouth had abducted her. When they caught up with the two of them, Narmouth was on top of Alex, forcing himself on her. Tarsea wanted to personally punish the asshole for attacking his soul mate.

Since Narmouth had no honor, rather than having a fair fight with Tarsea, Narmouth pulled a knife. He proceeded to stab Tarsea and had been arrested for assault. Since Troyk medical technology was so advanced, Tarsea was healed by a med-tech within minutes of his arrival.

"Calm down, Alexia," Solfa said. "Since he caused a concussion, you could not communicate through the communal pathway when Raine attacked you. As far as anyone knew, you were with him on that gathering place trail of your own free will. Tarsea's presence could be viewed as threatening and Raine claimed self-defense when he stabbed him. Since Tarsea's injuries were healed, no one wanted to go through the hassle of charging him. We could not use you as a witness, since as far as anyone is concerned you are from this world. We did not want you coming back to the attention of Jeryl Jarlyn. Your cover story is working so far. I do not want to tempt fate."

"Well, crap! That sucks! You sure we cannot accidently send him to another universe?" Starc had to grin again at the expression on Alex's face. There was an endearing mischievous smile on her face. It never ceased to amaze him how resilient Alex was. He only hoped that Shirl shared that same characteristic.

"Sorry, baby, not going to happen," Tarsea replied. Starc watched as Tarsea tightened his grip around his soul mate's hand.

Alex addressed her friend. "As far as everyone is concerned, my name is Alexia Montiff. I am from Starling Province. Since they know you are from Ginkgo Terra, you don't have to watch how you talk. They do not use contractions in this world. So I cannot say 'don't' but 'do not' in public. I constantly have to watch myself. When I talk telepathically to Tarsea I just talk the way I always speak."

Shirl gave her friend a radiant smile. Starc wished he had caused that smile upon her beautiful, if not currently ravished, face. "Alex, I am just happy to be here with you. I will watch my language as well, so we can go through this together."

"Tomorrow we will introduce you to your brother," Darden informed Shirl. "Either Starc or I will be present anytime you are with him. Koel, you will be our back up."

"I will be happy to play nursemaid to such a lovely lady." His cousin got up and went over and kissed Shirl's hand. "Although it pains me, I have an appointment this evening and have to leave."

Starc did not know why, but he wanted to punch Koel for kissing her hand. Everyone else generally desired to hit his cousin because of his smart mouth, not Starc. But tonight, for the first time in his life, he wanted to do some serious damage to Koel.

"I will walk with you, cousin," Starc said. He knew he needed to leave Shirl's presence for the time being. "Darden, we will coordinate what time to meet tomorrow to deal with Cianan."

As he wished everyone a good night, he thought he saw the disappointment in Shirl's eyes. He did not know if he was taking a leap, hoping that look had been caused by his departure. One thing was clear, he needed to determine what his feelings were for this woman.

Chapter 5

The roar of male voices overwhelmed Shirl, as she walked into crystal telepath headquarters. She was glad that both Starc and Darden were at her side. Had she come alone, she did not know if she would have continued into this male dominated room. Darden had explained the crystal telepathic gene primarily appeared in male children. It was rare for a female to have the ability. Since her mother was a crystal telepath, it was generally believed that all her children would be born with the power to manipulate portal energy. Shirl had an ability out of legends, the rare female crystal telepath.

Once again, she wished Alex was by her side. Although Alex tended to fade into the background, her presence generally invigorated Shirl. She spent most of the night catching up with what had happened to her best friend since coming into this parallel world. She could not believe the changes in Alex. There was a confidence about her that she never had. They would have talked all night, had Tarsea not come in and carried Alex out of the room. Shirl had never heard Alex giggle like she did as Tarsea absconded with her.

Her eyes surveyed the room and stopped on a tall male about thirty feet away. She would have recognized him anywhere. There was no question, the man was her brother. He had the same champagne blond hair and light brown eyes she had. They could have been twins. His face was alight with a broad smile, sharing a joke with whoever he was talking with. As soon as he made eye contact with her, the smile was replaced with a frown.

She must have made some kind of noise, because Starc placed his hand on her shoulder. Through the tunic's material, she felt the heat generated from his touch. Shirl wondered what it would feel like if they touched skin to skin. Regardless, his touch brought her renewed confidence.

"Let us get this over with," was all Starc had to say as the three of them walked toward her brother. She could not agree more. With all the things she heard about her brother, she was not excited about meeting him.

Shirl heard various comments about her appearance through the communal pathways as she made her way toward her brother. There was nothing communicated she had not already heard. She was grateful that Tolfer had spent time with her last night. Shirl had no issues navigating from pathway to pathway. Alex said he was a great teacher and she had not been exaggerating.

Leenea kept pumping the herbal beverage down her throat, relieving what pressure she felt in her head. Shirl had been migraine free since coming to this world. It appeared she had an easier time managing the communal pathways than Alex. Although she listened to what was being discussed in the pathways, she did not join any of the conversations. Alex was still recovering from her earlier attack and did not join her and Tolfer as they surfed through the different channels.

"Cianan," Darden addressed his fellow crystal telepath, "I want to introduce you to Shirl." He had not bothered to explain she was his sister, Cianan already knew. Shirl stood a little taller, not knowing what to expect from her brother.

There was an awkward silence between the siblings. She did not know if she should hug him, shake his hand or just stand there. If looks could kill, there was no doubt she would be dead. She figured a hug was out of the question. Things were going as badly as she expected.

Darden let out a frustrated, loud sigh. "She was a baby when your parents left. Do not be an ass. Say hello to your sister." Shirl could tell that Cianan did not appreciate Darden's involvement or opinion. She had never seen such a look of aggravation cross anyone's face, as she saw reflected on her brother's.

Cianan merely looked her square in the face and turned around to leave. He had not gotten far when Starc stopped him. She could not hear what transpired between the two men. Shirl was generally the center of attention wherever she went. Men flocked to her like flies to honey. She did not necessarily like being judged by her looks, but she had never experienced the hostility that her brother directed toward her.

"This is not about you," Darden told her. His words did little to soothe the hurt of her brother's rejection. She could not admit she secretly hoped her brother would be thrilled to see her. "He has always been a moody son of a bitch. On the rare occasions I had been paired with him, I would count the minutes until our mission was over. Unfortunately, Jeryl Jarlyn wants you paired with your brother during your training. I have no idea why, but it is not my place to countermand his orders. I doubt you are in any physical danger from him. Starc or I will be with you at all times, so you have nothing to worry about."

The first of a flock of men approached to be introduced to her. Darden did the honors, but she was too distracted by the conversation still going on between her brother and Starc. Shirl heard blurbs of speech as different men came up to her. She saw Cianan's face go from anger, to disbelief, and finally to acceptance.

"Let us head to meeting room 108," Starc communicated through the communal pathway. Shirl saw her brother walk along with Starc. At least their first words to each other would not be in public, but the confines of a secured room. She was grateful that both Darden and Starc were there to support her. Alex had told her they were trustworthy and everything that had happened so far confirmed Alex's belief.

Shirl walked beside Darden. She admired the various crystals worn by the people she passed. It was hard to believe these beautiful gems controlled portal energy, taking her anywhere she desired. As they approached the room, she knew her reprieve related to dealing with her brother was over. She took a deep breath and walked into the conference room. This was worse than entering a dental office for a root canal. Once again, she grabbed her crystals to give her courage.

Although there were a table and chairs in the room, everyone continued to stand. She had never felt more awkward in her life. This was her brother, her flesh and blood. Although she had Alex and Candy, she had always wanted a brother. It shattered any dream she may have had when she stared reality in the face and it spit at her.

Enough of this silence! Shirl approached her brother and extended her hand. "I am Shirl, your sister."

If it was possible, Cianan looked even angrier. He took one step toward her and slapped her across the face. "I do not have a sister and I do not want one." The power behind the blow sent her flying back into Darden's arms.

⤸〇

A rage the likes of which he never experienced came over Starc. Although Cianan was his height, Starc had a good forty pounds of muscle on the crystal telepath. He grabbed Cianan and slammed him into the wall. He felt the contact tremors come off Cianan's body.

"Do not ever touch that woman again. You so much as look at her the wrong way, I will make sure you are not able to lift a hand again as long as you live." Starc had his left arm bracing Shirl's brother's chest and his right forearm against his throat. Just a little more pressure and he could crush the bastard's neck. He could imagine the sound of the bones breaking in his mind. It would be so easy.

Without releasing the pressure he used to pin Cianan against the wall, Starc called over his shoulder to Darden. "Is she all right?"

To his surprise Shirl came up right next to him. He now saw determination on her face. It was the same look on Alex's face when she faced a challenge. There was a lot more to this woman than he originally thought.

"Listen, you piece of shit, I want nothing to do with you. I am going to chat with Solfa Theffar. I will ask her to talk Jeryl Jarlyn out of this insane idea of us working together. You may be my biological brother, but you are a coward." Shirl leaned toward her brother and whispered in his ear and then walked away. She brushed against Starc's shoulder, once again, not making skin to skin contact with him.

Starc could see Cianan pale as she walked away. "Wait," Shirl's brother cried, as she continued on her way out of the room.

"Let him go, Starc," he heard Shirl call to him. She then addressed her brother, "What do you want?" She stood taller than he had ever seen her. The woman looked invincible, nothing could touch her. He had been afraid she was going to cower in response to her brother's rejection. That slap shook something out of her.

"It is not true, what you said. They did not leave me behind because I was a bastard." Her brother looked crushed as he said those words. He could not imagine what Cianan had been through growing up. However, there was no excuse hitting Shirl. It appeared his sister was considering how to respond to her brother's statement.

"No, they left you behind because they did not know what they were walking into leaving this world. What they got was a world with an atmosphere that attacked their brains and brought about their ugly deaths. It is my understanding the gatherers shy away from Ginkgo Terra because of the headaches short exposures to our atmosphere caused. I was heading in the direction of dying the way our parents did, before I accidentally opened the portal. That still does not change the fact I don't want to have anything to do with you. From Darden and Starc's response, smacking a woman is not the norm here."

"Please, give me another chance. I have had so much built up anger toward our parents. You were just a convenient outlet." He started to walk toward his sister, but Darden got between them. Cianan raised his hands in surrender.

"I will sleep on it and have Starc give you my answer in the morning. In the meantime, Darden can start my lessons on how to use our mother's crystal to navigate within the portal." Shirl proceeded to take a seat at the table. She had a regal bearing about her. Shirl had dismissed her brother from her presence.

"Time to leave," Starc said, as he shoved Cianan out the conference room door. He then joined his twin and Shirl.

Shirl sat, holding her crystals in her hand. The bravado that she showed standing up to her brother was gone. She looked wiped out. And she was the most beautiful woman he had ever seen. He cursed himself for not stopping Cianan from hitting her. Starc had not expected that response from him. Regardless of Shirl's decision, he was going to have to keep an eye on Cianan Thork.

"How can I navigate the portal?" Shirl asked Darden. There was fire in her honey brown eyes as she questioned Darden. The gold next to her irises seemed to shine. Starc continued to examine her face. She had a mole just below her right eye, which only added to her beauty. Her lips were full and kissable. His eyes perused the left side of her face that was a light shade of red from the slap she had received. Everything about Shirl captivated him.

"We will start with you learning the different pitches energy will emit within the portal. There are simulators that will allow you to adjust the sound frequency to navigate different worlds. They are located in this facility. You will need to master those frequencies before you can enter an event horizon alone. I will take you with me on some test runs. This way you can hear and adjust the energy within the portal." Shirl's eyes became more golden as Darden explained how to manipulate sound.

"Can you hear the frequencies, Starc?" He was a little surprised when Shirl directed the question to him.

"I hear the different pitches. I just cannot manipulate them through crystals. I am just a Crystal Telepath Guard."

"Just," Darden laughed. "You always had my back as we were growing up and as I started my training. I do not think I would have been able to go through my first solo trip without you by my side. For some reason, you always discount your role in our lives and what you do for Aster Province."

Starc did not respond to his brother. After Darden discovered he was a crystal telepath, family life revolved around Darden and his training. His twin brother was the first crystal telepath his family had produced in generations. Their fortunes changed with the prestige of having one in the family again.

Starc was never given a choice about what he wanted to do with his life. As soon as Darden started his training, his parents put him in Crystal Telepath Guard training. Starc had never resented his twin. He loved him more than life itself. From time to time, though, he looked at his life and realized it still revolved around Darden.

His closest friends were Darden's. He even roomed with Darden as an adult. The one thing he had that was his own was his relationship with Elzbeth Southam. Unfortunately, his involvement with Elzbeth had become a disaster he never wanted to experience again. It fueled his non-existent social life and his passion for overthrowing the mind control telepathic government.

Darden and Shirl were both looking at him. They were expecting some kind of response to what his twin said. He thought how bitter Cianan had been and was blessed that had not happened to him.

"We should be heading back. I figure Alex has been pacing for the past hour and is driving Tarsea mad. Although I have shared information with her telepathically, she will not relax until Shirl is back in her sight." Starc knew this would change the subject and he would not have to answer his brother.

Shirl laughed. "Alex would wait up whenever I was on a date. My apartment was just down the hallway from hers. I stopped dating, fearing she would get a bleeding ulcer. Besides, I have some thinking to do regarding Cianan."

The idea of Shirl spending some time with her brother scared Starc to death. He did not know how they were going to prevent that from happening. If he was sent to some hellhole of a world, at least Starc would be there to protect her. He would rather not deal with the unknown that Cianan represented.

Chapter 6

~

"He did what?" Alex shouted, as she looked at the angry red mark that marred her best friend's face. Although the left cheek was a little sore, Shirl felt she ended up with the upper hand in her first encounter with her brother. She had stood up to him and prevailed. Shirl just had to determine what type of relationship she wanted with him going forward.

"Calm down, Alex," Shirl said. Her friend was so angry, Shirl would not have been surprised if Alex started exhaling fire. "I am fine. I scared the shit out of him, telling him that Solfa was going to Jeryl Jarlyn and ask him to change my tutor to Darden."

"It is still not right. I have met my extended family here and they are wonderful. You have a blood brother and the first thing he does is slug you! My cousin will make sure that Cianan does not darken your door again. I will not rest until that bastard of a brother is no longer part of your life."

There was Alex again, fixing what was wrong with Shirl's life. One of these days, she needed to take control and fix her own messes. She actually thought she had done a good job today of doing exactly that.

No sooner than Alex finished those words, there was a knock at the front door. Within moments the subject of their conversation was standing before them. Starc and Darden immediately buffered themselves between Shirl and her brother. She felt Alex back off. It was imperative that Cianan remain ignorant of their relationship prior to entering the Troyk universe. Her best friend also seemed surprised by her brother's appearance. Shirl had not mentioned to Alex how similar they appeared.

"We have an assignment for tomorrow," Cianan said without any preamble. He did not seem to care about the looks the people around him were throwing in his direction. The tension in the room could have been cut with a knife.

"A simple 'hello' would have been nice," Shirl growled at her brother. Where did he learn his manners?

"She is not ready," Darden replied. "We have not even sat in the simulator and listened to the frequencies of the different worlds she can explore."

"This frequency is not in the simulator," her brother responded. "Besides, the best way to learn how to navigate the portal is by being next to someone who is actually doing it. I will walk her through the particulars before we leave." Shirl could live with that. She was excited about learning to navigate the portal. Spending hours in a simulator would not satisfy the need she had to travel to parallel universes.

Darden looked concerned, "What world are you going to that does not have a frequency programmed into the simulator?" Shirl had an idea he already knew the answer to that question. She could see the color slowly draining from Darden's face. That did not bode well.

"Nightshade" was all Cianan said.

"Alex, go to our room and I will join you later," Tarsea instructed her best friend. Those words scared the shit out of Shirl. Where was the Prime Ruler sending her that would cause Tarsea to shelter Alex from the discussion?

Alex looked between her soul mate and her best friend. "I am not going anywhere. What is going on? What is the significance of the Nightshade universe?"

"It is where we take prisoners who are going to be executed. They are taking Chartail and Stephano there for their involvement in the attempt on Jeryl Jarlyn's life. Alex, I did not want you to find out this way. I certainly do not want Shirl involved in this operation." Tarsea put his arms around his soul mate. Shirl had never seen Alex look so content, regardless of how angry she currently claimed to be. She longed for that type of relationship.

Starc made his way to Cianan. "What kind of sick bastard are you to take your sister on such a mission?" He said as he jabbed Cianan's chest with his finger. The fervor that consumed Starc after Cianan attacked her yesterday had returned. Starc looked like he could do her brother serious injury. Had Starc made the first move, she doubted anyone in the room would stop him.

"I have direct orders from Jeryl Jarlyn himself," Cianan said. "Those orders include taking Shirl along with me. Fire under pressure, I suppose. I am not in a position to go against the Prime Ruler's orders." Her brother was not going to win any popularity contests. There was an arrogance in the way he communicated his orders to the group. The Prime Ruler's name would get no respect, but only condemnation within this household.

Shirl stood as her life played out before her eyes. She was just a spectator. It was as if she had walked into the middle of a play and had no idea what was going on, only that she was now the main character. This place and situation were so foreign, she was at a loss concerning how to react.

Tempers continued to heat. Tarsea ran his palm down his face. It appeared he had lost patience. "Koel, can you take Cianan for a walk around the block?" Shirl imagined Tarsea wanted Cianan out of the house for more reasons than to calm emotions.

Koel who had kept quiet until now, smirked at Cianan. "Come on, Mr. Congeniality. Let us get some fresh air." She never knew what was going to come out of Koel's mouth. Alex had filled her in about her new friends. Koel seemed the quirkiest of the bunch. He barely spoke a word in her presence. Cianan did not balk at leaving with Koel. It seemed he needed a break from the discussion as well.

As Koel left with her brother, Shirl got everyone back on track by asking, "Who is Chartail?" There had been a silent reaction when Chartail's name had been mentioned earlier. She noted the reaction, especially where Alex was concerned.

"Chartail," Alex answered, "is Tarsea's former girlfriend. Her father is a mind control telepath and a member of the Prime Council. She got tired of feeling defective for not having that ability. She went berserk and planned an unsuccessful assassination attempt on Jeryl Jarlyn."

Shirl knew her friend well enough to know she was not telling the whole story. She figured she would help her friend along with the explanation about Chartail. *"And—"* She used their shared communal pathway, not wanting anyone else to be part of the conversation. She knew she had to use it sparingly, until Alex fully recovered from the concussion.

Last night Shirl and Alex experimented with communal channels. They wanted to see if one had opened when they were children. Through trial and error, they found their closed communal pathway. Over time, others would link into it, but for the time being, it was all theirs. While they were experimenting, Alex got a nose bleed. It had concerned Shirl, but Alex just waved it off. Tarsea's mother made more of the herbal drink that helped Alex manage her telepathic abilities.

"And I was involved in helping to uncover that she was the mastermind. Another of the evolutionary telepathic enhancements is the ability to read another's thoughts. I can read minds, but not manipulate that person's decision like a mind control telepath." Alex made sure she differentiated between what she could do and the government's manipulation of their citizen's minds. She wasn't sure how she felt about Alex's new ability. It was just another oddity about this world she had to come to terms with.

Shirl once again spoke out loud. She still was not comfortable using telepathy, although she did not have the issues Alex had using the communal pathways. Shirl felt her friend was conveniently editing what she told her. "What I don't understand, Alex, is why you look so guilty when you talk about it."

"She and I were at a luncheon together. A man who had attacked me earlier came up to the table. Chartail confronted him and protected me. After the episode, I read her mind and discovered Chartail had planned the attack on the Prime Ruler's life. I had to betray the woman who aided me." Shirl could see how upset Alex was on this subject. Unshed tears formed in her best friend's eyes.

"What is it with weak minded men striking women in this universe?" Shirl wondered out loud.

"It is not the norm," Darden replied, "I assure you." Shirl could tell by Darden's tone a man striking a woman disgusted him. It was clear the men currently surrounding her would never raise a hand against a woman.

"What Alex did not share," Tarsea added, "was that two innocent palace guards were killed in the failed assassination attempt. We are trying to peacefully overthrow the government, but Chartail crossed the line. Although I had been dating her, she did not know I was working against the government. I was clueless she was plotting against the government as well, taking the violent approach."

"Shirl," Alex continued, "no one stood beside Chartail when she was caught. Her father did not even appear at the hearing in front of Jarlyn. She is bright and beautiful, but alone. I could not help but feel sorry for her and feel partly responsible. If I had come to Aster Province earlier, maybe I could have been the true friend she desperately needed."

Shirl knew Alex well enough to know that she would try to fix everyone's problems. She and Candy had certainly gone to Alex over the years to fix their issues. Part of Alex's self-worth was always gauged on how she helped her friends. Shirl often felt guilty that she did not reciprocate more. Taking her shopping to make sure she wore colors that flattered her hair color and complexion, did not come close to what she owed her.

"Alex, you can't fix the world alone. It appears to me you now have people around you who will finally help carry part of the burden." How she wished she was talking about herself. She was once again in a situation where Alex felt responsible for providing her aid.

The brightest smile graced Alex's face. "I know." Alex went into Tarsea's arms and kissed him. She turned, addressing Darden, "Back to the situation at hand. Anyway we can get Shirl out of accompanying her brother tomorrow?"

Darden shook his head. "I do not see how. Since we do not know what to expect, I will tag along."

"I will not let her out of my sight, Alex. I promise," Starc replied. Shirl was overwhelmed by the support her friend received from these men. She was grateful it spilled over to cover her as well. Shirl wondered what would have happened if she had opened the portal and entered this universe without Alex preceding her. "I will protect her with my life."

Starc said those words as he looked at Shirl. That strange heat she felt yesterday spread through her body. It warmed her heart, but also parts of her anatomy that were not accustomed to feeling anything. She recognized it for what it was. For the first time in her life, she was reacting sexually to a man. She was not sure if it was a true feeling or longing for what Alex and Tarsea had together.

"I guess it's settled then," Alex concluded. "I will accompany Shirl as far as the portal. It will give me a chance to properly say goodbye to Chartail."

With Alex's words, the room broke into a symphony of voices arguing back and forth. Shirl stood back and watched in fascination. Koel and Cianan returned and joined the mayhem.

Starc observed Shirl watch the scene in front of her. She looked at Alex in wonder. He imagined that she noticed the differences in her friend since she came to the Troyk universe. Starc had noticed the changes in Alex himself. Shirl's involvement in tomorrow's trip was one of the items that was still being discussed, but she was not involving herself.

"Let us go into the kitchen and talk about tomorrow," Starc said to Shirl. "I do not believe we can hear ourselves think, let alone have a conversation where we presently are." He took his role as a CT Guard seriously, always had. Although assigned to protect other crystal telepathic individuals before, protecting Shirl was something altogether different. There was so much more to lose if something went wrong.

He was glad Shirl willingly left the room with him. She was so different from her friend. Shirl let things happen to her, while Alex fought to control her life. He figured as Shirl stayed in the Troyk universe, she would come into herself, as her best friend had. For some reason, Starc wanted to witness that change and be an active participant in her metamorphosis.

"Wow! I have never seen Alex like that. She generally fades into the background. Now she's front and center." Starc saw Shirl was a little shell-shocked from the conversations going in the other room.

"She is a firecracker. Alex knows her strengths and weaknesses, although I think she is still experimenting a little to see how far she can push Tarsea. She can blend into the background when it suits her. I am guessing it was the way she reacted to her environment."

"Yes, with other people. However, when she was with me and Candy, she had the confidence to step out of the shadows. I have always respected Alex for her calm exterior, now I am in awe. If I could have a fraction of her inner strength, I would be delighted."

Shirl suddenly looked uncomfortable. Starc thought she had revealed more than she intended. He also wondered if this was the first time she had internalized that thought.

"I am not comfortable that your brother will adequately prepare you for tomorrow. Do you have any questions?"

Shirl laughed, "Where do I start?" She poured herself a drink and rejoined him. "I do not even know how I opened the portal. One minute I am walking and the next my crystal was glowing."

"That is a normal reaction a crystal will have to a natural portal. I am surprised it never happened before," Starc commented.

"I had not been on that trail before," Shirl answered. "Alex hiked with Candy or alone. It was the last location they could place her, so I had to explore the area for myself."

"Like in Sedona, tomorrow the portal will open automatically. Once your brother partially enters the event horizon, he will set the energy signature to open a gateway to the Nightshade world. At that point, we will enter. There will probably be an additional guard or two who will join us."

"I remember falling and twisting. Will that happen again?" She looked like she was going to break into tears.

"No, it will feel like you are just walking through a door as a gust of wind descends. You entered the portal without setting the destination. Unfortunately, without a gateway open on the other side, you had a very rough ride. Alex had experienced just a fraction of what you went through. She was actually pulled into the event horizon as it was closing. It had the destination, but was in the process of finishing its cycle."

"How am I going to learn how to navigate the portals this way?"

Starc took a deep breath, "Darden will teach you." He looked into the other room. From where he sat, things seemed to have calmed. "When you enter the portal, listen for the frequency. Hopefully, it is a frequency you will never hear again or will have to set yourself."

Shirl looked at him and frowned. "Have you been to the Nightshade world before?"

Starc shook his head. "No. Anyone who has been to that world does not speak of it." He did not want to scare Shirl, but she should know what she was up against.

He figured between entering the portal again and going to a world shrouded in mystery, Shirl must be on the edge of a panic attack. She was several shades paler since they entered the kitchen.

Alex appeared and sat next to her friend. "It's all settled. Chartail and Stephano will be delivered to the portal at ten tomorrow morning. Your brother will come here and pick us up on his way to the mountain. Starc and Darden will be here early. We will all have breakfast and Darden will give you your first portal lesson. Solfa told us about your bleeding earlier today. Darden wants to make sure your brain is rested and you have had a healthy breakfast before entering the portal."

"Will Tolfer be here tomorrow morning?" Starc asked. The prospect of eating breakfast prepared by Tarsea's mother or father was not an appetizing thought.

He saw humor light Shirl's face. She was stunning, it was almost painful to look at her. Tarsea's parents' lack of cooking skills was now legendary. She must have found it humorous that he reacted to having breakfast here, rather than the plan Alex communicated.

"Yes," Alex laughed. "Tolfer does most of the cooking. Although I have been accepted as third choice in cooking if he is not available. My aunt Norri, who is an excellent cook, is everyone's favorite right behind Tolfer. She will be here tomorrow morning to help out and to meet you."

Starc got the impression it was time for girl talk and he was a third wheel. "I will see you tomorrow morning. I should get back to the common room and see if there are any last minute items that need to be addressed."

He left the two women to their chat. The men had their heads together and were talking quietly. No doubt they did not want the girls to overhear what they were planning.

"I would not go against Alex's plans if I were you. Besides, she is too smart to fall for any lame plan you may put in place to prevent her involvement." With Cianan present, Starc could not comment that Alex could hear everything that was communicated in the warrior telepathic channel.

"You cannot blame me for trying," Tarsea said. "However, we could not come up with anything. With Shirl staying here, Alex will be super aware of her comings and goings."

Starc saw Cianan's questioning look regarding Alex's protective stance regarding Shirl. "Alex just arrived in Aster Province. She does not have many girlfriends yet. Last night she bonded with your sister. The two have been attached at the hip ever since."

"We have figured out everything we can for tonight," Darden said. "Let us head on out. Cianan, make sure you say good night to your sister. Be as charming as you can, you have a lot to make up for."

Starc followed alongside his twin as they walked to the door. Koel waited for Cianan. Once they were outside, Starc could not hold back the question he was dying to ask. "How do you think tomorrow is going to go?"

"It is going to be a disaster. We cannot trust Cianan, neither of us have been to the Nightshade universe before, and Alex is going to be a wreck. To top everything off, although she will not admit it, Shirl is scared to death of the portal."

Chapter 7

Shirl walked up the mountain trail behind Alex. Her friend hiked on a regular basis and was handling the trip with ease. Shirl did not know if it was her lack of conditioning or the amount of food she ate for breakfast, but she was panting as she continued to make her way up the trail.

"Step it up, Shirlyn. You are lagging behind," her brother complained. Although he was now acknowledging her presence, she wished he would call her Shirl. He probably called her Shirlyn, just to annoy her. Everything about her brother bothered her. That may have been the name she was born with, but it was not her. She had always hated the name Shirley, Shirlyn was just as bad.

Breakfast had been lovely. She met Norri, Alex's aunt, and fell instantly in love with her. Shirl could understand why Alex felt she was blessed with her extended Troyk family. Norri was accompanied by Solfa's mother, Pattrice. Now that woman was a piece of work. Pattrice cried throughout breakfast. She continually hugged Alex and Shirl, exclaiming how happy she was that the girls were home. Although Pattrice got on her nerves, Shirl was touched by how strongly she felt about them. Shirl was unofficially adopted by both of the older women. Pattrice continually tried to get Shirl to move in with her and Norri. She did not have to reply, with Alex foiling her cousin's attempts. It was hard to fathom Solfa was Pattrice's daughter.

Shirl took another moment before complying with her brother's request. She watched him as he continued up the path. His familial bracelet caught the sun, shining in response. Everyone in the Troyk universe wore one. It depicted the history of the family the wearer was a member of. Norri had given Alex her twin sister's bracelet, which she had held onto all these years. Alex finally had something that belonged to her mother. Shirl wondered what had happened to her parents' bracelets. She felt she stood apart from the others not having a bracelet, including Alex.

She increased her speed, regretting the second muffin she ate this morning. It felt like a ten pound weight in her stomach. The discomfort was partially due to overeating, but primarily due to nerves. She was going back into the portal, to a world that caused everyone concern. On top of everything else, they were accompanying two people to their deaths. Why didn't she just stay in bed, feigning a relapse of portal sickness?

Earlier, the prisoners were not present when they reached the trail. Cianan decided they would begin their ascent anyway. The Palace Guard had either started without them or were delayed rendezvousing with them. Shirl was thankful they were not making the trek with the prisoners. The less time she had to spend with the condemned individuals, the happier she would be. She was also concerned about Alex and the guilt she carried related to Chartail.

"We are stopping here," Darden said. "We do not want to activate the portal until the prisoners are present." Although he had never accompanied the condemned to the Nightshade universe, Darden was knowledgeable about the protocols.

Shirl looked down at the Aster Province, her new home. She was taken in by the beauty of the city and the layer of purple haze that hovered over it. When she first arrived, she had only been conscious for moments. Now she was able to bask at the magnificent sight before her. She noted a group of people coming up the trail, about half way to their destination. They would leave shortly for the Nightshade universe. Although Darden spent time with her before breakfast, Shirl was still nervous about stepping into the portal. Traveling to other worlds both thrilled and terrified her. Dreams were one thing, reality was something else.

There was a grumbling among the men. Shirl rejoined the group to see what had happened.

"What is going on?" she asked Alex. Shirl noted that Tarsea had positioned himself between Alex and the approaching party. The man was overprotective where her friend was concerned. Shirl could not help but like Tarsea and appreciate everything he was doing to keep Alex safe.

"Raine Narmouth is leading the group," was Alex's reply. She could feel her friend's body stiffen next to her. Shirl instinctively joined the group of men who stood between Alex and her approaching stalker.

As Narmouth approached, Shirl was surprised how good looking he was. She could not understand why such a man would have issues getting dates and had to resort to abduction. Raine was one of eight guards who accompanied Chartail and Stephano.

Chartail was as beautiful as Alex described. Rather than wearing a tunic, she had on a midriff and a pair of leggings. The material was black, which further brought out the fairness of her skin. Her blond hair was pulled into a bun at the back of her head. Stephano just wore black leggings. Both prisoners had their hands tied behind their backs.

Alex started to move toward the new arrivals, but was stopped by Tarsea. He did not say anything, but in a world of telepathic people, that did not mean anything. Shirl imagined they were arguing through the pathway they shared. At one point Tarsea loosened his grip and accompanied Alex to meet up with Raine and say goodbye to Chartail.

Shirl focused on Narmouth's face as he watched Alex approach. She did not like the way the man looked at her friend. His eyes roamed her body several times and he licked his lips. He reminded her of a predator cat just before it sprang on its doomed victim. Tarsea's stance reflected that he, too, saw the response Narmouth had toward Alex. Since Tarsea's back was to her, Shirl could only imagine the look on his face.

"Alexia, you look beautiful this morning," was all Narmouth said. He stood his ground, not taking a step toward Alex. The man's eyes continued to consume her best friend.

"I am here to see Chartail before she enters the portal," Alex addressed Narmouth. She walked past him. Several of the guards stepped aside, allowing Alex to stop in front of the condemned woman. "May I touch her?"

"Yes, as long as you stay clear of her bound hands," one of the guards answered.

Alex carefully positioned her hands and hugged Chartail. "I wish we had met earlier. We would have been friends." That was all her friend had to say through the tears she shed.

"We are already friends, Alexia," Chartail responded. "It means a lot that you came today. I do not know what will be on the other side of that portal, but I face my death, knowing at least one person cares."

Tarsea came closer to Chartail, kissing her on the cheek. "Make that two people, Chartail. I am so sorry I failed you." Shirl knew, like Alex, Tarsea was filled with guilt related to the woman's fate.

"Just treat Alexia right," Chartail said to Tarsea. "I will come back and haunt you if you discard her the way you have all the other women you dated." Shirl imagined Chartail would find a way to come back to keep her word. The woman seemed a force to be reckoned with. She could understand the strong attachment Alex had for Chartail after such a short period of time. Alex would always bear the guilt of turning in Chartail and Shirl would be responsible for delivering her to her death. At least they had each other to share the weight of their actions.

Raine Narmouth approached Cianan, "I turn the prisoner over to you for transfer to the Nightshade universe. Four of the guards will enter the portal with you. Only you, your sister and her guard may enter the event horizon. As the agreement with the Nightshade government dictates, all weapons must be left behind." Once again Raine Narmouth's eyes were on Alex. "The rest will join us on our journey down the mountain."

Starc handed his weapon to Darden. Shirl could tell they communicated telepathically when Darden nodded to his brother. Starc made his way back to Shirl, ready to enter the portal beside her.

Cianan approached the area where the natural portal existed and as with her crystal, her brother's quartz started to glow. An event horizon came to life and Cianan partially entered the portal. Shirl could not help herself, she stepped into the portal next to her brother. She listened as Cianan adjusted the frequency. Her crystal was reacting to his. Her brother grabbed her upper arm and they both stepped out of the portal.

"We are ready," Cianan said. "The trip will be easier if we enter the portal as close to each other as possible. I will enter first, followed by the guards and the prisoners. Starc, you bring Shirlyn with you."

Shirl stepped back, as the four guards came forward with their charges. Stephano started to struggle and two of the guards had to forcefully move him forward. Chartail walked with dignity to her death. Shirl watched as each entered the portal. It was time for her and Starc to enter. He placed his hand on her hip and gently steered her into the event horizon.

Chartail was facing her death. Shirl was not sure what she would find on the other side of the portal. Just prior to stepping into the event horizon, Shirl thought of a typical *Star Trek* episode. Whenever the "away team" was beamed to a planet, an unnamed security team member would meet his death. She was so glad she was not wearing red today.

Chapter 8

~

The Nightshade Universe

Starc was correct, moving through a portal correctly opened, was like walking through a door on a windy day. She had barely finished that thought, when she stepped onto solid ground. Although the portal was a dark void, the world she entered was just as dark. It took a minute for her eyes to adjust to the near absence of light. They had entered a room or a cave, she was not sure which. The air was cold, but wet with moisture. She felt a shiver of foreboding.

"I claim the female offering," a deep voice said. Shirl turned and stared into glowing red eyes. There were a number of men standing around a man seated on a throne. "Have the male offering brought forward." The men did not hesitate following orders. Shirl stepped back, closer to Starc.

As two of the guards pushed Stephano forward, she continued to survey her surroundings. They were in a large cavernous room with torches ablaze in the distance. Her eyes went back to Stephano and the guards, as they brought him to his knees and chained him to the floor.

"Turn around, Shirl, you do not want to see this," her brother stepped closer to her. The fact he called her Shirl should have warned her what was to come. Although she knew she should have listened to her brother, Shirl could not take her eyes off the chained man.

"Let the decorated soldiers of our Nightshade Force take their reward," the man on the throne continued.

Shirl watched in disbelief as three men with glowing red eyes slowly approached Stephano. Stephano started to struggle, but was helpless against the chains that bound him to the floor. As they opened their mouths, their eye teeth elongated. She had to be dreaming, there were no such things as vampires.

While her mind struggled with what it saw, the three vampires attacked the kneeling prisoner. One ripped at his throat, while another attacked his torso. The slowest of the three had to be content with a flailing arm. Her ears were assaulted by the sound of crushing bones and Stephano's cries. Shirl screamed and backed up in horror, as Starc braced her with his hands on her sleeveless arms.

As her eyes reacted to the horror before them, her body reacted to Starc's touch. Every nerve ending was on fire. What little capacity her brain had, she remembered what Alex told her about the extreme reaction soul mates had the first time they touched. It was within the gore and terror of this encounter that Shirl discovered who her soul mate was.

Starc felt like he had been struck by lightning as he held onto Shirl's arms. This woman could not be his soul mate, not here, not this way. Tarsea had confided in him how he felt about Alex from the start. He had not reacted to Shirl in such a manner. She was beautiful and he felt protective of her, but he was not consumed with lust for her as Tarsea was for Alex. Yet again, Elzbeth had destroyed his capacity to love.

"What can we do?" Shirl asked through the soul mate channel, even though she continued to scream. Starc imagined she did not know she was communicating to him, just thinking to herself.

"There is nothing we can do," Starc replied through their private channel. *"Calm yourself, we will leave this God forsaken world behind us."*

"We cannot leave Chartail here, to die in the same manner,"

Starc brought Shirl into his arms, sheltering her from whatever was left of Stephano's torment at the hands of these vampires. He had heard tales of such creatures, but did not believe they were true. How many of the Troyk Prime Council knew what a death sentence truly meant? Did Prime Adholm know what his daughter was going to face in the Nightshade universe?

Cianan shifted positions to stand in front of his sister's back. Although he had been violent and hateful to his sister in the beginning, Starc was moved related to the protective manner with which Cianan treated her since they entered the Nightshade world. Cianan had not admitted to having been to Nightshade, but Starc thought based on his reactions, he had.

"Take the female offering to my quarters. I have much to discuss with the representatives of the Troyk world." The master vampire rose from his chair and approached. Starc took Shirl deeper into his body, encasing her in his arms.

Chartail walked beside her vampire escorts. Smart girl. After witnessing what happened to Stephano, it was a good idea to follow the instructions given. She may or may not be facing the same fate as the man whose bloody corpse lay before them. Best not to upset these creatures.

"I am Yorik. You three are guests in my home and members of my nest for as long as you are here." Starc imagined that the vampire was addressing him, Cianan, and Shirl. "The Troyk are behind in their offerings to me. Quite a bit behind, actually."

"Capital crimes are becoming rare in our world," Cianan responded.

"It has been too long since you have traveled here and provided me my tribute. I have provided your Prime Ruler with his bounty, but you fall short in providing mine." Yorik walked around their party, assessing them as he would had he been purchasing cattle.

Starc and Cianan did their best to hide Shirl from the master vampire's gaze. There were too few of them and so many vampires. Even if they had weapons, they were grossly outnumbered.

"I have a way to even the stakes," Yorik said. Shirl turned around in Starc's arms. He held her closer to his body, if that was possible. "You will travel to the world you know as Ginkgo Terra and retrieve my daughter. Her mother stole her from me fifteen years ago. The girl should be fully grown and of use to me now. Crystal telepath and your guard will find my daughter and bring her here. I will hold the second female as assurance you will return. The four remaining men will help to reduce the shortage in the offerings owed to me."

A swarm of vampires came upon them and the guards protected themselves and their charges for all of five seconds. The men who accompanied them were attacked in the same manner as Stephano had been. Although they were not bound and chained, there was little they could do to stop their terrible fate. In the chaos that ensued, a second vampire's voice cut through the mayhem. "I claim the female crystal telepath for the duration of her stay."

The vampire that spoke walked from the shadows and into view. Where the other vampires had eyes that exhibited their blood lust, this new vampire had clear dark brown eyes. He was pale, but still had color to his cheeks. He was also dressed differently. The vampires in the room were clad in black, this vampire wore blue slacks and a dark green shirt. The man resembled what Darden would look like when he returned from Ginkgo Terra. Starc would never have mistaken him for a vampire.

"It is not your place to make such a claim," Yorik growled.

The other vampire merely shrugged. "Blood says otherwise. The girl will be placed under my guardianship."

Starc looked around him, their four guards were on the ground, dead. He did not have any options as far as he could see. Death was all around him and his soul mate was in his arms. His only hope of keeping her alive was turning her over to this vampire. He seemed to have some kind of power over Yorik.

"We deliver your daughter and you release us, as well as this woman." Starc communicated with Cianan through a communal link, *"We have no choice as I see it. Tell me you have another way to deal with this situation and I will follow you."*

"I see no alternative to get out of here in one piece," Cianan replied.

Shirl turned in his arms and faced the vampire who claimed her. "There has been too much death already. I will go with you willingly." His soul mate walked out of his arms and stood before the vampire who claimed her. She showed the same courage and intelligence Chartail exhibited earlier.

"My name is Drake, my lady. You will be safe in my care while these two men accomplish their mission. In the meantime, you do not need these." The vampire proceeded to remove Shirl's crystals and placed them in his pocket. "We do not want you to leave prematurely."

For an instant Starc was afraid Shirl was going to fight to get her crystals back. He saw a short-lived spark in her eyes, then it was extinguished. "You will return them upon my brother and his guard's return." It was not a question, but a command.

"Naturally," Drake answered. He snapped his fingers and two women came to collect Shirl. These women were covered with vampire bites in various degrees of the healing process. They were dressed scantily, probably to provide the vampires easy access to nourishment. It made him sick to think Shirl would soon be in the same condition as these women.

"I will be back for you as soon as I can. Do not fight these creatures. Whatever you have to do to survive, do it. If you can, find Chartail. She is more cunning than I ever gave her credit for. We will come back for you and her. Tell her that." Starc communicated everything he could think of through the soul mate channel.

He watched as Shirl was taken away. She did not respond to him through the channel. Starc glanced over and saw Drake watching Shirl being taken away as well. There was lust in his eyes toward his soul mate. Starc barely contained the anger he felt related to this situation and his inability to protect her.

Yorik handed over a piece of paper to Cianan. "This is where you will find my daughter. Only her presence here will get that woman released. You go back to the Troyk universe and enlist assistance to rescue your sister, you will all die." Starc did not doubt his words for a moment.

"Have you been to Gingko Terra before," Starc asked Cianan.

"No."

"I have one request, Yorik," Starc said. "Neither of us has been to the world where your daughter lives. My brother goes there regularly. There is only one portal we are familiar with in that world." Starc took the paper from Cianan and read it. "My twin brother will be able to navigate a portal to Chicago. With his aid, we will bring her back faster."

Yorik considered Starc's request. "I am not unreasonable. You may go back to the Troyk universe and leverage the use of your crystal telepathic brother. It has been too long since I have seen my daughter. You have two risings of your sun to bring her to me. If you fail, you will forfeit the female crystal telepath." With those words, Yorik left the room. All the vampires left, except Drake.

"Take your time, gentlemen. Your sister is very beautiful, Cianan. I would not mind adding her to my female slaves if you fail. Besides, she will find more pleasure in my arms, than in yours." Drake said those last words directly to Starc. Once again, Starc had to hold himself back.

Cianan opened the portal to the Troyk universe.

"We will be back for Shirl. She is my soul mate and is precious to me. Treat her like the rare gem she is, or so help me, I will drain you dry of every drop of your precious blood." Starc then stepped into the portal.

Shirl followed the servant girls. She heard what Starc communicated through the soul mate channel. Surprisingly, Cianan shared some final words with her through their familial link before he entered the portal. They both said the same thing. Do whatever she had to do to survive. They would be back for her. She could only pray that was true. Shirl could not help but worry they would not find the girl in time. What future were they dooming Yorik's daughter to if they were successful?

She was so scared, she could barely function. Her feet felt weighted with cement, as she continued to walk down a long corridor. Visions of the horror she just witnessed kept flashing in her mind. Shirl had only seen Stephano die, but had heard the cries of the other men as they met their terrible deaths. She was yet again alone in a strange new world. Well, not exactly alone.

"Chartail," Shirl asked, *"are you all right?"*

"Yes, for now. It appears I am not the only one they decided to claim, whatever that means." Shirl did not want to think about what being claimed by Drake entailed. Better Drake than Yorik, was her only consolation. The vampire ruler seemed put out by Drake's interference.

"Starc said he would be back for both of us. He said to do whatever we had to do to survive. We can do this! You are not alone, Chartail. Alex befriended you and so will I. We will see this through together." Shirl did not know if she said this to make Chartail feel better or to convince herself things were going to work out. She was grateful for the telepathic ability to converse with Chartail. Had she been alone, she was not sure what she would have done.

After a short break, Chartail communicated through the communal channel they linked through earlier. *"Alexia is special. You are her friend?"* Shirl witnessed how close her best friend had become with this woman. It was time to come clean.

"They fooled everyone, Chartail. Alex and I grew up together on Ginkgo Terra. We are the offspring of Benko Jarlyn's followers. He is alive. You and I will live to see him take control of the Troyk government." She was not sure she should have divulged this information to Chartail. It was unlikely either of them would ever return to the Troyk universe. What harm did it do to give Chartail a little hope?

"I will live to see that day, Shirl. We will do whatever it takes to survive, just as we were told. Use this pathway whenever you need me."

The women Shirl followed stopped before a door and motioned for her to enter. Only one woman accompanied her into the room. Warmth engulfed Shirl as she walked into a small spa room. There was a lovely pool with a waterfall, massage table, and several chaise lounges. The air smelled of lavender. A variety of plants were strategically placed around the room, to provide the natural aroma. After the horrors she just witnessed, this slice of paradise was so out of context, she was confused.

"Remove your clothes and lie face down on the table. I will help you relax. They find the blood sweeter when a woman is not stressed." For the first time in her life, Shirl thought about passing up a massage. However, whatever was going to happen to her was out of her control. She might as well enjoy a nice massage before whatever hell she was going to experience began.

Shirl removed her tunic, leggings and underwear. The massage table was heated and she instantly felt better just lying on it. Oil scented with lavender was spread over her body, using long Swedish massage strokes. Shirl had a number of knots that deep tissue massage techniques would loosen. The woman working on her continued with the relaxation method.

On the worst day of her life, she was getting the best massage she had ever experienced. Something was fundamentally wrong with that. The woman completed another long stroke and then took a short break. Then large cold hands caressed her back and continued the massage. She almost jumped off the table, with the shock those icy hands caused.

She intuitively knew it was Drake. As he caressed her back, his hands warmed slightly. A shiver ran up her spine as he continued to touch her. She was burning up, reacting to whatever magic he manipulated. Shirl caught her breath as he worked his way down her back, past her derriere to her upper leg. He kept his hands from the apex between her legs. She took a deep breath and held it every time he came close to the juncture. To her complete horror, her body was actually being turned on by Drake's actions.

"Stop glamoring me!" Shirl demanded. She had seen enough vampire movies to know how these supernatural monsters were able to captivate their female victims. Shirl was not going to let this creature have his way with her, regardless of how her body was reacting to his touch. It was not natural how his presence was arousing her, making her long for him.

Without skipping a stroke, he laughed. "How can I glamor you when I am not looking into your eyes? Your body is merely responding to my caress."

He slid his hands to her inner upper thighs. Shirl moaned and caught her breath as he continued to touch her. Somehow he was able to create heat from extreme cold. Her body was craving more and her mind had stifled any protests. She was not sure how he was bringing about her reaction, but there had to be something supernatural underlying what he was doing.

He slowly turned her over and she stared into his deep, rich brown eyes. Drake smiled down at her and she thought her heart skipped a beat. Her soul mate had touched her for the first time today and she was lusting over a filthy vampire.

"I am many things, but I am not filthy," Drake responded.

"Are you telepathic?" Shirl knew absolutely nothing about real vampires. Her knowledge of movie lore was not going to protect her against Nightshade vampires. She just knew she wanted this one like nothing she had ever experienced before in her life. Including what little time she had with her soul mate. Shirl continued to struggle against the strong attraction.

"We have a connection. It will grow stronger once I take your blood. To fulfill our union, I will give you my blood as well." Drake took his finger and ran it along her left breast until it found her nipple. He then made circling motions with his finger along its tip. Her traitorous nipple hardened under his continued attention.

"There will be no union. Starc and my brother will find the girl and bring her to her father. Then I will leave this place and never see you again." Shirl barely got out those words as his tongue replaced his finger. She cried out at the sensation, as he continued to lick and suck at her breast. Shirl was terrified she was going to come right then and there.

Drake dragged his tongue along her upper breast, her chest and then ultimately to her neck. Shirl pushed her head onto the table's small pillow, exposing her neck to him. She wanted him to take her, drink from her. The thrall, he had induced made Shirl's mind shut down, only her body was functioning.

"Just a taste, my lovely," Drake skimmed his fang along her neck. She could barely breathe, reacting to what he was causing. He bit into her carotid artery, missing bones. It should have hurt, but it felt unbelievable. Drake drew her blood into his mouth with small pulls against her neck. She almost purred as he drank her life force into his body.

Once again Shirl took in air as she gasped, trying to get control of her own body and emotions. Her mind was slowly winning the battle to override what the vampire was doing to her body. The realization of what was happening crashed into her brain. "You cannot do this, I belong to someone else." Guilt consumed her.

"My sweet. You belong to no one, just whomever you choose to give yourself to. Your blood is ambrosia. I have never tasted its equal. You now carry my mark. No other vampire will dare touch you. Through the door behind you, are the women's quarters. You will find all the luxuries your little heart desires. For willingly sharing your blood, we will be generous. Unfortunately, it is not all given willingly. I am truly sorry for that. I promised you would be safe and you are. Beyond your safety, I can do no more."

Drake left. She walked to the pool and stuck her toe in the water. The temperature was perfect. Shirl immersed herself into the soothing liquid. She felt dirty and needed to wash his scent off her body. Shirl floated, trying to make sense of what just happened. Was she seduced by a vampire? What did she owe a soul mate, she just met?

"*Oh, God! Help me, Shirl.*" Shirl sprung out of the water when she heard Chartail's cry for help. The poor woman was screaming within the communal channel.

Drake's words came back to her as she listened to Chartail's weeping. Beyond Shirl's safety, Drake could not offer any assistance. She crawled from the pool and fell onto a lounge chair. Shirl curled up and cried as she listened to Chartail's misery. She also had to come to terms with how she had reacted to Drake and ultimately what she would tell Starc when they were reunited.

Chapter 9

⁓

The Troyk Universe

Starc exited the portal onto Troyk soil. There was a commotion on the narrow mountain pass. Tarsea was being held back by Darden and Koel, while Raine Narmouth was being restrained by two of the CT Guards. He noted that Alex was sitting on a nearby boulder watching the exchange in disgust. When she noticed him, she stood and walked over to him.

"Where is Shirl?" It was a simple enough question to answer. Starc just could not find the words to tell her that he had not protected his soul mate. He felt so guilty leaving Shirl, he could not make eye contact with Alex.

Fortunately, Cianan answered Alex's question for him. "The Nightshade ruler is holding her captive until we deliver his daughter to him." What he said was factual. Starc was glad he had not mentioned the type of world where Alex's best friend was being held. He should have offered himself as a captive, allowing Shirl to go free. It would have been doubtful Yorik would have agreed, but Starc did not even try.

The confrontation between the men ended as it became clear there were greater issues at hand. "Where are my men?" Raine Narmouth inquired. The information was too sensitive to communicate through any communal pathway. It was unlikely anyone in the city would pick up the conversation, but Starc could understand why Raine vocally asked the question.

"They are dead," Cianan replied, "along with the male prisoner. The Nightshade ruler took them as punishment for our not keeping up with the quota for their blood sacrifice. My sister is being held as a bargaining chip to guarantee our return."

"What blood sacrifice? Where is his daughter?" Alex asked the obvious questions. Concern written all over her face.

Starc found his voice; he could no longer hide his failure from his friends. "Jeryl Jarlyn has a trade agreement with the Nightshade ruler. He gets his damn crystals and we provide our condemned prisoners to feed his people. I am sure you have heard legends of people craving blood. Legends are generally based on fact. Today they became very real to me."

"Are we talking about vampires?" Alex asked in disbelief. "You left Shirl with a bunch of bloody vampires?" There was shock in Alex's expression, not condemnation.

"I had no choice, Alex. They would have killed her and the rest of us. We had no defense against them." Starc ran a hand through his wavy hair. "*Alex, she is my soul mate. Does that give you an idea how difficult it was to leave her behind?*" He shared this though the warrior link, so Raine Narmouth would not hear.

Alex paled before his eyes. She staggered backwards, falling into Tarsea's arm. "Where is the vampire's daughter?" It was clear Alex understood the no win situation he had been placed in.

"Chicago, in the Ginkgo Terra universe," Cianan answered Alex's question. "Darden, you are the only crystal telepath I know that has been to Ginkgo Terra. Are you familiar with where Chicago is?"

"*I know where Chicago is,*" Alex communicated once again through the warrior path. "*Is Sedona the only natural portal on Earth?*" Starc knew nothing would keep Alex from joining them and saving her friend. Tarsea would no doubt try to stop Alex, but Starc needed her to help save his soul mate.

"*I will have to open a portal between Sedona and Chicago. It has been a while since I was forced to open a temporary event horizon. My crystal should have the energy to accomplish the task. We need to get rid of Narmouth and start planning our trip.*" Starc saw his brother eye both him and Tarsea. Darden knew they both hated Narmouth. His twin was going to leave it to one of the two men to dismiss the bastard.

"We will take it from here," Tarsea addressed Raine Narmouth. "Your mission is complete. The girl is in my parents' care. She is my responsibility to rescue. Starc had also been assigned to protect her."

Narmouth did not look eager to leave the group of men. Starc imagined Narmouth was thinking about how he could leverage the rescue of Shirl to some political advantage. After all, she was a surviving daughter of one of the followers of their Prime Ruler's son.

Alex must have had the same thought. She walked up to Narmouth and put her hand on his arm. "I did not have a big breakfast and I am really hungry. Will you buy me lunch again, Raine? You have a lot of explaining to do related to how you have been treating me." As far as Raine was concerned, Alex barely knew Shirl. It would not seem strange that Alex would be willing to leave the men who were planning Shirl's rescue.

Starc knew Alex was sacrificing herself to get Narmouth off their backs. He could not afford to let her soul mate hinder Alex's plan. *Let her do this, Tarsea. Time is of the essence and we need every precious moment to save Shirl. Koel will accompany them to lunch to assure Alex's safety. As soon as we are ready, they will meet us back here and we will get the girl.*

"I am still not comfortable being alone with you after the other night," Alex informed Raine. "My head still hurts from the pounding you gave it. But I do feel there could be something between us. Koel will join us for lunch. That will make me more comfortable." He was amazed at how well Alex could lie. If he had not known better, he would have felt Alex genuinely had feelings for Raine Narmouth.

There was no doubt that as Alex was verbally talking to Narmouth, she was soothing Tarsea through their private channel. Starc had briefly experienced the soul mate channel with Shirl, shortly before he abandoned her. He was sick with worry about what his soul mate was suffering at the hands of the vampires.

If anyone had told Alex she would be walking down the portal mountain trail holding Raine Narmouth's hand, she would have told them they were insane. She could not think of another way to separate Narmouth and the remaining CT Guards from Tarsea and the others. Her primary concern was rescuing Shirl from the Nightshade universe. She still could not believe there was a parallel universe populated by vampires.

When she first came to the Troyk universe, Darden had told her about the portal. Over the years different species used the gateway to travel between parallel worlds. Legends such as vampires, the Fae, and the Greek Gods came from past portal travel. Over time the portal between one world and another would close. That was why the Greek Gods vanished into thin air. Alex had wished it had been those gods that held Shirl, not a band of blood sucking vampires. She would have liked to compare Adonis's body with her soul mate Tarsea's. There was not a doubt in her mind Tarsea would win, hands down.

"I want shrimp for lunch, Raine," Alex communicated through one of the communal channels. She wanted as many people as possible to know she was with Raine Narmouth, so he would be less likely to drag her off somewhere. If she was stuck having a meal with Narmouth, she would have her favorite food as compensation.

"You can have whatever your heart desires, my love," Narmouth whispered in her ear. She wished she could swat him away like the gnat he truly was.

Alex hated when Raine used endearments when he talked to her. He had assaulted her twice, both times she had been saved by the men in her life. She looked over her shoulder to make sure Koel was still with them.

"What do you like to eat, Koel?" she asked her latest body guard. Koel had beaten the crap out of Raine the first time he attacked her. Alex felt better with him along. Hopefully Raine remembered every punch.

"Anything, as long as it is not cooked by Leenea Childers," Koel replied with a laugh. "Raine, how about *Leftovers*? It is close to the bottom of the trail. You will no doubt need to report back to work and explain the deaths of four of your guards."

Raine mumbled something to himself that Alex could not make out. The man had recently been promoted to captain of the Crystal Telepath Guard. She was sure it was not going to look good to lose men on one of his first missions. In addition, he had not entered the portal, as she was sure he had originally planned. His obsession with her had saved his miserable life. He stayed behind to be with her, shirking his duty to the men he was supposed to lead.

Word of what had happened this morning in the Nightshade world had hit the communal pathways. One of the CT Guards who accompanied them must have broadcasted the discussion before they split company with the men. The secret deal that Jeryl Jarlyn had with the vampires of that world was now common knowledge and the people were horrified. It was not widely known that the Troyk condemned were executed by vampires for nourishment.

Alex started to have issues managing the telepathic traffic within the pathways. The concussion that Raine caused the other night had negated what healing her brain had done after her rough ride through the portal. She could no longer contain the telepathic static. Blood ran from her nose.

"Crap," Alex said, "we have to cancel lunch. I cannot go into a restaurant when I am hemorrhaging from my nose. This is your fault, Raine Narmouth! You go back to work. Koel will take me back to the Childers. I need to rest." The nose bleed was really just a trickle, but Alex was going to milk it for everything she could get.

"I will take her back," Koel told Raine. "They are calling you back to headquarters. The communal pathways are buzzing with news. It appears you have quite a bit of explaining to do."

Raine appeared to be in a panic. He looked between Alex and Koel. "I will make this up to you, Alexia. Please get her back safely, Koel. I will check on you later, babe." With those words, he hurried toward the center of town.

"He calls me babe one more time," Alex said under her breath, "I am going to kick him in his jewels! We need to head back to the Childers's home. Some herbs will help with this damn nosebleed. It would not be a bad idea for us to get our fill of the herbal mix, since we are going to Ginkgo Terra. Everyone will struggle with headaches while we are there. The beverage will hopefully reduce the severity of the pain."

They started toward home. Koel provided a report status to the rest of the men still on the mountain. The group needed to formulate a plan to kidnap an innocent woman in order to save her best friend and Starc's soul mate. Right or wrong did not factor into the discussion.

Starc sipped on the herbal concoction, preparing for his first trip to the Ginkgo Terra universe. They determined the location of the Sedona natural portal and where they needed to go in Chicago. The woman lived in a northern suburb of the city.

"It will be easier to manage the girl if she comes willingly. That means we need a mind control telepath to go along with us." No one responded to what Tarsea had said. They had been fighting the use of mind control most of their lives. There was no question it would be easier on everyone if they used the telepathic power, but they would be giving up their principles. Where did you draw the line regarding when mind control was acceptable and unacceptable?

"We are talking about Starc's soul mate, my sister Tarah will do it," Koel responded. Half the group looked at Koel, while the others were still glassy eyed, fighting their own internal battle with right and wrong. "We are family. You do what you have to do for family."

Tarsea considered what Koel said. "Tarah is thirty-two years old. Supposedly a mind control telepath is immune to the mind destroying element in the Ginkgo Terra atmosphere, but I am not willing to take the risk of losing Tarah. Benko Jarlyn has already adapted to the universe's air, we will use him. He has been protecting Shirl most of her life. Besides, it is time to see what this man is really made of." Benko Jarlyn had been the rallying cry of every group against the Troyk government for the last twenty plus years.

"Phoenix is at least a ninety minute drive from Sedona," Alex said. "We may not have the luxury to wait for Benko to join us. That is assuming we can even contact him. Darden cannot waste any of his crystal's energy making a side trip to pick-up Benko either."

"I was due to join up with Cassie yesterday," Darden shared with the group. "Benko was joining his daughter in Sedona this time. If I am late, she will wait several days before heading back to Scottsdale. Odds are, he will still be there when we arrive."

"It is settled then. We are going through the portal to Sedona, and with Benko, we kidnap that poor girl." Tarsea did not sound happy, but was resigned to what was necessary to save Shirl. Starc saw the acceptance of that fact in everyone's expression. Several of his friends and family nodded in agreement.

The plan was in place, but Starc did not participate in its creation. He had failed his soul mate. Alex must have picked up on his mood, since she came and sat next to him. She did not say anything, just took his hand and held it. Starc glanced at Tarsea to see his reaction. Her soul mate merely nodded, understanding that Alex needed to be close to her best friend's soul mate. She knew that Starc did not wish to talk.

Starc thought he and Alex would sit in silence until it was time to go to the portal. He needed peace, to wrap his brain around everything that happened today. That plan was shattered when Darden said through their familiar link, *"We need to talk. Meet me in Zane Childers's study."*

He looked at his twin brother and knew he was not going to like what his brother wanted to discuss. "I need to talk to Darden," Starc said to Alex. "Thank you for the downtime. I figure it will be the last either of us will have for some time." He released her hand and followed his twin.

Starc entered the study and took the chair next to Darden. They both faced Zane Childers's cherry wood desk. The room was filled with heavy wood furniture. There was a rich green and brown blanket on the sofa, a decorative container with facial tissues, but that was the extent of Leanea's influence on her husband's refuge.

Starc wondered what the future held for him and Shirl. Would he have his own space where she would put small touches in decorating the room? A warm sensation filled his heart. He knew what he felt for the girl, he was just concerned it was not enough.

"We need to discuss the legends associated with soul mates and crystal telepathic powers," Darden said, using their familiar link from being twins. *"There are things you should know. It could mean the difference between rescuing your soul mate or condemn her to a short life in the Nightshade universe."*

"I am listening," Starc said.

There was a knock on the door and Alex entered the room. "I am standing in for Shirl," she informed the brothers. She made her way to the chair behind the desk. Due to her diminutive size, she was swallowed up by the chair. Before either Starc or Darden had the time to respond to her presence, Alex continued. "I know you are talking about what happens when soul mates make love. No one knows Shirl better than I do. Her voice needs to be heard."

It was not too long ago that Zane and Tarsea had a similar talk in this room. Alex was in the common room with Starc, as Tarsea had an argument on the same topic they were about to have. The poor girl looked so embarrassed. She ended up walking in on her soul mate and his father's discussion and basically took matters into her own hands. Starc could not fault Alex wanting to represent her best friend.

"All right, you stay, Alex," Starc replied. "Go on, Darden, you were saying." With Alex present, they ceased using their telepathic familial channel.

"No telepathic side conversations between the two of you," Alex warned. "I want to hear everything said."

Starc loved Alex's spunk, "You have it, darling." It was easy using an endearment addressing Alex, since he felt comfortable with her. He still struggled with his feelings concerning his soul mate. Now that she was here, he was interested in what she thought Shirl's feeling would be. He chided himself for not thinking of having her part of the discussion from the beginning.

"Legend states when soul mates have sexual relations the first time, the hormone that brings about the next evolutionary stage of their telepathic powers is excreted." Darden looked at Alex as he uttered those words.

"Darden," Alex responded, "we know that. What we need to know is what those additional powers will mean to a crystal telepath. The additional telepathic abilities I received will not help in Shirl's situation. Are there stories particular to females with her gift?"

"I read all the tales when I was younger," Darden said, "after I found out I was a crystal telepath. The most interesting stories dealt with the rare female crystal telepath. Legendary tales tell of her being able to navigate natural portals without crystals, once mated. She would be able to open a temporary gateway, as easily as she opens a natural gateway." If what Darden shared was true, it would make their escape from Nightshade that much easier.

"Would the talents be more intuitive?" Alex inquired. "Shirl has virtually no experience navigating the portal, let alone opening a temporary gateway."

Darden stared at Alex, considering her question. "I do not know, Alex. These are merely stories. I have no practical experience in these matters. Your experience using telepathic powers shortly after having spent... time with Tarsea would be our best indication."

Starc laughed at Darden's inability to voice that Alex and Tarsea had sex regularly. The momentary release of his laughter helped relieve a little of the stress that overpowered Starc. Almost from the start, they had to pry Alex and Tarsea apart. His experience with Shirl was very different. They would be virtual strangers, forced to have sex to possibly enhance Shirl's crystal telepathic abilities. He was as reluctant to question Alex on that topic, as Darden was to talk about his best friend's sex life with the woman in front of them. They did not have the luxury of time, Starc had to know.

"Alex, I have had one momentary physical contact with Shirl. I feel protective of her, but no sexual desire. She has shown no signs of being attracted to me, as you were attracted to Tarsea. How would she react in a rescue mission if we needed to have sex in order to escape confinement?"

Alex paled before his eyes. She had been forced to have relations with Tarsea before they would normally have had it, in order to trigger their enhanced abilities. Tarsea told him Alex's body was one raging hormone, but her brain fought the attraction. It was Alex in the end who seduced her soul mate.

"Shirl is no virgin, but does not have a lot of experience. Sex has never been pleasurable for her, probably because her partner was not you. I told her what happened between me and Tarsea. If you need to have intercourse with her at a moment's notice to save each other, don't hesitate. You can wine and romance her later. She will understand what needs to be done and not hold it against you." Starc was sickened they were even having this conversation. The woman was his soul mate and deserved so much more than quick sex for a purpose other than love. They might not have time to discuss their actions like Tarsea and Alex had. The last thing he wanted was to rape his soul mate.

Tarsea communicated through the warrior link, *"We have to get going. Finish up whatever you are talking about. It is time to leave for the portal."*

Alex got up from the gigantic chair and made her way around the desk. She walked up to Starc and embraced him. "Bring her home safe. Everything can be worked out when she is out of danger. I wish I was going with you. Tarsea does not want me going because of the concussion. For once I am not arguing with him. He is right." Starc knew how much Alex wanted to go with them and how much staying back cost her.

"I will not come back without her, Alex," Starc said, as he looked at his brother. Darden nodded, understanding what his brother was truly saying.

Darden handed Starc a crystal on a sterling silver chain. "In case she cannot get her crystal back from the vampire, she may be able to use this as a substitute. Keep it close to your skin. The crystal was partially phased to her this morning. Since you are soul mates, I am hoping contact with you will complete the phasing. I plan to be by your side, but you need to give this to her if we are separated."

Starc held the crystal in his hand. It was an amethyst, not too different from the one Shirl wore. He put on the necklace and tucked the crystal under his tunic. Rather than feeling cold against his skin, the amethyst was warm. For an instant he felt closer to his soul mate. He knew she still lived and was depending on him to rescue her. Starc was determined not to fail her again.

Chapter 10

~

The Nightshade Universe

Shirl woke naked and cold. She was still on the chaise lounge she had crawled onto earlier, as she listened to Chartail's screams. Guilt consumed her as she thought how her body reacted to what Drake had done to her. Chartail had been violated by the vampire that claimed her. She was not sure how she was going to face the other woman. Shirl knew she needed to find Chartail and see what she could do for the poor thing. They promised each other they were there for each other.

A robe was draped on the chair next to where Shirl had fallen asleep. It must have been viewed as showing too much compassion to have actually covered her. They would find no allies in this terrible place. She rose from the lounge and wrapped herself in terry cloth. Shirl had a similar robe hanging in her closet at home. Drake pointed out earlier that the women's quarters were through the door just behind her.

She reluctantly placed her hand on the handle of the door that led to where she would possibly find Chartail. Secretly she hoped the door would be locked, but it opened easily. She left her small spa and entered into a large elaborate one. Women in various states of dress were spread around the pool and surrounding areas. Shirl felt she had somehow landed in a harem straight from some movie related to *The Arabian Nights*. She fully expected Scheherazade to start telling enticing tales. No one spoke to her as she made her way around the large pool. She could not help but stare at the women she passed. As with the ones who escorted her earlier, they all showed signs of vampire violence upon their skin. She became more anxious, not finding Chartail among them.

"Chartail, where are you?" Shirl called to her. She continued making her way around the pool, then heard moaning behind an area draped in red satin. Cautiously, Shirl followed the moans, pulling back the fabric. There lay Chartail, in a semi-conscious state. She was naked, bleeding from numerous wounds that covered her body. Shirl stood in shock, not knowing what to do.

"Move away, girl," a woman said behind her. She moved aside to allow the woman access to Chartail. "Make yourself useful and help me clean out the wounds this poor girl received. We do not want them to get infected. That is a worse death than at the hands of these monsters."

Shirl took a warm cloth and watched as Florence Nightingale cleaned the wounds. She cared for Chartail in the same manner she had witnessed. "She needs a doctor," Shirl told the woman.

"All a doctor will do is give her an injection that will allow her body to replace the blood she lost ten times faster than normal. That will give this poor child no relief from Yorik's blood lust. I see Drake's mark on your neck. You got off easy. No vampire will dare touch you."

"Who are you?" Shirl could no longer contain her curiosity. The woman appeared to understand how things worked around here. She looked to be in her late forties and did not have any bite marks on her body. She had salt and pepper hair, gray eyes and was still very attractive. Shirl wondered how she managed to ward off the vampires.

"My name is Rosemarie. I live in the city outside the Nightshade structure," the woman responded to Shirl's question. She continued to administer to Chartail as they talked. "They pay me to take care of the girls brought here." Whatever employment arrangement they had included not taking Rosemarie's blood.

"I came through a portal to this world, so I am unaware of what city or structure you are talking about. Are you free to come and go from this place?" Shirl had so many questions she wanted to ask. She needed to be careful and get critical information before the woman left.

"There is a structure several miles wide that filters out the sun," Rosemarie said. "I suppose you could call it a large tarp that allows the vampires to walk outside during the day. The city is a short train ride away. We barter our labor or blood to survive in this parallel universe. There are similar setups throughout the Nightshade world."

"Can I walk out with you and accompany you to this city?" Shirl asked. She was not optimistic she was going to like the answer, but she had to ask.

"You belong to a vampire. There is no leaving this area without being accompanied by Drake. As I said, you carry his mark. Every woman here belongs to either a single vampire or the collective."

"What is the collective?" The more information she gathered, the greater chance she had of surviving. She prayed Starc would make it back, but she had to make contingency plans.

"Those who are members of Yorik's nest are considered the collective," Rosemarie responded. They finished caring for Chartail's wounds. The woman covered her with a blanket. "The girls that service the collective do not last long. It is better to catch the eye of a vampire and have him claim you. Then you feed a single vampire."

"Where do these women come from? You said you offer labor or blood to survive. I cannot imagine anyone would willingly offer their lives, to die in this fashion."

"Nightshade is at war," Rosemarie said. "The girls who belong to the collective are those vassals the vampires cannot protect. This world also has three portals. Random people fall through the portal several times a month from different worlds. They provide immediate blood or are used to strengthen the gene pool. Humans in some parts of this world are bred like cattle. Anything to keep the blood flowing and not contaminated."

A chill ran down Shirl's body. If Yorik or Drake lost a battle, she and Chartail could be sold to another vampire lord and end up belonging to a collective. Their life expectancy would possibly not be long enough for Starc to return with Yorik's daughter.

"You do not need to worry, you belong to Drake. Royalty is not involved in this war." Rosemarie left Shirl, as she pondered the woman's words. She looked at Chartail, pale from the loss of blood. Shirl sat in the only chair in the small area they occupied. She was not sure how effective she would be, but Shirl would do her best to protect Chartail from further harm. Chartail would not survive another attack.

Shirl woke as two vampires entered their area. Yorik followed closely behind his guards. She stood without thinking, placing herself between Chartail and the master vampire. It might turn out to be a losing cause, but Shirl would not sit by and let Yorik violate Chartail again. Shirl needed to gather what courage she had.

"She has barely recovered from your last attack," Shirl confronted the master vampire. "Chartail needs more time to garner her strength." Shirl was extremely nervous, she was afraid she would vomit. Her knees were shaking so badly, she was surprised she was still standing.

Yorik stood in front of Shirl, placing a hand on her throat and the other at the back of her neck. His hands were cold and dry, nothing like Drake's. Rather than being turned on, she was repulsed by Yorik's touch. He had fury written all over his face.

"I see that Drake has marked you," Yorik snarled. "That is the only reason you are standing and not dead at my feet. The woman you foolishly try to keep from me belongs body, blood, and soul to me. You will leave now, or I will do to this woman what I would have done to you. I can get my blood from any of the slaves who occupy this harem."

For some weird reason, Shirl would have stood her ground if the vampire had only threatened her. Since the warning was targeted at Chartail, she had no option but to leave. She was about to exit when Drake entered. Shirl stood back, closer to the bed, where a still unconscious Chartail lay.

"Not taking proper care of your new toy, I see," Drake addressed Yorik. He said those words with no emotion. His face, however, showed outrage. "You should learn self-discipline. The woman is a prize and she will be dead before the day is out if you continue."

Warmth spread through Shirl's body. She was not sure if it was a reaction to Drake trying to save Chartail or another reason all together. As much as she was repulsed by Yorik, the opposite was true regarding her reaction to the Prince of Vampires.

Yorik left without another word. His guards followed, not daring to look at Drake. He went to Chartail and lifted her wrist. "Her pulse is weak, but steady. Yorik will not return this evening. Your friend will live through the night. Now, my beauty, you owe me a bounty for saving her life." Unlike the other vampires, Drake's eyes were clear of the blood lust. However, a different type of lust shown from his eyes.

Shirl followed him without a word. They walked toward the entrance to the small spa area, she had originally occupied. Relief spread through her body, there was no bed present. She feared his sexual advances more than she feared his taking her blood. Blood was nourishment, while sex with Drake would be very personal. Starc had told her to do anything it took to survive. Her mind started justifying the act of sex with this vampire, would be in the pursuit of saving her life. If she kept telling herself that, maybe she would believe it.

They entered the small spa exactly as it had been when he first touched her. She needed to get her mind off her attraction to him. "Yorik is the master here, but he fears you. One of the servants said you are royalty. What influence do you hold over him?"

Drake smiled, his face appeared to have more color with that simple action. "For a vampire, blood is everything. The life force that pumps throughout my body contains the oldest blood of our kind. We do not have to fight over petty things such as land and fealty, our blood gives us ultimate power." As he spoke he ran his hands up and down Shirl's arms. The motion was both distracting and turning her on. Blood was power where Drake was concerned, knowledge was what would ultimately save her. Shirl needed to focus and gather as much information as she could.

"I do not understand. Do you have the ability to set me free, regardless if my friends bring back Yorik's daughter?" Shirl moved away from the friction his attention caused. She was too hot and wanted this man too much. When had she started thinking of Drake as a man, not a vampire?

Drake moved to once again place her body within his reach. His hands caressed her lower back. "I have claimed you, no harm will come to you if your friends fail in their mission." Once again she wondered what his claiming meant, if she could ever escape this man. How many had been in her position over the centuries. He said his blood was the oldest of their kind.

"How old are you?" Shirl inquired.

"You are from the Ginkgo Terra universe. You could not comprehend how old my blood is. Your species were not standing erect when my master made me. I do not have words to describe how the cosmos created such a creature as he. Such an oddity that would feed off any living thing it could find. Over several millennia his diet changed to the blood that feeds my body today."

Her life and her story seemed so insignificant compared to the man who stood before her. She had lived twenty-three years. The things he must have seen over that time. It was flattering that one such as he would be interested in her. His eyes drank in her essence, as if he was drinking her blood.

"What happens when my brother and my soul mate deliver the girl? Although you said you have claimed me, will you allow me to leave?" Shirl wondered if she wanted to leave this man. She desired to leave the world Yorik ruled, but not necessarily Drake. If he offered to take her elsewhere, would she choose him over a soul mate she had known for such a short period of time? Alex had a violent reaction to her soul mate even before they touched. There was no such connection to Starc.

"That, my love, is up to you. You say he is your soul mate, but could that be the case with the reaction you had to me?" Drake ran his tongue along her throat. Her legs were barely holding her up. She had such an all-consuming fire building within her. He must have sensed her weakness as he guided her back to one of the lounges. "I have had more partners than I can remember, with a very few I can actually say I loved. You will join that elite group if you stay."

"What happened to all the women over the years?" There must have been so many. He was truly immortal. It was likely that one day he would not remember her, as he had forgotten so many of the women in his life.

"Immortality is a curse that most cannot handle. Mortality. The shorter the life span, the more one appreciates what one has before him. Few make it more than several centuries." Shirl considered his words. She hated being bored, always looking for something to occupy herself.

When the headaches started, all she did was lay around and do nothing. Would life with Drake eventually result in such inactivity, minus the pain? She had been so excited about the possibility of traveling to other worlds. The idea of such travel caused her pulse to react.

Drake gently removed the scabs that had developed over the wound he caused yesterday when he drank from her. His fangs entered her neck once again. He drew her blood into his mouth. His bite still did not hurt. However, she did not feel the thrall take over as it did before. Was he losing his control over her? When he finished, he backed up and leaned against the wall.

"I have recently started to live again, Drake. My mother's crystal will open worlds I did not even hope to dream about. I cannot imagine just lying here, waiting for you to visit. There is a strong attraction to you, but I know it would wither with the life you offer."

A strange look crossed Drake's face. It was as if he had come to the realization that what he had hoped would develop between the two of them was lost forever. "Even with the strength of the soul mate bond, I have lost you."

Shirl did not understand what he was saying. "Starc is my soul mate. There was something else between us which I was helpless to fight." There was no condemnation in her voice, just the truth.

"I am one of the most powerful vampires you will ever encounter," Drake continued. "When Starc mentioned the existence of a soul mate connection, I merely leveraged that psychic wave length. Everything you felt should have been exactly what you would have experienced with Starc. There must be something within your bond to him I was not able to recreate."

Shirl stood mute. He had manipulated her mind, as well as her body. She felt betrayed. All this time she felt guilty about being disloyal to her soul mate, Drake had used that connection and used it for his own gain. Shirl hugged herself, as a cold wave of shame engulfed her. Although they had not had sex, she had reacted to his touch. Part of her rationalized what she would have gone though, had he not tricked her. However, the greater part of her was angry and close to tears.

Drake placed his hand in his pocket and pulled out her crystals. He walked to her. Drake lifted the necklaces over her head and placed them around her neck. Gently he lifted her hair so the delicate gold chains would not snag. "Let us hope your brother and the mate of your soul are successful in their mission. If he does not become the mate of your heart, you know where you can find me."

"I am never returning to this hellish world, Drake," Shirl informed him. The mere thought produced goose bumps along her arm.

Drake rubbed her arms. Although the soul mate bond was no longer being manipulated, Shirl did feel something as Drake continued to massage her. She felt it best not to explore her reaction.

"Never is a long time," Drake responded. "If you return, wear this gem. It will give you free passage within the Nightshade universe until you are once again at my side." Drake slipped another necklace around her neck.

Shirl looked in wonder at the blood opal Drake had given her. The stone was primarily black and red with fragments of green at the top. "Opals are water stones. They help ease handling change in one's life. They enhance memory and decrease confusion. I find it ironic you have given me the love stone, since it was never love you offered."

"I only offer what I can give, Shirl. I am a man of action, not words."

He walked toward the exit. "Drake," Shirl said as her voice broke with emotion, "I have one request of you. When they bring the girl, you will offer her your protection, as you offered it to me. Yorik may be her father, but that does not mean he will not brutalize the poor thing." The guilt associated with trading her life for the other woman's would be less burdensome if she knew Drake looked out for her. "You owe me that much. Who knows, maybe she will be the woman you can spend eternity with."

Drake looked at her with an intensity, drinking in the sight of her. It felt like a goodbye, even though he would continue to protect her as long as she was in this universe. Shirl knew he would no longer try to seduce her. His quest for someone to spend the loneliness of forever with would continue.

He merely nodded and left. Shirl sat on the lounge and pondered where Starc was. Drake's words about Starc becoming the soul mate of her heart made her long for the man for the first time since their initial touch. Would their coming together be as explosive as what she felt with Drake? The vampire had hijacked what she would have felt for her soul mate for his own benefit. It was clear he had not fully captured what she would ultimately have with her soul mate. She could now only hope that Starc would make Yorik's deadline.

Chapter 11

Starc took a sip of the caramel colored beverage that Alex said was Shirl's favorite. The cloying taste of sugar coated his taste buds and he wanted to gag. He watched his brother drain his glass and order another one. Alex had said that taking caffeine with headache medication helped to further relieve tension-type headaches. He decided to chew on herbs and have a shot of alcohol while they waited for Benko Jarlyn to arrive. Darden had immediately contacted Benko with the cell phone he carried when he traveled to Ginkgo Terra. The technology was foreign to him. Anything and everything could be broadcast through communal pathways at home. There was no need for technology that carried voice.

"What is the closest drink to stoak?" Starc asked his brother. Stoak was distilled keen, a drink all three men drank when they went to a bar in the Aster Province. He needed something that would calm his nerves. Benko Jarlyn was taking too long to meet up with them. Time was running out for Shirl.

The waitress dropped off another sugar water. His brother asked the waitress, "Bring him a shot of your house whiskey, please."

The waitress glanced at Starc and smiled, "Would you like anything to eat?" In the Troyk universe, orders in restaurants were given telepathically. Generally, as soon as you ordered your drink, it was immediately delivered to your table. He was not used to waiting, as he did in this world. There was no question, his anxiety regarding Shirl had eliminated any patience he usually possessed.

Darden looked at the three men that shared the table with him. He considered the menu and then ordered an item called wings and fried something. Starc could not help glancing toward the entrance of the restaurant, waiting for

Benko Jarlyn and his daughter Cassandra. The man was a legend and he would soon meet him. Shirl's life depended on Benko helping them, as did the future of their universe.

His drink was delivered and Starc drained the glass. The liquid burned as it made its way down his throat. He considered ordering another when a middle-aged man and a young woman entered the bar. Without introductions, he knew who the man was.

Benko Jarlyn did not resemble his father, but the mother who had been a one night stand with the Troyk Prime Ruler. Jeryl Jarlyn had taken his son and raised him in what he hoped would be an image of himself. Like Jeryl, Benko was a mind control telepath. Unlike his father, he did not feel the gift should be used to manipulate others. When he was barely twenty years old, he staged an unsuccessful rebellion against his father. Benko could no longer tolerate the choices that were taken away from the Troyk populace. Mind control tele-paths directed what they purchased, where they lived and how they spent their time. Free will existed only where someone had no doubt regarding what they wanted or if the mind control telepath had no desire to sway opinion. There had been no restrictions over what they influenced, including the act of sex.

Starc examined Benko as he walked toward their table. He had rich brown hair, graying around his temple. The man walked with confidence, as if he owned the establishment. Every woman in the restaurant took note of him, as he crossed the room. Benko had a short conversation with the waitress and finally arrived at their table. As he joined them, Starc noticed Benko had light honey brown eyes.

He had been so focused on Benko Jarlyn, he had not noticed the girl who entered with him, until she walked into his brother's embrace. Cassie Jarlyn was his brother's soul mate. Like Tarsea and Alex, Darden and Cassie looked like they fit together. Starc had never embraced his soul mate, as Darden was holding Cassandra Jarlyn. He had only held Shirl as terror presented itself before their eyes.

"We have a situation," Darden said to Benko Jarlyn. He released Cassie and proceeded to introduce the new arrivals to Starc, Tarsea, and Cianan. They still did not know where Cianan's allegiances lay, so Darden provided more information through the warrior link. *"I will introduce you as Ben Clark. We do not know if Cianan is loyal to your father. You are simply the father of my girlfriend, who knows Chicago."*

"I have procured a small dining room where we can talk in private. The waitress will bring another round of drinks and the food you ordered." Benko gestured for the group to follow him. Starc left the remains of the soda he had ordered on the table. He could use another whiskey.

Darden looked in deep thought as they made their way to the separate room. He must have been trying to figure out what he could share orally and what he had to share through the warrior channel. It would be so convenient if Cianan started to pick up their conversation in that channel. They would know he could be trusted. Only people that were loyal to the true leader of the Troyk universe would be able to converse in that private telepathic channel.

"Cassie's father is aware of where I am from and my telepathic gift to travel through the portal. When I contacted Cassie, I asked her to bring her dad. He is familiar with Chicago and the suburb where Yorik's daughter resides." Darden explained to the group, establishing the cover story for Cianan.

"Shirl opened the portal while searching for Alexandra. She was interviewed by your father and then released. He knew of her crystal telepathic abilities and sent her to the Nightshade universe. She is being held captive there until we deliver the master vampire's daughter. We will need you to travel to Chicago and convince the girl she needs to come with us. I know this goes against everything you believe in, but it is Shirl's life we are talking about."

Starc could see that Benko was trying not to react to what Darden was telling him. The drinks were delivered and the legend took a healthy sip of his beer. "I understand what you are up against. I will do everything in my power to assist you in getting your friend back." He shared more information with the group through the warrior path. *"When my father made that unholy alliance with the Nightshade rulers that was the friction point that caused me to unsuccessfully rise up against him. Your friend is in peril because of my father. I do not like to use my skills, but in this case, I can do it with no guilt. Besides, I owe it to her parents to continue to look after her."*

"You seem awful familiar with our world," Cianan commented.

"I did not like my daughter dating an older man. Darden was forthcoming with me concerning who and what he was. Naturally, I did not believe him. When he took me on the trail where the natural portal between worlds exists, I wanted to know more. We have so many legends of gods, monsters, and other creatures. It made sense that such beings came to our world at points in time through such portals. With a telepathic being who could control portal travel in front of me, why would I not believe in a world of vampires?"

"Who said anything about vampires?" Cianan responded. Starc knew that Cianan was suspicious of who this Ben Clark was. He was a member of Jeryl Jarlyn's gatherers, men who searched for Benko Jarlyn.

"Darden mentioned it when he called us and requested our help," Benko replied. "Listen, we are wasting valuable time. I understand the girl is your sister. You should be doing everything in your power to rescue her, not cross examining a friend who is here to help." Starc could not help but admire Benko. The man was more than what legends depicted him to be. Here was a man who spent his adulthood in a world that was not his own. He offered to assist them without hesitation.

Their food arrived and Starc realized he was starving. He had barely eaten earlier this morning before they ventured to Ginkgo Terra. Starc rationalized he also needed energy to rescue Shirl. Before he knew it, he had a pile of chicken bones sitting in front of him. The Troyk universe brought back food and inventions from other worlds. He wondered why chicken wings were not served in his world. His mouth was still on fire from the hot sauce placed on the chicken. Alex or Shirl would have to help Tolfer reproduce the recipe. For the first time, he felt confident they would rescue his soul mate. He did not know if it was Benko's presence or that they were one portal trip away from their quarry.

As they were finishing their meals, Starc could feel a headache coming on. He grabbed more herbs and chewed on them, something he noticed the others were doing as well. He could not believe that Darden would spend days in this world, fighting constantly with the headaches. Yet again, he thought of his soul mate and what she must have suffered as this world's atmosphere attacked her brain.

Darden stood and addressed the group. "We should find an isolated spot and I will open a portal to where Yorik's daughter lives. Once we have her, I will take Cassie and Ben back to Sedona."

"That will not be necessary," Benko responded. "We will find our way back. Your first priority is rescuing Shirl. Cassie and I do not want her spending any more time in that world than necessary. We'll enjoy the sights of Chicago for a day or two. It would be a shame to travel there and not enjoy their deep dish pizza." Once again, Benko did not disappoint Starc. When he had Shirl home and settled, Starc wanted to return here and work with Benko to plan his campaign back to the Troyk universe. What was a little headache when it came to creating a better world to raise his children? He had never really considered the future before, his support in the past had been to seek out vengeance.

Tarsea shook Benko's hand. "It was a pleasure meeting you, sir. I hope the next time we meet, it will be under better circumstances. Darden has mentioned you and I had looked forward to meeting you. I am sure my girlfriend, Alex, would like to eventually meet you." Starc knew that Tarsea would want Benko to know that Alexandra, whom he watched over her whole life, was safe in the Troyk universe. *"She is my soul mate. Thank you for keeping her safe after her parents died. She has thrived in our world, but you need to come home and take your rightful place. We will be prepared when you want to make your move, but do not wait too long. There are more uprisings and we cannot get to everyone in time."*

Benko stood, "We should be on our way. Chicago is two hours ahead of us. It would make sense to arrive when it is still light out. Dusk is the perfect time to arrive and grab the girl."

Starc had expected Benko to respond to Tarsea's words. It should not have surprised him when he did not. One battle at a time. This time he would be fighting for Starc's soul mate. The next time, perhaps a world.

In all the years Starc had been a CT Guard, he had never been through a forced portal. Within this portal, he could barely make out the frequency emitting from Darden's crystal. The crystal that his brother gave him for Shirl, lay cold against his chest. Like a natural portal, there was little turbulence within the void they traveled. It was not lost on him that Darden had control, otherwise they would be falling through nothingness until a random portal opened.

They emerged in a wooded area, just outside a city teeming with people. Yorik's daughter, Afton, attended Northwestern University in Evanston. The shadows created by the trees and the time of day, helped to cloak them from pedestrians along the sidewalk. They just had to find their way to McCulloch Hall on Sheridan Road.

Before they left Sedona, they decided that Cassie would approach the girl. Cassie would represent herself as a high school senior, who was going to attend Northwestern in the fall and wanted to check out the campus. Like her father, Cassie was a mind control telepath. She would use her telepathic gift to bring

Yorik's daughter to the rest of the group. Benko would then convince Afton that she wanted to see her father. No one was proud of what they were doing, but Shirl's life was in jeopardy.

Starc watched as Cassie entered the dorm. He wondered where Shirl went to school and if she lived in similar student housing. They were running too close to the time that Yorik had given them. If the girl was not in her dorm or had taken off with some boy, they would not meet the deadline to save Shirl. Darden was as agitated as he was, as he watched his brother pace.

He exhaled a breath of relief, as Cassie exited the building with a tall, pale, dark haired girl. The two young women were dressed similarly. Under different circumstances, the two could be going out to a bar to have some fun, since neither were carrying books.

They had decided that Darden and Benko would emerge as soon as they saw Cassie walking onto the well-lit sidewalk. Cassie would introduce her father and say Darden was her older brother. The plan was dependent on Afton having the slightest desire to see her father. Everyone knew a mind control telepath could not force someone to do something they did not want to do. They prayed on indecision, even if it was just a smidgen of desire or doubt.

Starc could hear his heart pounding as he watched the small group conversing under the street lamp. He saw Afton nod. That was a good sign. The girl smiled in response to something Cassie said. Guilt consumed Starc. He was sending this young woman to God only knew what. Shirl was depending on him to save her.

The small party made their way toward the rest of the men. "Afton, this is Starc, Tarsea, and Cianan. They are coming with us to see your father. Remember I told you we were going through a portal to another world. There is nothing to be afraid of."

Under normal circumstances, finding out you were going to be walking through a portal, would tend to cause a great deal of anxiety. Benko's control of the girl's mind was strong, she actually appeared to be excited at the prospect. Afton had a huge smile on her face and walked forward to stand near Darden. She took his hand as he opened the portal that would take them to the Nightshade universe. Cianan and Tarsea followed the two into the portal.

"Thank you both for what you did," Starc said. "I know it was not easy to manipulate the girl's mind. Had Shirl not been in danger, I would never have asked such a thing." Starc did not wait for a reply. He walked through the portal, knowing his soul mate would be on the other side.

Would Yorik be true to his word? Did a blood lust vampire attack and kill Shirl while they were gone? Drake had promised he would protect her. Had the vampire kept his word? What condition would he find his soul mate in? So many questions and concerns crossed his mind, as the void within the portal consumed him.

As Starc emerged from the portal, he was greeted with screams coming from a female. Afton was in her father's embrace and was hysterical. Even a mind control telepath at this point would not be able to convince the girl her father was not a monster. Darden and Tarsea stood close to the girl and her father, but did not attempt to separate the two. As before, the room was full of vampires with blood lust showing in their eyes.

"We have delivered your daughter. The female crystal telepath should be returned to us and we will leave your world. This is simply what was agreed to." Starc said, hoping the master vampire would stick to their arrangement.

Yorik did not hear him or did not wish to respond to. The creature stroked his daughter, as someone would a cat. Two women came for the girl and took her away. Afton yelled for Darden, as she was dragged from the room. Starc could only imagine what his brother was feeling at this point.

"I now have two males and a female with crystal telepathic abilities. What a treasure I have been able to obtain. My people are starving and you hold the ability to bring people to my world to save my dying race. The friend you brought with you can return to your world." Yorik spoke with regal bearing, but it did not seem to faze the four men before him.

"A deal was struck. My sister, for your daughter. We delivered our end. A ruler such as yourself would naturally be true to his word. Let her return with our friend," Cianan sucked up to the master vampire. Starc hoped Yorik would consider Cianan's words. The butterflies in Starc's stomach wildly fluttered as a menacing grin crossed the master vampire's face. He knew before Yorik voiced a word, he was not going to like what he was about to say.

"My word is my bond. The female crystal telepath may leave. However, the three of you will stay. Your world still owes me tribute and two crystal telepathic men will support the efforts to feed my starving people. The brother who travels with you will stay as insurance that you both will return." With a simple gesture, the vampire guard came to remove them from the room.

"Wait," Darden yelled, "let us at least see the woman. She is new to her telepathic powers and I want to assure she will be able to navigate the portal. It would be a waste to both our worlds if she loses her way within the void." Starc could see that Darden's request was being considered by Yorik. The vampire must have been weighing what he would gain allowing the three of them to be re-united with Shirl. Most off-world people did not know that a crystal telepath, under certain conditions could open a portal anywhere.

Yorik appeared to be wavering. Starc decided to continue where his brother left off, hopefully tipping the scales in their favor. "A threat is only as good as your word to follow through. How do we know Shirl is alive? Holding me hostage to assure my brother's compliance is worthless, if he cannot trust I will still be breathing upon his return."

The vampire approached them. It appeared the blood lust impacting his eyes had weakened. They were now a lighter shade of red. "There is logic in what you say." Starc almost laughed. Logic seemed to be the last trait he would imagine a vampire, who was barely holding back his hunger, would possess. "You will be taken to the female telepath. For the time being, however, you will not be needing these." The master vampire removed the crystals that both his brother and Cianan wore.

Yorik motioned once again for the guards to remove them from his presence. Starc held his breath, as the guard escorted them from the room. He prayed the crystal he wore underneath his tunic would remain undetected. Shirl would be able to harness the power of the crystal to open a temporary portal out of the Nightshade universe. The only hurdle that remained, was making love to his soul mate. The thought of forcing her to have intercourse with him to save their lives was abhorrent. He just knew no other means to leave this world.

Chapter 12

〜

Shirl paced her small haven within this hellish world. She wore a short white toga that draped over one shoulder. It was what the women in the harem wore, if they were allowed to wear anything. The bare shoulder allowed the vampire easier access to their victim's life blood.

Her neck had barely healed before Drake reinforced his mark on her flesh. During his last visit, Shirl was able to convince him to have Chartail brought to her room. She had used the promise he had made her to the best of her ability. Shirl knew if she asked too much, her words would eventually fall on deaf ears.

Chartail moaned, bringing her attention back to her new friend. Her body was ravished with more bite marks than Shirl cared to count. The drug they gave her replenished her blood at an alarming rate, allowing Yorik to harvest her several times a day. The last time Yorik came, he took Chartail's blood and raped her in front of Shirl. Fortunately, Chartail was in such bad shape, she was oblivious to being violated.

Drake held her back from any feeble attempt she could make to protect the woman. All Drake could do was stop Yorik from killing his tribute. Shirl started to think maybe it would be a blessing if Chartail died from one of the attacks. Although Shirl had no sense of time in this place, she knew time was running out for both of them.

Shirl adjusted the blanket covering Chartail. She was not coming back to consciousness, merely vocalizing the tormented dreams she was enduring. The sound of the wood door scraping against the stone floor grabbed her attention.

It was too soon for Yorik to visit Chartail again. The woman would not survive another attack at this time.

She turned toward the entrance, prepared to hold off Yorik. Shirl was at the point where she was prepared to offer him her blood. Perhaps with the master vampire's mark on her as well, Drake would take more decisive action toward her and Chartail.

She almost did not believe her eyes as they basked on Starc, Darden, Tarsea, and her brother. Whether it was sheer relief or the soul mate connection, she immediately went into Starc's arms. Shirl had been used to cold turning to heat when Drake held her. This was something quite different. Starc's skin was scorching hot against hers. It felt as if her blood was boiling.

Shirl kissed him, as a thirst for his taste overwhelmed her. Her body craved his. Starc's strong hands grabbed her hips and lifted her to his body. She wrapped her legs around his waist, as Starc carried her the short distance to one of the stone walls. Shirl felt the cold stone against her back, but it did little to relieve the intense heat coming off her body.

Shirl continued to devour Starc. She became aware of male voices at the edge of her consciousness. Her body disregarded what little her brain was capable of communicating. Only the urgency to have this man inside her mattered. The fact there was an audience was completely lost to her. Shirl had never reacted this way to a man in her life. She could barely breathe for the need that engulfed her being. Her one coherent thought was that the mating bond was righting itself, after Drake's manipulation of it. Presently it was overcompensating, as it tried to find the right balance.

The ripping of her panties, away from her body, barely registered within her overwhelmed brain. Starc adjusted his hold on her and entered her with one thrust. Her mind flashed to a scene from *Wild Orchid* where the Carrie Ottis character witnessed two people making love against a wall in a ruined resort.

Shirl had wondered what it was like to be so overcome with desire. She now knew. Starc released his claim on her mouth. Shirl took in air, replenishing the oxygen in her lungs. Breathing was overrated. She placed her mouth back on his, needing Starc like Drake needed blood.

Her universe narrowed to just this man and what he was doing to her body and soul. He drove in and out of her. No words penetrated her mind, his cock did all the communication necessary. Nothing existed to Shirl except her soul mate and the urgency building within her. She was on the cusp of something she knew would be mind-blowing magnificent. There could have been an eighty piece marching band playing in the room, she would have been ignorant of their existence.

Starc kept thrusting, filling her to the hilt. She met his frenzied rate. Shirl could feel him deep inside her womb. There was a part of her that needed him deeper. Reaching where no man could ever go physically.

Shirl adjusted her body, trying to accommodate even an additional centimeter of him. She pounded on his back for more. There was an itch inside of her, she never knew existed, but Starc was satisfyingly scratching it. He continued to drill inside of her. The static within her body was building until Shirl was not sure she could take anymore. He exploded in her, relieving his body of his seed, as she cried out with her own release.

She had never climaxed with a man before. There was nothing she could compare to what they just shared. She knew it was more than most women on Earth would have experienced. Shirl had barely steadied her breathing when her brain sizzled. There was no other way to describe it. She started to panic, as the euphoria of making love with her soul mate wore off.

For the first time, Shirl purposely linked into the soul mate channel. *"What is happening to me? It is as if my brain is frying."*

Starc held his soul mate, as his brain excreted what would trigger the next evolutionary stage of their telepathic powers. He was barely functioning again mentally. A biological need took over his body and mind, as soon as Shirl came into his arms. His animalistic need to mate, overcame any rational thought he possessed.

He reassured Shirl that what was happening to them both was a natural process. *"A hormone is generated the first time soul mates make love. You will be able to manipulate your crystal in new miraculous ways. That includes being able to open a temporary portal with little effort."*

Starc had been dreading how he was going to talk Shirl into making love. However, as soon as they touched, a combustion occurred like nothing he had never experienced before. He did not know if it was them or something magical with soul mates that caused the frenzy that just occurred.

"Are you two finished yet?" his soul mate's brother bellowed. As he made love to Shirl he lost the reality that three men were just a few yards away. That was how consuming his passion for Shirl exhibited itself. He stood in front of Shirl, shielding her from their eyes. Too little, too late in his opinion.

Starc could see Shirl's face redden with embarrassment. She had been so overwhelmed, she must have lost her perception too. He glanced at Cianan and saw him leaning over Chartail Adholm. Tarsea was on the other side of Chartail, administering what aid he could. Had someone described her condition to him, Starc would not have believed it. The woman looked like she had been attacked by a pack of wild dogs.

As Shirl adjusted her toga, she said, "We should not communicate through the communal pathways. At least one vampire was able to hear a telepathic conversation I had with Chartail." She stepped around Starc, facing the men present when they performed the extremely personal act, moments before.

Although she did not look them directly in the eye, Starc knew Shirl was ready to move forward and leave this terrible place. More color returned to her cheeks, although she was still dreadfully pale.

Starc took his soul mate's hand and walked toward the injured woman. Chartail's condition allowed him to concentrate on something other than what had just occurred between him and Shirl. No words of love or telepathic connection existed between them while they had sex.

"What in the name of all that is holy happened to her?" Starc stared in disbelief at the woman lying before him, then whipped his head toward his mate. He noticed the mark on Shirl's neck. He was torn between hatred and appreciation for the man who claimed Shirl. Drake had violated his soul mate's neck, taking her blood. Looking at Chartail, he shuddered to think what Shirl would have looked like if Drake had not intervened.

"Yorik," Shirl said. "I did everything I could to help her. That animal was relentless. Drake stopped him several times from ripping her to shreds." At that point Shirl started crying. The tears were not for what she had endured, but for what the woman in front of them did. Starc took her into his arms. Heat once again generated between them. He released his soul mate, they could not afford to lose their minds and bodies again.

Darden approached Shirl and touched her crystals. "Drake returned them to you. We will not need the back-up crystal Starc wears. I was afraid Yorik would discover it when he took ours."

"I am not leaving without Chartail," Shirl stated. "Regardless of her crime, no one deserves what she has had to endure. Darden, just tell me what I need to do to open a temporary portal." His soul mate had a determination he had not seen her display in the short time he had known her. Pride for Shirl warmed his heart. This experience, although horrific, had given her an inner strength he had not witnessed from her before.

Tarsea lifted Chartail into his arms. "Seeing her like this, we could never leave her here. We will figure out what to do with her once we get back to the Troyk universe. Starc promised we would get you both out of here, and that is what we are going to do. Darden, let us get on with it!"

"Shirl," Darden said. "Buried within the usual static of the communal pathways is a faint frequency. That frequency is always there for a crystal tele-path. When you are near a natural portal, your crystal picks up the frequency and opens an event horizon automatically. You need to find that frequency and increase the volume. The louder that frequency, the less power your crystal will need to open the portal."

Starc watched his soul mate close her eyes and concentrate. Her fore-head wrinkled as she deepened her efforts. He expected she would be frustrated since she did not immediately open a portal. However, Shirl remained calm. Starc was not sure how quickly the hormone would work to accelerate her natural crystal telepathic gifts. Darden and Cianan watched Shirl, as Tarsea whispered into Chartail's ear. Although only moments had passed, Starc was becoming agitated. He was not sure when the vampires would return.

He grabbed the crystal underneath his tunic. "Darden," he said, "can you use this crystal and open a portal yourself?"

Darden shook his head. "When I was teaching Shirl about portals and crystals, I had that crystal partially tuned to her brain frequency. It will take too long to re-adjust. Give her a little more time, she will do it. Her brain automatically opened the portal in Sedona with no previous training. She is a natural."

Starc was about to respond when a loud frequency in his head brought him to his knees. "What the fuck!" Starc did not bother to cover his ears. He knew that deafening sound came within his own head. The crystal he held within his grasp started to glow. Shirl's crystal responded in the same manner. He gazed from her amethyst, to her lovely face. She had a look of utter amazement in her eyes. They were as large as a captivated cat's. An event horizon had opened.

"Take her hand," Darden communicated through the link that existed since they were born. He knew only their link and the soul mate channel would break through the ear shattering frequency he was experiencing. *"I had heard stories about soul mates being able to navigate together, even if one was not a natural crystal telepath. You know the frequency for home, you can navigate for her."* Darden communicated to Cianan and Tarsea they were leaving.

They were about to step through the temporary portal when the door opened and a single vampire entered. Drake. Starc did not know if more vampires were behind him or if Drake would attempt to stop them leaving the Nightshade universe.

"You do not have to leave, Shirl. I will take you to another location within the Nightshade universe where you will be safe," Drake spoke to Shirl through the communal pathway. When the event horizon opened, the volume of the frequency reduced, allowing Starc to hear what the vampire said to his soul mate. There was an intimacy in the delivery Starc did not like. "If you do not find your heart, return. I am here if ever you are in need of me."

Shirl turned and gave the vampire a weak smile. She tightened her grip on Starc's hand. *"Let us leave this terrible place,"* Shirl communicated through the soul mate channel. *"Help me find the frequency that will take us home."*

Starc glanced behind him as he entered the portal. He looked past Tarsea, who held Chartail in his arms. Drake was holding back a number of vampire guards, helping to assure their escape. Darden and Cianan were ready to enter the portal right behind him.

They left the Nightshade universe, but what had Shirl done to survive? Chartail looked close to death and Shirl had a single mark on her neck. He knew he told her to do whatever it took to keep living, he was just not sure he could ever trust her again if she had sex with Drake.

Starc hated himself for how he felt. The betrayal of Elzbeth Southam, once again haunted him. Did he have a future with his soul mate beyond the physical craving that clearly existed between them?

Chapter 13

~

Shirl finished off her glass of wine. She telepathically ordered another. Before she finished chewing the bite of salad she placed in her mouth, the wine arrived. She did not think there was enough alcohol to soothe the hurt she felt.

They had been back in the city for two days, and Starc had barely spoken to her. There had been no physical contact between them as well. It was almost as if their wild sex escapade had not occurred. She started to question Starc's motives related to their interlude. Had he merely had sex with her for her brain to excrete the hormone needed to escape the Nightshade universe?

Chartail was hidden away in the safe house the men used to ferry dissidents to another world. Alex and Tarsea spent most of their day caring for Chartail, pretending to have mid-afternoon interludes. Solfa and Darden took the evening shifts. The communal pathways were abuzz with chatter about the two couples.

When the group was together at Tarsea's parents' house, they spoke about what to do with Chartail. The poor woman's father had earlier proved he did not care for his daughter. Most of her friends had disowned her. Shirl could not really blame them.

Guilt by association must have paralyzed them with fear. The Troyk universe had little tolerance for people who spoke or acted against the government. There was no *Bill of Rights* here. No freedom to speak against governmental policies, a right that was sometimes taken for granted in the United States. Here, little dissension murmurs that arose were quickly rectified by mind control abilities.

Their first priority was to get Chartail physically healthy. Her mental health was another matter. Shirl could only imagine the terrible dreams that plagued the woman's sleep.

Shirl did not dream. She half expected Drake to dominate her dreams, as vampires did in the series *True Blood.* That series did not come close to what she saw in the Nightshade universe, until the Hep-V vampires entered the picture. The savagery and blood lust was closer to the reality she experienced there.

She did not dream of Starc either. The incredible sex they had should have fueled weeks of wet dreams. It had also been performed in public. Shirl half expected a dream where they were making love, as the Super Bowl's half-time entertainment. Exposed for all to see, as she had been in the Nightshade universe. Maybe her subconscious was still coming to grips with what had happened.

"Shirl," Alex said, as she broke through Shirl's thoughts. Her friend knew she needed a distraction, so she dragged her to lunch with two friends she met through Chartail. As if having lunch with the girls was going to fix what was ailing her.

Alex looked at Shirl, with concern on her face. Today, Alex was wearing a non-descript tunic and leggings, allowing her to blend into the background. Her friend was a true chameleon. Alex wanted to make as little of an impression as she made her way to and from the house Chartail was recuperating in.

"We want to know if Cianan is seeing anyone," Sondra said. Like the other woman sitting at the table with them, Sondra was tall, blond, and beautiful.

"My brother and I are not exactly close," Shirl shared with the women. That certainly was an understatement. Her brother barely tolerated her. Although he had been protective of her when they were in the Nightshade universe, as soon as they returned to the Troyk universe, Cianan went back to being an ass. "I will covertly find out and get back to you." That seemed to satisfy Sondra.

"It was so nice of the Childers to take you in. You have a built-in friend with Alex. Sondra and I were so pleased when Chartail introduce us before…" Jessalyn did not finish her sentence. She did not have to. They all knew what Chartail had done.

There had been an uproar when the citizens of the Troyk universe found out about Chartail's supposed fate. The protests were short lived, as Jarlyn's mind control telepath squad convinced the populace of the commodity a condemned prisoner presented to the population. Shirl was immune to mind control tactics, but pretended her acceptance of Troyk policy. She did wonder if anyone would be sentenced to death and sent to the Nightshade Universe in the future. One thing was clear, she would never again accompany anyone to that world. The severity of her experience there would negate any mind control telepath from trying to convince her otherwise, mind secretion or not. The blood opal Drake had given her was hidden in her underwear drawer.

The discomfort caused by the discussion was relieved when her brother communicated through their familial link. *"We have an assignment for tomorrow. Jeryl Jarlyn wants us to go to the Terra Flora universe and acquire some rare agates. I will pick you up at ten. Inform Starc about the assignment."* Yes, inform Starc indeed. They were barely speaking. She even wondered if Starc would go with them. He was assigned to protect her, but she was afraid he would find someone to cover for him.

"What is it?" Alex inquired. Her friend could always read her like a book. She never was able to hide anything from Alex.

"That was Cianan letting me know we have an assignment. I hope Terra Flora is a better experience than the last hell hole where I was sent."

"Terra Flora!" Alex exclaimed, as she stood and threw her napkin on the table. "That does it! We are going to the zoo." What going to the zoo had to do with Terra Flora was beyond Shirl's comprehension. Alex had a committed look on her face and Shirl knew there was no talking her out of this trip. "Ladies, we will see you next week."

Alex placed money on the table and hugged each of the women before they left the restaurant. Shirl wondered if the zoo had polar bears. She realized how little she knew about the geography and the temperate makeup of this world. Shirl never remembered Alex being so melodramatic. She figured she was not going to like what was at the zoo.

"This is the terrifying Giant Larma beast from the Terra Flora universe. That is the world Jarlyn is sending you for some rocks," Alex said in disgust.

Shirl stared at the animal that even her most terrifying nightmare could not have conjured. "It supposedly only eats rodents," Alex continued, "but I have no idea how aggressive these beasts are in their natural habitat. This one came through the portal. It took six CT Guards to bring it down. Raine Narmouth told me all about it, when I was stupid enough to go on a date with him."

Her friend had telepathically asked Tarsea and Starc to meet them at the zoo. The men replaced Koel who had been watching over them from a distance during lunch and their journey here. Raine Narmouth still presented a threat to Alex. She never left the house without one of the men accompanying her. Koel had stayed behind to help Tolfer guard Alex while the rest of the men were working to rescue Shirl and Chartail.

"Not stupid," Tarsea said, as he kissed the top of her head, "misguided." It was obvious that peck on her head was not enough for her friend. Alex grabbed her soul mate's tunic and brought him down to her level, so she could kiss his lips. Tarsea deepened the kiss. Shirl re-directed her attention back to the Giant Larma beast, giving them a little privacy. Starc seemed unaffected by the amorous display. He and Shirl certainly had gone a lot further than just a harmless kiss.

"I have been to Terra Flora before," Starc informed her. "Although I have never seen one of these in the wild, we will be prepared to fend one off if the need arises." Those few words were more than any other conversation they had in the last two days. Starc had become the king of one word answers.

Feeling hurt all over again, Shirl wanted to do the one thing that always made her feel better. Shop! Leenea had given her money to buy tunics and leggings, but she had been too depressed. Now, that was saying something, too depressed to shop!

"I've seen enough," Shirl said. "There was a cute clothing boutique I saw as we made our way here. Let's check it out." Alex cringed every time Shirl used a contraction in her speech.

Starc and Tarsea moaned at the prospect of accompanying their soul mates shopping. It must be a universal male trait. Shirl wondered if Tarsea was talking to Tolfer through their familial link to see if he could relieve them.

Starc walked beside Tarsea as they followed their soul mates into the quaint shop. He figured Shirl thought he dreaded the idea of shopping with her. Nothing would be further from the truth, regardless of the groan he had performed for

Tarsea's benefit. He could not wait for Shirl to model the different outfits, as she tried them on, especially the evening wear.

Troyk women dressed quite elaborately for the second dinner seating at restaurants. Where daytime fashion was quite conservative, what women wore later in the evening was quite revealing.

Tarsea was continually trying to get rid of the sheer outfits Alex's aunt and cousin purchased for her. His friend did not want men to ogle his soul mate. Starc knew he would behave in the same manner, if his reaction to Drake was any indication.

Shirl grabbed a number of outfits for both her and Alex from the racks. Starc perched himself right outside the dressing room that Shirl occupied. She would have to walk past him to see herself in the mirror. Tarsea was in a chair nearby, mumbling to himself.

Alex came out first. Her soul mate took one look at her barely-there outfit, sprang from his seat, and dragged her back into the dressing room. He heard some scuffling and then Alex's laughter.

Shirl came out wearing her first outfit. Starc was speechless. His mouth became dry, he could barely swallow. She was stunning in the sheer silver and gold tunic, with matching leggings. The metallic color made it look as if Shirl was a jewel placed in a setting. The translucent material hugged her every curve and his eyes traveled to her breasts. Bead work covered most of the area, thank the Supreme Being.

"You are absolutely beautiful in that outfit," Starc told Shirl. "I know Leenea gave you money, but please, let me buy this outfit for you. Until my dying day, I will always imagine you in this outfit when I think of you. Would it be too bold to ask you to go to dinner tonight, allowing you to bring other women to shame?"

Shirl stared at him for several seconds. Starc had been so angry with himself over the jealousy he felt related to Drake, he barely had spoken to Shirl over the last few days. He could only imagine what that silence had communicated to his soul mate. She finally replied, "I would like that."

He walked to her, brought her into his arms and kissed her passionately. *"I am so sorry for the way I have been behaving. It has nothing to do with you. Just old issues I cannot seem to let go of. I realize that is not fair to you. We need to get to know each other, rather than just letting the heat we generate take over."*

Alex and Tarsea emerged from the dressing room. She was dressed in her tunic and her hair was a mess. "We are going to head back to the house," Alex said. "It is hopeless trying to buy evening wear with Tarsea nearby. I think it is best for Norri and Pattrice to buy my clothes. Those outfits at least make it out of the store in one piece." She lifted a torn tunic. Tarsea gave Alex's butt a gentle pat and she started giggling.

"I am buying the tunic and leggings for Shirl. We are going out tonight for the second seating at Gerard's," Starc informed his friend. Tarsea gave Starc an approving wink as he accompanied Alex to the front desk to pay for the shredded outfit. Shirl went back into the dressing room to change. He could not wait to take her out on their first date.

The two couples exited the store and walked back to the Childers's residence. Starc took Shirl's hand and she did not shake him off. He had to tell her about Elzbeth Southam and how his experience with her would cripple their relationship until he came to grips with his trust issues.

Chapter 14

~

Shirl floated through the restaurant, as the hostess showed them to their table. She was so happy to be with Starc. The early difficulties between them seemed to work themselves out. As they made their way, she could not help noticing the looks she was getting from men. The outfit she wore was like a neon sign to gaze at her.

Norri spent twenty minutes messing with her hair and makeup. Alex's aunt was compensating for the time she lost, separated from Alex, and now with Shirl. Starc tightened his grip on her waist, sending nonverbal communication that he was proud to be alongside her.

They were seated at the back of the restaurant. It provided the privacy a young couple would crave when first dating. Shirl liked being out of the limelight. Alex had told her what to order, so she did not bother to look at the menu. Her friend had become obsessed with food since coming to the Aster Province.

Shirl was too nervous to care what she ate. Something set off Starc's earlier foul mood and she needed to understand what. There was still an awkwardness when they were alone that needed to be resolved. The waiter came and they both telepathically ordered their dinners. Starc ordered a bottle of wine to accompany their meal. As usual, the wine was delivered almost immediately after ordering.

Shirl took a sip from her glass. She traced her finger around the top of the glass and it hummed. Crystal. Starc watched as she continued to draw a strange type of music. The song of crystal soothed her soul, helping to cut the edge off her frayed nerves. She wondered if all crystal telepathic individuals had an affinity for the stones or if it was just her. Shirl could not fathom just using them for the utility of their power.

She gathered her courage and broached the question she had been dying to ask. "What did I do that made you so angry at me earlier?" Shirl took another sip of wine, rewarding herself for jumping in the deep end of the pool. The wine also helped to relax her.

Starc stared at Shirl. He must have been trying to figure out what to say. "I had a relationship a couple years ago and was betrayed. Ironically, it was neither of our faults, but I cannot get past being cheated on."

Shirl took in his words, but they made no sense. "I do not understand. If both of you were guilt free, why do you feel betrayed?"

Starc rubbed the scar over his left eye, shaking his head. His gaze returned to Shirl. "We had just decided to become exclusive. The next night she had sex with Rayne Narmouth."

Shirl nearly spit out the sip of wine she had just taken. This was the same Raine Narmouth who had assaulted Alex twice. "Did he rape her?" she whispered. "How could you possibly feel she cheated on you if she was forcibly taken?"

"It was not rape in the normal sense," Starc replied.

"What other sense is there?" Shirl asked in disbelief. What kind of world had Alex and she entered? The men's reactions to the attacks on Alex made it clear a woman's consent was required for sexual relations. "I am lost!"

"She had been approached in a bar the day after we had decided on exclusivity. Raine had been dating her as well casually off and on for several months. We were friendly rivals back then. Narmouth and his brother walked up to her when she arrived. Shortly after, the three of them left the bar together. I received a telepathic communication the next day, telling me she had changed her mind, she was now with Raine. Several days later we ran into each other and she changed her mind yet again. Her behavior made no sense to me. She seemed so committed to me when we made the decision. It kept bothering me that both Raine and his brother were together with Elzbeth."

"Why did the brother's presence bother you?"

"He is a mind control telepath," he shared with her through the soul mate channel. *"She had committed to me, then left the bar with the Narmouth brothers and then as soon as she saw me again she changed her mind. It is classic mind control. She must have had some doubts about our relationship and Narmouth preyed on that doubt. A mind control*

telepath can take any indecision and make the decision for you. It is only after a new stimulus is introduced that the mind will re-evaluate a decision made. We have no idea if the decision we originally made was ours or one made by someone with mind control talents."

Shirl considered his words. The real victim here was the poor girl. She was violated mentally and physically. Shirl did not know what to say regarding the rape. Anything she said would be overcritical where Starc was concerned. She considered his behavior toward her and what may have caused Starc's temporary withdrawal of affection. The requirement to continue the discussion was delayed when their dinners were served. What little appetite she had was gone after hearing the story. She moved food around the plate with her fork. Tasting a bite here and there.

"Talk to me, Shirl," Starc begged her.

Shirl could barely contain her anger. "Your behavior recently was more of a reaction to what may have happened between me and Drake. I was in a life or death situation and I chose to live. Drake did not force me to do anything. Yes, we kissed, but that was it.

"You and I had been basically strangers, but a single touch told us we were soul mates. A concept, by the way, that is foreign to me, not having grown up here. I owed you no fidelity. You held all the cards, Starc. I was ignorant of what being a soul mate was. If you had a question regarding what happened between me and Drake, you should have asked before you took me against that wall. You tried and convicted me without even letting me offer a defense. Actually, I should not have had to offer a defense at all!"

She did not feel it necessary to explain how Drake used their soul mate bond against her. The situation was so close to what happened with Elzbeth, it was scary. At least she had not made love to Drake, if that act could have been described in those words.

It was a matter of trust and forgiveness for an action, neither of them had any control over. Was anything felt with full commitment? Wasn't there some doubt in everything people did? She was being judged on something she would always fail, with no fault of her own.

Her eyes burned, she was so consumed with anger. She could not get her emotions under control. She wanted to get out of the restaurant and away from Starc.

"Alex, can you and Tarsea come get me?" she communicated to her friend through what still remained a closed link. "Starc, I cannot sit here anymore and talk to you. If we continue this discussion, I am afraid I will say some things I will never be able to

take back. I should be fine going to Terra Flora tomorrow with Cianan. We should not see each other for a couple of days. I have a lot of thinking to do, and so do you."

Shirl stood on legs that barely held her weight. She somehow made it to the restaurant's exit and sat on a nearby bench. Alex and Tarsea would be there soon, based on how close the gathering place was to the Childers's residence.

In a matter of minutes, Tolfer sat next to her. "I was on the way to my parents' when Tarsea asked if I could pick you up. Looks like you had a rough evening. Let us get you home so you can talk to Alex."

Shirl looked at Tolfer. He was always so cheerful and caring. "Alex has been getting me out of one problem after another all of my life. I think it is time I deal with things on my own."

Tolfer grinned and placed his hand over hers. "It is commendable that you want to be more self-sufficient. Your world has been turned upside down. No one understands that better than Alex. Why not talk to her as a sounding board. Do not ask her to fix things, but tell her some of the things you are thinking about doing. She will then give you feedback. Ultimately, these are your decisions to make, if you truly plan to stand on your own two feet."

The man made a lot of sense. It would be helpful to talk to Alex. The idea of using her to run ideas across was sound. Shirl could not figure out why she had never thought of that before. She guessed it was always easier to let Alex make the decisions. Shirl figured it was finally time to grow up.

"Can you tell me the tales about soul mates as we walk to your parents?" Shirl asked her escort.

"It would be my pleasure," Tolfer replied. "Although, Darden would know more tales related to crystal telepathic soul mates. I just know the basic fables."

Shirl felt so much better as she walked alongside Tolfer. He was so easy going, so nurturing. He was like the brother she never had. She finally realized she was hungry. "I did not have a lot to eat at dinner and it turns out I am starving. How about preparing a mid-evening snack for me. Plus, Alex would be more than happy to eat again."

They both laughed at that last remark. Her laughter hid the devastation she felt regarding her relationship with Starc. She did not think there was going to be a simple fix. It may have been doomed from the beginning.

Starc finished off the bottle of wine and then ordered a couple shots of stoak. The distilled keen went down smooth, warming his body. Getting drunk was not going to solve any of his problems, but it sure was a nice way to delay the inevitable.

In telling his story, he managed to hurt Shirl. He could not blame the anger she felt toward him, which was why he did not follow her out of the restaurant. Tarsea had communicated to Tolfer through the warrior link, rather than the familial channel. It was Tarsea's way of letting Starc know Shirl was being taken care of.

He downed his third shot of stoak when Darden joined him, carrying two more shots for the brothers to share. Since Darden was part of the warrior link, he knew this evening had blown up in Starc's face. Darden had been the only person he had ever shared every detail about what happened between him and Elzbeth Southam. Without a word, he grabbed the shot his brother steered in his direction and drained the glass. He had already accepted the fact he was going to feel like shit tomorrow morning.

"She does not want to be near me, not even on tomorrow's mission. I cannot blame her any more than I can blame Elzbeth. Shirl is my soul mate. It is supposed to be easy with soul mates, like Tarsea and Alex."

Darden laughed at his comment. "There is nothing easy about Tarsea and Alex's relationship. Alex gets mad, she tells Tarsea how it is going to be, and he copes. That girl is always trying to see how far she can push Tarsea before he lays down the law."

"There is real affection between them, like you and Cassie."

"You forget, little brother, I was there when the two of you were reunited in the Nightshade universe."

Starc hated when Darden referred to him as his little brother. They were separated in age by a mere five minutes. Regardless, his brother was missing the point.

"That was just biological," Starc replied. "A relationship has to be more than raging hormones." Starc thought how easy it would be if that was not the case. As soon as he started thinking was when he ran into problems.

"I cannot speak for Cassie and myself, since our relationship has not progressed to become sexual. I do know that Tarsea says he cannot let things fester too long with Alex. If he does not address what is wrong with their relationship, he ends up sleeping on his parents' couch.

"Can you think about the grief Tarsea goes through when Leenea finds him sleeping in the common room after Alex throws him out or he walks out on her? Those two are so much easier to be around after they work out their frustrations." His brother did not have to elaborate on how those two worked out what was troubling them. They argued and then they made up. In short, they communicated.

"So," Starc answered, "what you are telling me is I should have gone after Shirl. Easier said than done. Darden, I do not know what to say to her. Besides, she asked me to leave her alone for the next couple of days." Starc was miserable and there was no more alcohol on the table.

"I wish I knew what to tell you, brother. What I do know is you need to go through the portal with her tomorrow, regardless of what she says. Your job is her safety, period. If you cannot work out what is wrong, at least get to the point where you are talking to each other. Odds are she is talking to Alex and Tarsea is agitated not having Alex to himself. For Tarsea's sake, go talk to Shirl and try to start the mending process."

⌒◯

"I am keeping the two of you up," Shirl said. "You should go to bed. I will be fine." She had spent the last hour talking to Alex and Tarsea. At first she was not comfortable talking so intimately with Tarsea present, but Alex was adamant he stay. Alex's rationale was that Tarsea knew Starc, all the stories about soul mates, and the Troyk universe. Her friend reasoned, if they were going to have a real conversation about their relationship, if Starc was not present, Tarsea was a competent replacement.

Shirl could still picture Tarsea's face when Alex referred to him as a 'competent replacement.' It took everything she had not to break down and laugh. Bottom line, Alex was right. Having Tarsea there resulted in a more balanced discussion. There were so many questions she wanted to ask Starc, but could not do so. She had shut him down before he had time to further explain things.

"You need to talk to Starc," Alex said. "In the meantime, you cannot go through the portal alone tomorrow. We still do not trust your brother. They have CT Guards for a reason. Terra Flora presents several hazards, if the Giant Larma is not enough for you. That thing still gives me nightmares."

103

Evelyn Lederman

Shirl had already been regretting calling Starc off the portal trip tomorrow. It was a decision made in haste, her emotions overtaking her good sense. She would have Tarsea or Tolfer communicate tomorrow to Starc and have him go to Terra Flora with them. Spending time with him on a mission might help foster a good discussion between them, even with her brother present.

"I am going to have a glass of herbal tea to help me sleep," Shirl said. She rose and hugged both Alex and Tarsea as they left the common room.

Shirl was making her way to the kitchen when there was a knock on the front door. She heard voices in the hall, as she prepared her tea. Tomorrow was going to be a stressful day. Maybe the tea would prevent her mind from replaying her discussion with Starc at dinner over and over again. She needed to quiet her brain and get some sleep.

Footsteps made their way to the kitchen. She glanced in the direction of the hall and Starc stood before her. Shirl's first reaction was to fall into his arms. After what happened in the Nightshade universe, that probably would not be a good idea. Her body craved him like nothing she had ever experienced. It was her brain that kept raising the red flag, deservedly so. Sex was not the solution to their problems.

"I could not let things stand where they currently are," Starc said. "Everything you said to me in the restaurant, I cannot argue with. I already hate myself for these ridiculous things I am feeling regarding Elzbeth and you. The problem is, I cannot figure out how to get beyond those thoughts. Finally, I could not stop making love to you in the Nightshade universe, if I had even tried. I did not have a functioning brain cell, as soon as you came into my arms." He looked so defeated standing there alone. Her heart ached for him.

Shirl walked away from her tea and into Starc's arms. She knew she was giving up too easily, but she craved his touch. It soothed her soul. "Tarsea tried to explain what he thought was going on in that brain of yours. I should not have cut you off. The situation got me so angry and frustrated. It was my way of relieving some of what I was feeling. I am sorry for that. Leaving was the coward's way out." She felt pounds lighter, getting that off her conscience. It felt great telling him how she felt.

"I told you to survive in the Nightshade universe anyway you could," Starc told her. "Words cannot truly express how relieved I am that you are alive and you were not forced to do anything you find abhorrent. The thought that I could have found you as we found Chartail has haunted my dreams. I was out of line to suggest anything inappropriate happened between you and that vampire. Shirl, I just do not know where to go from here?"

"There is something I should have told you," Shirl admitted, "but I was so angry. Drake was able to manipulate the soul mate connection for his own use. I don't know if it was because he was not meant to be my soul mate or something was off kilter with Drake. I battled my feelings for Drake because they did not feel natural. In the end, I turned him down.

"When you and I were reunited, perhaps that frenzied reaction was the bond righting itself." That had to be the explanation why they both lost all control and made love with three other people in the room.

Starc paled. "My telling you about Elzbeth and the mind control telepathic impact must have taken you back to Drake and the nightmare you experienced. I am so sorry."

"Perhaps we should both stop apologizing and start moving forward. Maybe Elzbeth will always haunt you, but we can move beyond that together."

"I can do that," Starc said. "The explanation of the righting of the soul mate bond also helps to reduce the guilt at making love to you in front of everyone. I re-entered the Nightshade universe knowing we had to have sex to save our lives, I was just not sure how I was going to suggest it in such a way that I would not feel it was rape. The fact nature took that problem off my hands relieves me a bit."

"I guess it is a good sign we are holding each other," Shirl replied, "and still able to have a conversation. We have a big day tomorrow, let's head off to bed."

Starc looked at her in disbelief. "Shirl, are you inviting me to spend the night?"

Starc could not believe his ears. Was she letting him into her bed after all that had occurred this evening?

"I am inviting you to literally sleep with me," Shirl clarified. "If we spend the night together without making love, maybe we have something more than just lust. We dove right into hot sex, without knowing each other. For a one night stand, I guess that is fine. As soul mates, I expect that we would want something more."

Starc released her. She picked up the mug she had been sipping from and poured the leftover liquid into the sink. Shirl took his hand and together they walked to the room she was occupying.

"Shirl," Starc said, "you better put on a nightgown or something. I do not think I will be able to control myself if you are not wearing any clothes." Starc doubted he would get any sleep this evening, considering how hard his cock currently was. His desire for her had not waned since the time they had been together, he just had better control of it. He removed his tunic, but decided to sleep with his leggings on. They helped hide his desire for her, a little.

From the dresser, she pulled out a non-descript white shift. Shirl looked at him, smiled, and walked toward the washroom. Thank the Supreme Being she did not change in front of him. Nothing would turn him on more than watching her strip.

Starc pushed the sheets back and got between them. He was tempted to ask through the soul mate channel if he could get a rain check for the chance to watch her change. She seemed willing to work things out, even if he said something stupid.

The washroom door opened and a vision walked out. She was angelic in the white shift. Her blond hair cascading over ivory shoulders. Shirl had not buttoned the top three clasps. He could see her crystals falling between the tops of her beautiful breasts.

As much as he loved the way she looked in the night shirt, he would have given anything to lift the material over her head and bare her for his inspection. He would examine every inch of her amazing body. If it was possible, he grew even harder. It was going to be an agonizing night.

Without a word, Shirl joined him under the covers. Even though they were not touching, the heat they generated was incendiary. This was a terrible idea. The worst decision he had ever made. How he was keeping his hands off her was beyond him.

"Wow," Shirl said, "it is really hot under these covers." She proceeded to kick the linens down to the end of the bed. Her actions eliminated the material that helped hide his erection. "Was it this hot before?" She proceeded to pull the shift around her hips and then over her head. Shirl wore nothing under the nightshirt. He gazed at her perfectly shaped breasts. How he longed to take them into his mouth.

"Shirl," Starc growled, "you cannot do this and not expect me to touch you." He could barely contain the urge to caress those breasts. He was not sure what game she was playing, but she played dirty. He hovered over the invisible line on the bed that separated his half from hers.

"I changed my mind. A little exercise may help us sleep better." Shirl looked at him and gave him a provocative smile.

She had barely finished her sentence when Starc was on top of her. One hand covered her left breast, while his mouth explored the other one. He licked and sucked, unable to get enough of her taste. With his hand he squeezed and played with her breast's nipple. He was not making the same mistake as the last time of not communicating with her. *"Shirl, you are beautiful. If I do anything you do not like, tell me. All I want is to bring you pleasure."* Her fingers dug into his shoulders, providing an erotic massage as they reacted to what he was doing to her.

He shifted to place her left breast in his mouth. Its tip hardened as he continued to suck. He increased the pressure as he feasted on the nipple. Shirl arched her back, her body's response to what he was doing to her. Starc took his right hand and placed it under the small of her back. He released her breast and covered her mouth with his.

He continued to kiss her as his left hand made his way to the juncture between her legs. She further spread her long limbs to give him better access. Starc needed to make sure she was ready for him before he entered her. The first time they were together she was able to take all of him. However, he was not sure how physically comfortable she was during that act. He wanted this time to be perfect for her. First he entered her with one finger. She was wet and ready for him. He could not deny his body its relief another minute. Starc entered her with one thrust, as he had before. This time he would take it slow. He would cherish and worship her. She played to his rhythm. Starc treasured every gasp and moan that came from Shirl. His hands explored every inch of her body, he could reach. Her skin was as soft as satin.

For the first time in their relationship, Shirl initiated the kiss. It started sweet and innocent. There was a tentative quality about it, which was amazing since he was inside her. He deepened the kiss, as he had everyone he had ever given her. She tasted of spices and Shirl. She was unique. She was addictive.

Their bodies became slick with sweat as he continued to slide in and out. *"Faster,"* Shirl communicated through their link. As she requested, he increased the rate at he entered and withdrew from her core. Urgency overtook them, as it had the first time. They climaxed together. He had never experienced the magnitude of the orgasm he shared with his soul mate.

Rather than falling on top of her, he turned over on his back, taking her with him. "Are you thirsty? Would you like some water?"

"Let's just lay here a couple of minutes," Shirl replied. "Let me catch my breath. I know it's a cliché, but that was wonderful. My whole body is humming. I don't think I could stand if I tried. We should take a shower before we try to sleep. Cianan will be here at ten tomorrow morning."

Her body shimmered from the sweat generated from the exertion of their lovemaking. She made no attempt to cover herself. Starc drank in the sight of her. He needed to taste her again.

Starc nuzzled her neck, he could not get enough of her. He dragged his tongue up her neck and came across the mark she still wore from Drake. "Did it hurt when he bit you?" There were probably better times to have brought up her experience. He wanted her to know it was safe telling him anything. He had to garner her trust.

She looked into his eyes, taking his face in her hands. "No, it did not hurt. He was careful not to break any bones. I can still hear the bones being crushed as those vampires killed Stephano and the CT Guards. There was also a numbing agent in Drake's saliva. He licked and numbed my throat before he fed from me."

Starc considered what she said. He could not help himself, he had to know, so he asked her one more question. "Did he bite you anywhere else?" It would kill him if he took blood from her inner thigh.

Shirl got a knowing look in her eyes. "He wanted to take blood from my femoral artery. I would not let him. There was something too intimate about him biting me there that I was not comfortable with. Drake was true to his word. He protected me from the other vampires, as well as from himself."

"What did he mean when he talked about finding your heart?"

"I told him I was your soul mate and I belonged to you. If I set boundaries, maybe he would honor them. He said my soul may have been committed to you, but not my heart. For some reason, I think Drake is very lonely and perhaps was hoping I would fall in love with him. After he told me about manipulating the soul mate connection, I am not sure what I really felt for the man. I have seen dozens of vampire films, but nothing prepared me for the reality of it all."

Starc had never lounged in bed and talked to a woman. Talking to this woman was a salve to his soul. For the first time he really understood what having a soul mate meant. It was more than the incredible physical attraction. He was beginning to see Shirl touched him inside like no one had or would ever again. Starc hoped that Shirl felt the same way.

"How about that shower," Starc said. "Promise, I will not touch you while we are showering. I think we can both use some sleep. Terra Flora can be a dangerous place if we are not properly alert and prepared." Starc figured there was a good chance he was going to break that promise.

Chapter 15

〜

Shirl prepared two mugs of the herbal beverage that reduced the static in her head associated with the communal pathways. Where Alex drank it to prevent the nose bleeds she had been suffering, Shirl utilized the beverage to better hear the frequency in her head that allowed her to navigate the portals.

The idea that she could open a portal to anywhere within the infinite universe was overwhelming. She had asked Alex to join her in the kitchen as their soul mates slept. Shirl was still not comfortable communicating telepathically. Communication was so much more than words people spoke. It was how their bodies responded, if a person would make eye contact, and all the other non-verbal aspects as one conversed.

Alex dragged herself into the kitchen. She looked drained, as if she had not slept in weeks. "For goodness sake, Alex, doesn't that man ever allow you to rest?" Shirl asked in disgust. She blushed thinking about last night and being with Starc. They never should have taken that shower. It only led to them making love under the pulsating water and then again in their bed. It amazed Shirl how quickly she thought of it as "their" bed.

Her best friend's face blushed. "As little as possible." Alex let out a little giggle Shirl was now getting used to hearing. "Seriously, I have had difficulty sleeping because I was worried to death about you. When Starc and your brother talked about what happened in the Nightshade universe, I was petrified for you. Every time I closed my eyes, all I could see was some monster sinking his fangs into your neck. It was not a good looking vampire I imagined, but a rabid dog demon." Shirl saw tears well up in Alex's eyes.

She walked to her friend and kissed her forehead. "I was lucky Drake was there. He tried to manipulate the soul mate link between me and Starc. His touch was enjoyable, although I was plagued with guilt because of it. Compared to how Chartail was treated, I was handled like fragile crystal." Knowing what she was, Shirl felt that was an accurate analogy. They valued her in that world, as they did here, because she was a female crystal telepath. "Once we were reunited, something happened to the link between Starc and me. He touches me and I ignite, regardless of how annoyed I may be with him."

"I know what you are talking about," Alex replied. "Tarsea uses sex to either get his way or distract me. Unfortunately, it works every time. You and I never had a physical relationship that lasted for any length of time and then we are catapulted into these intense soul mate melodramas. Sometimes I feel like I'm trying to take a drink from a fire hose when I am dealing with Tarsea. I am more likely to get caught in the extreme stream of water than quench my thirst."

"I am definitely caught in a whirlpool of emotion where Starc is concerned. However, that's not why I wanted to talk to you. Rather than toss and turn, I needed to concentrate on someone other than myself." Shirl almost laughed at the look of horror that crossed Alex's face. "Relax, I was not focusing on you. I was thinking about how relatively easy I was able to fit into Troyk society, while you are still having to pretend to be someone you are not. It would be nice if Candy could have the same type of transition I had. She must be worried sick about us both."

"Funny, I was thinking the same thing. She probably made it to Sedona and is driving everyone insane," Alex said. "Candy is probably getting in their faces, telling them how incompetent they are. Our being dragged into a portal to another universe would not be on their list of possible scenarios."

Scraping footsteps sounded behind them. "It was the luckiest day of my life was when Darden opened that portal," Tarsea commented as he dragged himself into the kitchen. "You girls did not put any coffee on? I do not know how you are able to function without caffeine." He started his own brew after he kissed Alex.

Alex returned her soul mate's kiss willingly. There was a harmony between the two she had not been able to achieve with Starc. They fit together. It was almost magical. She supposed that was because they were soul mates. Could she settle for anything less with hers?

"It was always the three of us," Alex continued, recovering from the passionate kiss. "Candy will be exposed to mind control probes by Jarlyn, as you were. I cannot imagine Candy talking about you, without mentioning me. It is not a long stretch to associate Alexia Montiff with the other surviving daughter of the refugees, Alexandra Mann. I have already admitted to being part of the family. We are going to have to come up with a way to warn Candy, without compromising her ignorance of me in this world." The complexity of the story they were going to have to contrive almost gave Shirl a headache. She would have to think more on the subject.

Shirl heard the front door close and moments later Tolfer walked in. He hugged Alex and then came to her. "I could not let you run off to Terra Flora without properly feeding you. Do you feel like something sweet or savory this morning?"

Alex was the one with the sweet tooth, Shirl rarely bothered with desserts. "Savory. Can you make something that has a little kick to it?" She had always loved Mexican breakfasts with their flavorful salsas. Shirl especially liked green tomatillo sauce on her eggs. She was one of those people who could not get enough cilantro. If that herb was not present in the Troyk universe, she would have Darden bring some back with him from Earth.

"I am sure I can whip something up. Where is Starc?"

"Still sleeping," Tarsea answered between sips of his coffee. "He got a little unexpected exercise last night."

Alex kicked her soul mate under the table, "Ouch! What was that for? Our bedrooms share a wall."

"A little tact goes a long way, baby," Alex responded.

Tarsea looked at Shirl over the lip of his mug. "Sorry, Shirl. I did not mean to be obtuse and make you feel uncomfortable. As soon as things stabilize, we need to all move back into our apartments. There is not enough privacy in this house."

"I could not agree with you more," Starc said, as he joined the rest of the group in the kitchen. He gently caressed Shirl's shoulder, before he headed to the coffee. That intimate touch was a start. It was not an outright display of affection, as Tarsea had shown Alex, but it was a huge step for Starc. "However, for the time being, we have to be more aware of our surroundings." Starc made a side comment within their private channel. *"The shower in our room is next to the linen closet."*

Shirl could feel her skin warm, reacting to Starc's comment. The smell of onions frying in a skillet grabbed her attention. "That smells heavenly, Tolfer. When I cooked at home, I was more likely to set off the smoke alarm than produce something I could eat." Her stomach growled and she could not wait until Tolfer was done with his latest masterpiece. Discussion related to Candy would have to wait. It would be a good idea to have a substantial breakfast before they headed to Terra Flora. She had no idea how they were going to find the stones that Jarlyn wanted. To add to that, there was the Giant Larma beast and whatever other critters lived in that universe that created additional challenges.

Chapter 16

~

"Let us give Shirl the freedom to fly solo on this trip," his brother suggested. Starc was pleased that Darden decided to join them on their trip to Terra Flora. Alex showing Shirl one of the world's more unfriendly inhabitants had not gone over well with him. Everyone's nerves were a bit frayed and Starc still did not fully trust Cianan. Would her brother get between Shirl and a larma beast if one attacked? Until he could answer that question, the jury was out on his trustworthiness.

Starc had heard almost the whole conversation that occurred between his soul mate and Alex this morning. Tarsea had seen him as he made his way to the kitchen, but had not given away his presence. He had only wished his soul mate had discussed more of her feelings with Alex before the conversation shifted to their friend, still in the Ginkgo Terra universe.

There was no question they clicked sexually, it was everything else that worried Starc. All he wanted was Shirl to be comfortable in their relationship. It was obvious she had many doubts which Starc had been neglectful in address-ing. They needed time and a lot less drama. He could no longer sweep their problems under the rug. Starc had to aggressively deal with what had not been working so he and Shirl would have a future.

Shirl approached the natural gateway and the event horizon opened. As before, Starc's crystal glowed as his soul mate's did. She turned to him and smiled. That simple act eased his nervousness about this mission. They had worked this morning on the frequency that would lead them to the Terra Flora universe.

His soul mate would adjust the frequency and Starc would only intercede if she did not get it correct. He would be able to hear as she made adjustments, knowing if she was heading in the right direction. Darden and Cianan were just there for the ride and protection once they arrived. They entered the portal and Shirl started to adjust the pitch being emitted. Within seconds they entered the Terra Flora universe.

They were immediately assaulted by the heat and humidity of this parallel world. At least they did not have to deal with the almost constant rain that usually plagued Terra Flora. It was great for plants, not for humans. Starc's tunic was already sticking to his body and sweat trickled down his back. The sun beating down on them with no cloud cover did not help. They were not far from the jungle that would provide some relief from the sun. It presented a whole new variety of dangers. They brought insect repellent, he was just afraid they would sweat off the spray.

"Let us get Jarlyn's crystals we came for. The faster we find them, the faster we can leave," Cianan said. Shirl's brother's hair was already soaking wet and he was shaking off excess water. It was the first time Cianan had been to Terra Flora. Descriptions did not do justice related to the impact the heat and humidity had on their bodies.

"If we head to high ground, we would have a better chance of finding what we are looking for." Shirl seemed to have a natural instinct related to crystals. For someone who had never been in this world before, she spoke with knowledge born of confidence. *"If I was not afraid of being locked up, I would say the crystals were calling out to me."* She communicated to him through the soul mate channel. He loved the intimacy she was willing to share with him.

Shirl wet her handkerchief and tied it around her neck. Starc wanted to lick the excess sweat off her throat. He could almost taste the salt in his mouth. Shirl looked quite alluring, as she pulled her hair into a ponytail. He felt like a wet rat.

Starc knew he had to get the group moving. He needed to stop being distracted by his soul mate and focus on the mission. There would be time to spend with Shirl later. He looked around and decided best to head west, the same direction Shirl was looking. There was an inactive volcano that would provide a good place to look for crystals.

"Everyone needs to keep drinking," Starc instructed. "We do not want anyone to get dehydrated or start suffering from heat exhaustion. Take it easy, none of us are used to the humidity. The last thing we need is for someone to faint. If anyone starts getting a headache, let me know." Starc knew all the symptoms of heatstroke. It was his job to make sure everyone got home in one piece.

Darden led the way, with Starc bringing up the rear. As he suggested, they took it nice and slow. His brother set a moderate pace, balancing the need to accomplish their mission and still not get sick. The insect repellent was doing its job. He could see mosquitoes all around, but none landed on him to feast. They could not afford to bring back a disease transmitted by one of these insects.

He followed his own advice and took a drink of water from his canteen. As he drank, his eyes landed on his soul mate, who walked behind Darden. She seemed the least impacted by the extreme heat. Shirl had told him about Phoenix and the very high temperatures they would have in the summer. Unlike Phoenix, this world had humidity, instead of a dry heat.

"Tell us about the crystal we are supposed to find," Starc asked. He wanted to get his mind off how extremely hot it was. If his mind could concentrate on something else, it would stay sharp.

"Jeryl Jarlyn showed me the crystal when I visited with him," Shirl shared with them. "It is similar to the pinkish-red phantom crystal, although I had never seen one personally. On Earth it is extremely hard to find. I saw a picture of it once. It had been found in Madagascar. Never been there, but it was a cute movie."

Yet again, he had no idea what his soul mate was talking about. He used to laugh when Alex said something no one understood and Tarsea would mumble something under his breath. He found it charming, but he loved everything Shirl did. That thought stopped him mid-stride.

It was the first time he had thought of Shirl and love in the same sentence. The little things she did or said were the things that moved him, not the incredible sex. Every nuance of her was slowly working into his psyche. That thought was quite overwhelming, as he realized what having a soul mate truly meant.

"What is wrong?" Cianan asked him, noticing he had fallen behind.

"Nothing," he answered. He quickened his pace to catch up, without exerting too much effort. "What does the crystal do?" he once again asked Shirl. Starc had been amazed by her knowledge of crystals. Her love for those stones must have created a kind of kinship with Jeryl Jarlyn, which cut short his examination of her regarding Benko when they met.

"I am not sure about this one," Shirl answered. "The one I am familiar with helps with feelings of abandonment. It must have been difficult on our Prime

Ruler to have lost his son in the manner he did." She probably said those words for the benefit of her brother. *The one he showed me had very little power left. He has been obsessed with finding Benko and the rest of us. I would imagine this stone provides the same benefits as the one I know about.* Shirl communicated through the soul mate channel.

They walked for about an hour and then rested. There was no place to sit and it was too dangerous to wander off. Everyone finished their first canteen and refilled them with the water they ported. Conversations were held to a minimum, taking a mental, as well as a physical break.

After fifteen minutes they continued on their way. They probably had another hour to walk before reaching what they hoped was the first mine. If they were lucky, they would find the crystal there. The mission only called for a single type of crystal to be recovered. Anything else they could keep for their own use.

Starc's legs were getting heavy from the exertion when they came upon their destination. They pulled out their crystal powered flashlights and entered the cave. Various pieces of quartz lined their way, evidence that mining had already been done by a previous party. The question arose whether the other group had taken what they searched for.

Slowly and methodically they looked at the stones on the floor and within the walls. Fortunately, it was a little cooler in the cave. There was a small trickle of fresh cold water falling down the face of one of the walls. After they tested the water to determine if it was safe to drink, they enjoyed the cool life giving liquid. It had a mineral taste about it, fortified by all the elements contained in the mountain adjacent to the volcano.

He noted that Shirl had examined a couple of crystals and placed them in her pocket. *"Have you found what we came for?"* he asked her through their closed link. The fact she had not spoken aloud made him doubt that was the case.

"These are rare Faden quartz tabby crystals. They help to support physical, mental and emotional stability. Chartail could use them. She is still a mess, although that is not surprising."

"Shirl, come here," her brother called. "Take a look at this."

Shirl walked to where her brother stood and examined the stone. "Thank God!" Shirl sighed. "These are exactly what we are looking for. They also are emitting a lot of energy. Jeryl Jarlyn should be able to use these crystals for years before anyone has to come back to this world and gather more. Can we take a little longer and see what else we can find in here? We have come all this way, we might as well grab some additional crystals. This place is amazing."

Darden stepped out of the cave and returned almost immediately. "We need to be on our way within the hour. I want to be long gone before the sun sets. There are a number of large nocturnal animals that call this world home." His brother always did his homework and researched the different worlds he entered.

Shirl found a number of extra crystals, explaining their uses as she placed them in her knapsack. They found a small amethyst geode they decided to drag home with them. Amethyst were the best crystals for telepathic portal travel. A crystal telepath would go through several crystals a year. They gathered their findings and packed up. It was time to head back to the portal and home. The walk back would be harder because of the additional weight, but at least it should be a little cooler, Starc reasoned.

They made their way out of the cave, to the clearing just short of the jungle path they had taken earlier. "What is that cute little animal?" Shirl asked.

Starc looked in the direction Shirl pointed. His heartbeat accelerated as he looked upon a larma beast pup. "Shit! Where is its mother?" Before anyone answered, an animal larger than the one at the Aster Province zoo emerged from the jungle and headed straight for Cianan.

Shirl stood in mute horror as she watched the Giant Larma beast attack her brother. She was so petrified, she could not move. Starc and Darden pulled out weapons and ran toward the animal before it took off Cianan's leg. They placed warning shots next to the beast. The animal either was not hungry or no longer sensed its young was in danger. It removed the grip its mouth had on her brother's limb and disappeared into the jungle. Her soul mate and his brother quickly started to examine her brother's leg.

"It does not look like the femoral artery is impacted. Thank the Supreme Being," Darden said. "Your leg is still a mess. I cannot tell if any of the bones were crushed, can you stand?"

Her brother gallantly tried, but was unable to. Shirl was finally able to move and knelt near Cianan. "You guys will either have to act as crutches or we have to make some kind of litter and drag him back to the portal."

"Shirl, see if you can open a temporary portal," Darden asked. "I do not like how his leg looks. The crystal I am wearing does not have enough energy. I was not expecting we would run into this much trouble."

Shirl concentrated, as she had in the Nightshade universe. She did not seem to be able to pull up the right frequency. "Something is interfering with my ability to open a temporary portal. It must be all the crystals in the cave."

Darden swore underneath his breath. He looked up at the sky and then the surrounding area. "I do not think we have the luxury of time. We have to help you walk back through the jungle. Starc and I will alternate supporting the side with your bad leg. The path is too narrow for all three of us to walk. Plus due to the heat, the other can semi-rest when he is not supporting you. Everyone should have a healthy drink before we start on our way. We will walk for thirty minutes and rest for fifteen. That will still get us back to the portal before the sun sets."

Shirl always had a good sense of direction. Once she had been somewhere, she could always find her way to the portal. She took the lead, as they traced their way back. The crystals did not add that much more weight. However, it was not any cooler than before.

She pulled back her hair, allowing her neck to once again be exposed. The more skin she uncovered, the better job her body would do at cooling itself. Shirl turned around and the men were dragging along. Although it had not been thirty minutes, she decided they should stop. The trail widened and would be an ideal place for everyone to rest.

"Let's stop here," Shirl said as she arrived at the spot she designated as their first rest area. She helped the men remove the burdens from their backs and joined them sitting on the path. Her brother looked in bad shape and the other two men did not look much better. Everyone was drenched in sweat.

She stretched out her leg, leaned against a tree, and closed her eyes. Thinking she heard a rattle, she quickly moved her feet and opened her eyes to see a thick snake strike her lower calf. She screamed as a chill ran down her spine.

"Shirl, did that snake bite you?" Darden asked. Starc was already examining her leg. "Does anyone know what do about a snake bite?"

Darden's words cut through Shirl's shock. "You regularly hike a trail in Sedona and you do not know what to do about a rattlesnake bite? Arizona is swarming with rattlesnakes." It was a bit of an exaggeration, but she was permitted. After all, she was just bitten by a damn snake.

"Relax, Shirl," Starc said through the soul mate channel. *"Breathe with me. Tell us what we need to do."* Shirl could feel her heart rate decrease and got her breathing under control. It was as if Starc was directing her body's functions. She was once again amazed by the power soul mates had over each other.

"First thing, I need to remain calm." She looked at Starc and nodded. It was her way of acknowledging what he had done for her. "We need to immobilize my leg, so the poison does not spread. We need to wash the bite and cover it with clean, dry dressings. Lastly, I need my calf at or below the level of my heart."

Starc drew a knife from his boot and was about to cut her leg. "No!" Shirl cried. "The Internet site said not to cut or try to remove the venom." She looked her soul mate in the eyes, "You have to carry me and Darden will help Cianan." Starc nodded and started to do as she instructed.

After he washed her leg, he further bent down and kissed her calf, not far from the snake bite. He did not say anything. Shirl figured it was his way of saying it was going to be all right. Starc tore his tunic, to use the material to dress the wound. Shirl had never seen anything sexier in her life. His now exposed skin shimmered with sweat. She longed to wipe the wetness with her tongue. Salt after all, helped retain water. There would have been a perfectly good reason to do what she longed for. After a moment she discarded the notion. These men had already witnessed too much of what Starc and Shirl had done together.

After Starc did everything he could, they started their trek back to the portal. They took it even slower than before, knowing they probably were not going to stop again. Starc carried her as if she weighed less than a feather.

Darden soldiered along, assisting her brother. Slowly they made their way along the trail, but losing their race with the sun. With the diminished light she was not sure, but she thought her calf was starting to swell. She chanted, trying to stay calm.

Shirl grabbed her necklaces and concentrated on controlling herself. Blue stones were for calming. Shirl had an aquamarine among the crystals around her neck. Originally she had not worn that piece, but changed her mind at the last minute. She had the foresight that something could happen that required the crystal.

"This is not going to be easy," Darden advised the group. "We need to get off this path and make our way through the jungle. There is a nocturnal boar in this world and we have been walking on its trail. I have been noticing the bark of the trees showing evidence of boars. They are most dangerous during the dusk hours. Starc, you cannot wait for us any longer. Get Shirl to the portal and to a med-tech as soon as possible. Time is more of a factor with her."

"Go," her brother said, reinforcing what Darden asked. He looked terrible. What little rational capacity she had left, she was weighed down with guilt. Why had she not been able to open a temporary portal? That was what mated crystal telepathic females could do with ease.

"Sorry, Shirl," Starc said. "I think we are both going to get a little scraped up, but I need to get you out of here and fast." With those words, Starc increased his pace. Fortunately, so close to the boar's path, the foliage was not as thick. He made his way around trees, with some of the limbs ricocheting back at them. A few of them stung, but they were making good progress. She could still hear Darden and Cianan behind them.

Shirl closed her eyes and drifted to that annoying state between being awake and asleep. She struggled to keep her eyes open. Every time she jerked awake, she was overwhelmed with waves of nausea. The fever then came on.

"We are going to get trampled, Starc!"

"It is all right, it is the fever. There is boar activity on the trail, but we are safe from them. Your ears are just a little hypersensitive."

"I have never had sensitivity to sound when I ran a fever before," Shirl complained. She felt terrible and was getting scratched up as they made their way through the woods. Shirl knew she was whining. Was a comfortable bed too much to ask for when she felt like crap?

"Your thoughts are leaking into the soul mate channel. You are not whining, by the way. The sensitivity to sound is connected to your crystal telepathic abilities. Since you had not used them before, you did not experience this side of having a fever. Hang on a little longer, we are almost there."

She felt like she had been hit by an eighteen wheeler. Everything hurt. Shirl could not understand why Starc kept hitting her with some kind of rod. When she felt better, she was going to make him pay! Where was her blanket, she was so cold? Her teeth were chattering and it was really annoying.

"Cool! My crystal is glowing." Shirl found herself drifting into unconsciousness.

Chapter 17

~

Shirl woke up feeling absolutely terrible. Both Alex and Starc were hovering over her. She saw relief wash across both their faces. Shifting in bed was a big mistake, her body still ached from the fever. "How did we get back?" she asked.

Starc smiled. What a sight! "Your crystal opened the portal when we got in close proximity of it. Since we are soul mates, I was able to navigate using our telepathic bond. It is a very different experience being able to navigate the portal myself. Thank you, for that."

"You are welcome, Starc. I'll certainly look into getting bitten the next time we travel." Shirl knew she was being catty. She was parched, it felt like she had been in a desert. "Can I have a glass of water?" It was funny watching both Alex and Starc fumble in their attempts for one of them to satisfy the request.

If she wasn't so thirsty, she would have laughed. Alex handed her the glass, while Starc supported the back of her head and shoulders. She did not think she ever had water so delicious before. "Did Darden and Cianan make it back?" Shirl extended the glass and raised her eyebrow. Alex knew she was asking for more.

Starc nodded. "They were about thirty minutes behind us. As soon as we made it through the portal, I got medical assistance to you. When Darden and Cianan arrived a stretcher was right there. The med-tech worked on him on the mountain, but everyone felt more comfortable carrying him down. He is going to be fine. Cianan was very lucky the Giant Larma beast did not do more damage."

Shirl looked about her and did not recognize her surroundings. That happened more often than she cared for. "Where am I? This does not look like any hospital I have ever visited." The room was sparsely furnished and there was no medical equipment in sight.

"We are in the safe house we utilize from time to time," Starc informed her. "It is close to the trail head and we wanted you treated as quickly as possible."

She heard about this place. Because of the fever, she was still a little confused and disoriented. It then dawned on her why she knew about this house. "Chartail has been staying here. Is she all right? Where is she?"

"Right here," Chartail said. The woman walked out of the shadows. She must have been taking lessons from Alex. "I was able to take care of you for a change. You talk in your sleep. It can be quite informative nursing you back to health."

The surprise of seeing Chartail shocked her back into her right mind. "Did the medical team see her when they were taking care of me?" After everything they both went through, if Chartail had been discovered taking care of Shirl, it would be disastrous.

"It is all right. Chartail kept out of sight in the back room." Starc positioned a cool cloth on her forehead. It felt so good, she almost moaned.

"I brought you back some crystals from Terra Flora," Shirl told Chartail. "They may be able to help you with what you went through."

"While you were sleeping," Chartail said, "Starc gave them to me and explained their use. I am feeling a little better. Thank you." Shirl was amazed Starc remembered what she had told him about the quartz. He had paid attention. Starc concentrated on little things. That was important to Shirl. Big events were so rare, it was the small courtesies that had the biggest impact. Once again, her heart warmed thinking about her soul mate.

"Everyone will be meeting here later," Starc informed her. "Since the general population knows about our ordeal in the Terra Flora universe, it is safe for us to congregate here. Strangers have been dropping off flowers in the front of the house. You have become something of a folk hero. First, there was the Nightshade universe scandal and now this. We will discuss the possibility of moving Chartail if we feel her presence here has been compromised."

Chartail moved closer to the bed. She removed her copper bracelet and placed it around Shirl's left wrist. "You mentioned while you were talking in your sleep that you wanted a cuff bracelet. For some reason you thought it would make you belong in the Troyk universe. Keep mine safe for now. When events occur that allow me to come home, I will take it back. We will design one for you together."

Shirl was overwhelmed with emotion. After everything this woman had been through, giving Shirl her familial bracelet was such a selfless act. She looked forward to working on her own bracelet, together with her friends. One that depicted the friendships she forged with the incredible women in her life. Shirl glanced at Starc and wondered if their relationship would be part of the story the bracelet would tell.

⌒꩜

Starc was beside himself with relief, now that Shirl was awake and fever free. It had been a grueling couple of days. Starc had not left Shirl's side since he had carried her back from Terra Flora. Darden had delivered Jeryl Jarlyn his precious crystals. They had almost cost them the life of his soul mate. Chartail had started nursing her the moment he had brought her to the safe house. Troyk medical technology was quite advanced. However, it was easier to deal with physical injuries, like when Tarsea had been stabbed. Eliminating the venom from Shirl's bloodstream was a more time consuming task. A crystal telepath could travel to countless worlds, only generic anti-venom serums were available to med-techs. There was also the need to bring Shirl's temperature down.

Alex helped out as Shirl fought the fever. She was there to calm her friend, as Shirl came in and out of consciousness. Half the time Shirl thought she was back in the Ginkgo Terra universe. They talked about people and places Starc was unfamiliar with. No one slept until Shirl's fever broke. Once Shirl was out of danger, Tarsea was able to convince Alex to go home. He no doubt wanted to get his soul mate into bed, where he could hold her, as Starc wished to hold Shirl.

His desire to be alone with Shirl had to wait, as everyone arrived for their pre-determined meeting related to Chartail's future. Starc had never spent much time with the woman when Tarsea dated her. Over the last few days, Starc was overwhelmed with admiration for Chartail as she cared for his soul mate. He barely recognized her as she tirelessly administered to Shirl. Alex had noticed

Chartail's near fanatical need to aid her friend. She abdicated lead to Chartail, as they both nursed Shirl back to health.

The small group assembled in the common room in the safe house to come up with a plan. Solfa, Karlon Flonder, and Tarah were not present due to their close association with the Troyk government. Their presence noted by neighbors, would bring unwanted attention.

Chartail sat between Shirl and Alex. A strong bond had grown between the three. Starc knew that any strategy related to Chartail, would have to be endorsed by the two women for final approval to be given.

Majority rule was not going to fly in this case. Alex's healthy features made her stand out from the two women who recently lived through difficult ordeals. The woman who blended into the shadows, now shined from both physical and emotional strength. Starc knew with time, she would once again fade into the shadows when she was beside these incredibly beautiful and vibrant women. He noticed that Tarsea could not keep his eyes off his soul mate.

Starc started the discussion. The sooner they reached a decision, the sooner he would be able to spend time alone with Shirl. His arms longed to hold her, not to mention the rest of him. He would have to show restraint concerning his need for her.

"With all the attention this place has received since bringing Shirl here injured, I am afraid we may have compromised this location. It would be a danger to us, as well as Chartail, to keep her here."

"I have to agree," Tarsea chimed in. He further elaborated within the warrior channel, *"This location can no longer be used as a safe house for our activities."*

Chartail and Shirl looked at Tarsea and both asked, "What activities?"

"By, the Supreme Being, we have two more channeling the warrior path!" Darden exclaimed. Starc was not surprised Shirl had been able to link in. But Chartail's accessing the channel did surprise him.

"Chartail is one of us now," Alex said. "Any decision we come up with has to reflect that."

For the second time, Shirl spoke. "It is more than that. Chartail has also linked into the channel that exists between me and Alex. That channel does not feel like a communal channel, but something akin to the warrior pathway. She linked in as they were nursing me." Starc suspected that Shirl and Alex were communicating in that channel, bringing Chartail up to speed on everything that had happened since they both came through the portal.

"All right," Tarsea said, "we now know she shares powerful links with us. That does not change the issue at hand. Chartail cannot stay in the Troyk universe. It is too dangerous for her and the rest of us. If she is caught, we are all going to be sent to the penal colony."

"We are not sending her to that horrible place," Alex cried.

"Baby, we are not going to send her there. The question is where do we send her?" Tarsea answered his soul mate. Starc could hear the frustration in Tarsea's voice. He knew they had to come up with a solution that fully satisfied the needs of both their soul mates.

Had Shirl been stronger, Starc knew she would be right next to Alex challenging them. Starc could see that even with the lively discussion, Shirl was having problems keeping her eyes open. He caught Tolfer's attention and motioned in Shirl's direction. Tolfer rose and left the common room for the kitchen.

"How about either Terra Azure or the Standish universe?" Koel asked. "We have sent numerous dissidents to those worlds. They are safe and gatherers typically do not travel to those worlds." Terra Azure was a world that had little land mass, it was an aquatic world. There was a fairly large island inhabited by relatively technologically advanced people. The Standish Universe recently recovered from an ice age. Temperatures had warmed and the planet was once again livable.

"Perhaps Terra Azure," Tarsea answered. "The Standish universe requires a pioneer temperament, which Chartail does not exhibit. No offense meant. It is just my opinion."

"No offense taken, Tarsea," Chartail said. "I cannot see myself breaking my back to bring a planet back to life. What little I have heard about Terra Azure, it will be suitable for the short time it will take for you to bring Benko Jarlyn home."

The room got quiet, as everyone looked from person to person. Benko Jarlyn had not been mentioned in Chartail's presence as far as Starc was aware.

"It was me," Shirl sighed. "I needed to give Chartail something to live for when we were in the Nightshade universe." His soul mate was fading fast, she could barely sit straight in her chair. Where was Tolfer with the herbs that would give her some temporary energy?

Tolfer re-emerged from the kitchen with several mugs. He must have concocted several different beverages for the women, based on their individual needs. Shirl, Chartail, and Alex all received a mug and immediately started sipping their contents.

"Koel," Tarsea commanded, "put together an evacuation plan for tomorrow evening. Communicate what you come up with through the warrior channel midday tomorrow. There has not been any chatter regarding Chartail in the communal pathways. I want her safe in another universe before she is compromised." Koel was the group's logistical genius. Most of their operations were planned by Koel and executed by the remaining members of the group. Koel generally held back and observed, in order to make tactical adjustments where needed, once an operation was underway.

Tarsea left with Tolfer and Alex as soon as she finished her herbal beverage. Starc knew his friend did not like it when Alex was put in any type of danger. Tarsea had no choice but to allow Alex to be part of this operation, she demanded it. That, however, did not mean he had to like it. There was little doubt that when Tarsea got Alex home, he would find a way to work out all his frustrations.

Darden and Koel left shortly after the others. They had several words with Chartail before they took their leave. Starc noted that his cousin had touched Chartail, as he seemed to be touching every woman he had contact with. With three of the five friends having found their soul mates, he imagined Koel was growing frustrated. Although most people would not have noticed, Starc started to see a shift in Koel's personality. He still made stupid remarks, but now on fewer occasions. His cousin was becoming more serious and circumspect.

Shirl and Chartail were quietly talking as he re-entered the room. His soul mate seemed to have more color in her face and noticeably had more energy. She was swinging her legs and twisting a napkin, that Tolfer had handed her when he gave her the beverage. He had been worried sick about her and just wanted to wrap her in his arms.

Chartail must have picked up on his need. She kissed Shirl and stood. "It has been a very enlightening day. Tomorrow is going to be just as crazy, if not more. I better try and get some rest." She took a couple of steps and stopped. "I wish you and Alex had come through the portal years ago."

Shirl rose to embrace her new friend. "Use the crystals. They will help you rest. We are both going to need as much energy as we can for tomorrow's operation. Sleep well." Chartail walked to the second bedroom and closed the door behind her.

Starc wanted his soul mate in his arms. He could understand Tarsea's frustration when Alex put herself in danger. Now Starc was in the same position. Nothing would make him happier than locking Shirl in the bedroom during tomorrow's operation. Unfortunately, he knew that was not an option available to him. Shirl turned, she must have had an inkling of what was going through his mind.

Shirl was wired. She had no idea what had been in that beverage, but she had enough energy to run a marathon. Chartail had retired to her room. Shirl knew exactly how she was going to use her excess energy.

She got up and approached her soul mate. The same urgency that had hit her in the Nightshade universe was beginning to spread throughout her already charged body. There was a need she felt, one only Starc could fill. Everything except the man in front of her faded from her perception. All she wanted were his hands caressing her body. Her pores longed to soak up his touch. She was already wet, ready for their joining.

Starc watched her approach. She saw his anticipation reflected in his stare. The closer she got, the darker his eyes became. Dark, with need. He slowly rose, perhaps afraid he would scare her off. Silly man.

Shirl wanted to launch herself into his arms. She could let urgency take over her self-control, as it did before. It would be so easy to let insanity reign once again. Tolfer's beverage was not helping her control the frenzy overtaking her. The second time they had made love, it had been with her body and soul. She wanted to experience that completion again.

"I have waited for you my whole life," she told him, as she lifted her face to kiss him. The kiss started sweet. It could have been a first kiss had they met as teenagers. She would have liked that. They would have experimented with life together, as well as sex, as they grew up.

Starc deepened the kiss. He caressed her waist, as he brought her into his embrace. They were both holding back their passion, taking it slow. He probably proceeded cautiously because of her recent fever, while she wanted to experience every nuance of what they were sharing. She brought her tongue into his mouth, wanting more of his taste. His tongue met hers, as she continued her exploration. Shirl groaned as different sensations were overtaking her body.

She felt his hands move, as he lifted her into his arms. Without a word, he carried her into the bedroom. She knew from the Terra Flora universe, he had no issues dealing with her height or weight. Gently he placed her on the bed, as he turned to close and lock the door. As he made his way back to her, he removed his tunic. Shirl gloried at his magnificent chest, licking her dried lips. She grabbed the bed linens, trying to maintain control, as she watched Starc undress. It was not long before he stood before her nude. His erection grabbing her attention.

"Do you need help undressing, Shirl?" Need help, she thought, no. Want and desire help, oh yes! She wanted him to slowly and sensually remove her clothing. Some of her thoughts must have leaked through their closed channel. Starc smiled as he took hold of her leggings and undie waistband and slowly pulled them down her body. He littered kisses along her naked flesh, as the fabric pulled. When he got to her calf, he kissed and licked the snake bite. There was something unreasonably sexy about that.

Starc discarded her leggings and panties, tossing them on a nearby chair. He grabbed her tunic, lifting it above her head. He did not continue his voyage, but continued to linger at her chest. Starc took her left breast into his mouth, through the satin of her bra. As he sucked and pulled on her breast's nipple, Starc unhooked her bra. He released her breast and removed the material binding her.

Her right breast only had momentary freedom until it was captured by Starc's mouth. Never had captivity felt so damn good. Her nipple continued to harden as he sucked harder. She continued to control her passion, letting only near silent mews escape from her mouth. They had an audience before, she did not want Chartail to hear what was happening in this room.

Starc rose from her breast and made his way up to her neck. As with the snake bite, he kissed and licked Drake's mark. She would always carry the scar of the vampire bite, but Drake would never have her heart. It belonged to the man who was now kissing her. With that realization, the dam holding back her control broke.

She communicated through the soul mate channel, *"Change positions."* It was not a request, but a command. Shirl had always been a passive bed partner, but currently there was not a passive cell in her whole body. Starc merely smiled and grabbed her as he rolled over. She rose above him, straddling his hips, as she positioned herself. Shirl had never liked being on top, she had felt so exposed. Now she reveled in it.

Slowly she took him into her body, one exquisite inch at a time. Starc groaned, *"I am dying here, Shirl."*

Doubt crept into her heightened state. She did not have the experience to truly know the level of her soul mate's discomfort. *"How long can you hold out?"*

Starc gave her one of his wide smiles that warmed her heart. *"An eternity, if you can manage it."* Shirl returned his smile, continuing her slow-paced dominance over his body. When she had taken him fully into her core, she increased the pace at which she rode him. *"Faster, faster, baby,"* Starc cried out within their channel. Being able to communicate within the soul mate channel only further intensified the experience.

Whatever herbs she had consumed were wearing off. The energy that had earlier jump started her body, just as quickly phased out. She needed to keep up the pace until they both climaxed. They were so close, she needed to hang on a little longer. She found that last burst of energy which took them both into a shared rapture.

Shirl collapsed onto Starc, totally spent. He wrapped her into his arms and rolled over on his side. *"Do you have the energy to lift your arm?"* he asked. Starc knew she had overdone it after having been ill.

"No," she muttered into his neck. *"Don't bother to chastise me. I would have done it the same all over again, given the opportunity."*

"Really?" Starc communicated as he leered at her.

"Yes, just not now." She closed her eyes and drifted into a deep, cleansing sleep. Just on the edge of oblivion, she was not sure, but she thought she said one more thing to her soul mate. *"You have my heart, Starc."*

Chapter 18

Starc sat across the table from his soul mate. He had wanted to get her out of the safe house and into the fresh air. She needed to restore her energy. Brunch beside the gathering place park seemed the perfect solution. Last night had been incredible, but totally drained her. It was careless, after she just recovered from a high fever. He felt like an animal, preying on his weaker mate. There was no recrimination in her eyes this morning, when she finally woke. That did not mean he did not let himself off so easily.

He watched as she moved food from one side of the plate to the other. "Eat up, we have a full day ahead of us." She had complained of hunger this morning, but had barely touched her meal. "Is there something wrong with the food?"

Shirl gave him a reassuring smile. "The eggs are delicious. I guess I have so much on my mind I lost my appetite." She took several bites and placed her fork on the plate. *"I am worried sick about getting Chartail to the portal without being caught. They couldn't possibly send her back to The Nightshade universe and follow through with her sentence, could they?"* That was a frightening thought. No wonder she had lost her appetite. He wished he could reassure her that would not happen. Jeryl Jarlyn did not forgive or forget.

"You need to relax and stop thinking about all the things you do not have control over," Starc replied to her for the benefit of those around her. *"We are very good at what we do, she will not get caught. Even if something unexpected happens, I cannot imagine they will send her back. There was so much outrage at what the government was doing. If word got out that he had sent her back there, the protests would start all over again. People would question why they had thought such a sentence was beneficial to society. The mind control telepathic government wants to be covert in their manipulation."*

His soul mate must have considered what he said, she responded by nodding. She continued to pick at the omelet and home fries on her plate. He wished she had a healthy appetite, like her friend, Alex. Starc had finished his lunch and sat back and basked at Shirl's beauty. It was not the external beauty that made her glow, but the extraordinary woman she was on the inside.

He was concentrating on Shirl to such an extent, he did not sense the woman who approached the table until she spoke. Shirl seemed as surprised as he was. "Starc?" the familiar voice said. He turned to see Elzbeth Southam standing next to him. Her presence momentarily had him out of sorts. She was just as exquisite, as always. Elzbeth was the exact opposite of Shirl. Where Shirl was blond and had a fair complexion, Elzbeth had black hair and a swarthy complexion.

After an awkward silence, Starc introduced Shirl to his former girlfriend. "Shirl, this is Elzbeth Southam. Elzbeth, this is Shirl Thork." Shirl took in a startled breath of air. He was not sure it was due to meeting Elzbeth or being referred to with the last name of Thork. She had been called Shirl Tomlinson on Earth.

"That is a lovely amethyst you are wearing, Shirl. Are you a crystal telepath?" Elzbeth had not noticed Shirl's reaction. She seemed genuinely interested in meeting his soul mate. Starc had not been quite sure how to introduce the two of them.

"Thank you," Shirl responded, "it was my mother's. Yes, I am a crystal telepath. Starc is my CT Guard, although we have become quite close." The next words out of her mouth surprised and humbled him. "Starc told me about your relationship. I am so sorry you were used in that way. From the conversations we have had, I know he is truly sorry for the way he reacted."

Elzbeth blushed in embarrassment. She moved the hair that was tucked behind her ear, hiding part of her face. Starc knew Elzbeth did that when she wanted to change the subject of a conversation. They had been together long enough for him to know her various mannerisms and the way she reacted when she was under stress.

Shirl must have noticed Elzbeth's reaction to what she said. "I did not mean to make you uncomfortable. When Starc told me what happened between the two of you, I was very angry with how he handled the situation. I had a similar experience and his reaction temporarily negatively impacted our relationship. Men are slow to apologize, if they do so at all. I suppose I inappropriately apologized on his behalf."

"I do not normally like to talk about what happened. After the incident, I could not cope with what Raine did and Starc's rejection. Rather than trying to talk to Starc and work it out, I ran away. I moved to Starling Province and started over. My parents are still in Aster Province and I have been visiting them for a couple of days." Starc watched the tension drain from Elzbeth's face. His soul mate had a gift that allowed her to make people feel at ease. Starc had originally been horrified that Shirl would mention such a personal topic in public. However, after her initial shock, Elzbeth took the opportunity to voice pent up feelings. He knew Chartail would have been a basket case had it not been for Shirl, when she returned from the Nightshade universe.

Starc stood and embraced his former girlfriend. "I am sorry I was not willing to talk to you. It was only recently that I realized there was nothing to forgive you for. If anyone should ask for forgiveness, it is me. We had the start of something beautiful and I did not have enough inner strength to help you through your ordeal."

Elzbeth held him tight, kissed him and then stepped out of his embrace. "Thank you for that. I had debated whether to come and talk with you. Now I am glad I did. You have someone special here, Starc. Do not screw it up!" She glanced at Shirl, nodded and then walked out of his life for the last time.

"Wow, you do not take any prisoners, do you?" he said to Shirl. "I never would have had the mental fortitude to apologize to her. Thank you for forcing my hand." He returned to his seat, took her hand and gazed into her eyes. *"It means a tremendous amount to me that you have faith in me and our relationship to call me on what I did to Elzbeth. Your external beauty pales in comparison to the strong and incredible woman you are on the inside."*

They had several hours before they were going to take Chartail to the portal. Starc wanted to take Shirl to his apartment and make love to her. He wanted to reinforce to her the deep respect and burgeoning love he had for her. That plan was abandoned as soon as Solfa communicated through the warrior link.

"We have a critical situation. I have just been informed the CT Guard is on their way to the safe house to arrest Chartail. They had kept the operation out of my office, concerned we had a mole in the intelligence department. I am not sure if we have time to move her."

"I was just about to communicate through the warrior channel myself," Tarsea replied. *"Has anyone seen Alex? I have been trying to contact her and am not receiving a reply from her."*

"No," Shirl immediately responded to the news her best friend was missing. *"We were going to meet up at the safe house before we moved Chartail. She was supposed to be with you in the meantime."*

"She must have left the house while I was in the shower. Since she is not responding to me, I can only think that Raine Narmouth has her."

Solfa and Tarsea's words pulled Shirl out of her euphoric mood caused by Starc's sentiment about her inner beauty. Her whole life she had been judged and measured on her external beauty. To know her soul mate valued her inner qualities more than what nature provided, meant so much to her.

Now she was consumed by a sickening fear for her friends. Shirl heard about both the physical and mental impacts Narmouth's assaults had on Alex.

"What can we do?" she asked Starc. Although she was able to listen to what was being said in the warrior link, she did not feel comfortable yet communicating within the channel. If she had something worthwhile to contribute she would not think twice about adding to the conversation. Currently, she was just in a panic.

She listened as Tarsea gave orders. *"Starc and Shirl, head over to the safe house. Koel is already there. Do not enter unless it is safe."* Tarsea knew Chartail could hear what was being communicated. *"Darden, Tolfer, and I will go after Alex. Solfa and Karlon, provide backup for Starc. Under no circumstances do you compromise your standing within the Intelligence Department. Tarah, standby in case we need a mind control telepath."*

"There is nothing interesting being communicated in the communal pathways. Let us go back to the house and see what kind of trouble we can get into." Once again, Starc was communicating verbally to give an illusion of normalcy. Shirl figured what he was really telling her was there was no chatter in the communal pathways about Chartail's capture or military action around the house.

Starc threw some money on the table and they exited the restaurant through the gathering place park entrance. They took a shortcut through the park and headed toward the safe house. Shirl was communicating to Chartail through the channel they shared with Alex. She also tried to contact Alex through that channel. Her focus needed to be on Chartail now, not obsessing that Alex did not respond.

They slowed their pace, as they reached the street the safe house was located on. Shirl surveyed the people visible, nothing stood out as being out of place. She had seen most of these people in the neighborhood over the last day. Several had ventured up to her and asked about her health.

As they approached the house, she lost contact with Chartail. *"I cannot hear Chartail in any of the channels we have communicated before,"* she informed Starc.

Starc stopped in front of the house and started to pick dandelions. "I hate these damn weeds. If I pull one out, two seem to grow back in their place." She could see he was taking in his surrounding area as he pulled out more weeds. Shirl remembered as a child with Alex blowing on the weeds when they went to seed. There was still no news about her friend. Raine Narmouth still had not been found.

"I am two houses down from you," Koel communicated through the warrior link. *"Karlon gave me enough notice that the CT Guard was close. Chartail had a panic attack and I had to quiet her down. I left her unconscious on the bed before I climbed out the window. It would have been too conspicuous carrying her out of the house. The guards are inside right now. Back up and get out of there."*

Starc threw down the weeds he had collected in his hands, as a number of the CT Guard approached. *"Shirl, do not try and resist what the guards tell you to do. If we cooperate, we may be able to get out of this mess."*

Shirl stood her ground as Raine Narmouth and a number of the CT Guard approached them. She did not know if it was a good or bad sign Narmouth was here. *"Tarsea, Raine Narmouth is part of the operation to capture Chartail. I am not sure where Alex is, but she is currently not with him."*

"Shirlyn Thork and Starc Lours," Raine Narmouth said, "you are to accompany us and answer questions regarding your association with Chartail Adholm."

Chapter 19

~

Shirl had expected to be locked in one of the cells located in the basement of The Palace. Chartail had told her all about the subterranean prison, when they were in the Nightshade universe together. Chartail and Starc were led in that direction when they arrived, while she was taken to the fourth floor. She was led to the same room where she had her interview with Jeryl Jarlyn. Fear consumed her as she entered and came face to face with the Prime Ruler.

"Explain yourself," was all Jeryl Jarlyn said to her. He was seated in the same location they had sat just days before. His exterior did not reflect a man who was angry with her. It was almost as if she was explaining cutting class to the school's principal.

"I could not leave her in that terrible place," Shirl said. She was not going to bother to deny what she did. Shirl had not been caught with a smoking gun, but enough people had seen them coming and going from a house where Chartail was carried out of not thirty minutes ago. "She was sentenced to be executed for her involvement in the plot against your life. That did not mean she should be brutalized and raped by a blood lusting vampire."

"So you took it upon yourself to commute her sentence. Is that how things are done in the Ginkgo Terra universe?"

Shirl worked to control her anger. "If a person is sentenced to death, in civilized countries, it is done as humanely as possible. A number of countries do not allow death sentences any longer. Our government does not physically abuse and rape our prisoners. I was horrified at what I saw in the Nightshade universe." She was close to tears by the time she finished. Shirl knew her hands visibly shook.

The ruler of the Troyk universe just looked at Shirl. He took a deep breath and took a drink from the beverage he had on the table. He raised the glass, "Do you want one?"

"If it is alcoholic, yes I would." She could use something to numb the outrage and frustration of the situation. The fact the man was willing to drink with her was a good sign.

Jeryl Jarlyn stood and went to the small bar situated near where they sat. He put a couple of ice cubes in a glass and filled it with a caramel colored liquid from one of the bottles. He placed a swizzle stick in the drink and handed it to her. Shirl had been told that the Troyk universe took the best inventions they found in all the parallel worlds they visited and incorporated them in their everyday lives. She would never look at that little piece of plastic again in the same way. Shirl took a sip of the drink, coughing as it burned on the way down her throat.

The Prime Ruler laughed, as Shirl tried to control her coughing. "I gather you did not drink a lot in the Ginkgo Terra universe either." His smile vanished from his face, as a storm of dark emotion replaced it. "I did make the deal with Yorik, exchanging the prisoner blood for crystals and other commodities. It was supposed to be fast and painless. When your brother explained what he saw there, I was horrified. I know that in some factions within our world, I am considered a monster. Had I known what was in store for Chartail, I would have sent her to the penal colony."

"I am almost afraid to ask what that world is like," Shirl replied. She did not know if her brutal honesty was endearing her to him or getting her a one way ticket to that world. There were so many secrets she had to keep, but she also had to live in this world. She was a crystal telepath, she could leave anytime, once she found a better world.

"We only have so much land mass in our universe. There was no place to house the criminals that seemed to increase as time went by. Once we started to deport them off world to the penal colony, crime almost disappeared. We send monthly supplies to that world, including medicines. They make the best of an inhabitable world as they can. It is their choice to live in harmony with each other or try to kill one another. Their fate is now in their hands, not mine."

"That actually makes sense, in a warped kind of way." Shirl placed her hand over her mouth in horror. She probably went too far calling the Prime Ruler warped. She needed to recover from her lapse in judgment. If she continued with her thought, maybe he would let it pass. "I know where I come from, the jails are so overcrowded our sheriff had to set up a tent penal facility." Shirl sat back and took another sip of her drink. It went down easier this time around.

"Shirlyn, I know you have a lot of questions. Our world is so different from where you grew up, but you are one of us. This is the world of your birth. You also have a rare and special gift. A female crystal telepath has always been viewed as a blessing. I want you to feel free to talk to me. There will be policies you do not believe in, but give me the opportunity to explain my reasons behind what I do. The Supreme Being gave me my gifts in order to lead our people."

The Prime Ruler believed what he was doing was right. She knew she was not being manipulated. He was not attempting to use his mind control gifts on her. There was no pull on her brain. "What about Chartail and Starc?"

"Chartail will be sent to the penal colony. There will be no discussion on that. She did plan my assassination and feels no remorse for her actions. Starc will be released. A CT Guard follows the orders of his crystal telepath. You are personally responsible for his actions when he is guarding you. He brought you back alive from both worlds as his job dictates. That is all I can judge him on."

Shirl was about to throw caution to the wind. She needed to bring Candy to this universe. Alex had to hide who and what she was, while Shirl could live in the open. She wanted that for Candy as well. "I wish I could have helped you in your quest for your son. Although she knows nothing more than what I already told you about Benko, I believe I know of another descendant from your son's followers."

Jeryl's eyes grew large and he shifted forward in his chair. "Tell me about this person." She could almost see the Prime Ruler salivating.

"As you know, I grew up in an orphanage. There was a girl there I connected with. Although she was two years younger than I was, it was almost as if we could read each other's thoughts. Based on what I know now, I think it was a communal pathway. We had no idea about telepathy or how to navigate within pathways. I'm pretty sure she must be one of us."

"Tell me more." She knew she had Jeryl hooked. Shirl just had to bring him in slowly and steadily. She baited the hook, now she needed to complete the catch.

"Her name is Candace Phillips, but she goes by Candy. She is a little taller than I am, but more muscular. Candy is very good at sports. I have never met anyone who has more self-confidence."

"When you have fully recovered from your snake bite and the after effects, bring Candy home. I would imagine that Zane and Leenea Childers will be happy to foster her until you girls are ready to stand on your own two feet in our world. Things seem to be going along nicely between Tarsea and little Alexia Montiff. My head Intelligence Officer, Solfa Teflar, cannot seem to stop talking about her newly discovered cousin. I am glad you were able to have a friend until Candy can join you."

"She is a sweet girl. Alexia helped nurse me when I was running the fever. Things got a little dicey while Alexia was there. Chartail hid in the second bedroom. Neither of us wanted to put Alexia in a difficult position. I will bring Candy to you after she has assimilated to this world. When I bring her to the Troyk universe, I will send you word." Shirl hoped she had covered Alex and Tarsea's appearance at the house, in case more intelligence came in about their having been there.

"Do not overdo it, my lovely girl. You have a rare gift, but you have to take care of yourself. The crystal you wear receives its strength from you. It is worthless if you cannot draw from its energy because you have none yourself."

"Can I help to accompany Chartail to the portal?" Shirl knew she was walking a fine line at this point, but she still had an inkling of doubt where Chartail would end up.

"You still do not trust me?" the Prime Ruler asked. Shirl could see the man was not offended. He had the beginnings of a smile on his face.

"I have to sleep at night, sir. Any doubt will creep in and cause me insomnia. Chartail and I went through so much together in the Nightshade world." She rubbed the bite Drake had given her. She did not miss Jeryl Jarlyn temporarily down-casting his eyes, as she touched the physical proof of what occurred to her in the Nightshade universe.

Shirl had one more item to discuss related to Chartail. She hoped that guilt would cause the Prime Ruler to give her one more concession. "There is another request I have related to Chartail. Before she is sent to the penal colony, it would be nice for her father to see her and tell her he loves her. Prime Adholm is a good friend of yours and would do so if you request him to. There are no more tomorrows for those two. I would hate for Prime Adholm's pride to prevent his last chance to see his daughter. It would be a shame to let a lifetime of loving be overshadowed by one incredibly stupid move on her part."

Jeryl Jarlyn rose and approached her. He extended his hand and she took it. The Prime Ruler took her into his arms, giving her a fatherly embrace. "I will see that Chartail's father sees her before she is sent to the portal. Darden will set the coordinates if that will meet with your approval. That young man has been tutoring you on portal transit, according to Solfa. He also was one of those who rescued you girls from the Nightshade universe. I would imagine he has garnered your trust by this point."

"Thank you. That will all be acceptable."

The Prime Ruler chuckled at her approval of his actions. "See, I am not the monster some people will try to convince you I am. You have good friends in this world. Keep to their guidance and all will be well."

Shirl left his presence. She knew the people of this world had protested about what happened in the Nightshade universe and had been quieted. As charming and charismatic as Jeryl Jarlyn was, mind control telepathic rule was wrong.

Her friends had carefully supported efforts to overthrow the government and the Prime Ruler was ignorant of their involvement. That needed to continue. She needed to collect Starc and head back to the Childers's residence. There was still the question of where Alex was.

Chapter 20

Starc had finally released Shirl's hand once they reached their destination. The short detention he had in the basement of The Palace while Jeryl Jarlyn talked to Shirl, had felt like an eternity. She had communicated through the soul mate channel their conversation and at points he wanted to strangle her.

For some reason Shirl felt it was all right to taunt The Prime Ruler, as you would a hungry cougar. Fortunately, she left unscathed. He had been surprised at how accommodating Jeryl Jarlyn was. The man must have felt that Shirl was an untapped resource that would pay high dividends in the future. He kept focusing on Shirl being a rare female crystal telepath. Starc needed to talk to Darden and discover what other legends existed about women like Shirl.

They entered the Childers's home. Tarsea was in the common room, while Darden and Koel were still looking at various locations Raine Narmouth could have stashed Alex while he was fulfilling his duties.

"Any news?" Shirl asked Tarsea. Starc knew that Shirl had gone through hell in Sedona waiting for news about Alex. It was happening all over again. However, this time his soul mate was surrounded by people who cared for both her and Alex.

"Nothing. I have tried every telepathic channel she could possibly hear. We have learned from past experience that the soul mate channel mends itself first if she has any kind of head injury." Tarsea continued to pace as he drank from a glass. Starc went over to the bar and poured himself and Shirl a drink.

"I have kept trying to contact her through our channel," Shirl shared with Tarsea. Shirl was so close to Alex, Starc could not imagine how she would function without Alex in her life. Alex and Candy were the only family Shirl had. Starc had been shocked when she offered Candy to Jeryl Jarlyn on a silver platter. When she explained to him how different Alex and Shirl had to behave in the Troyk universe, he actually thought Shirl had made a brilliant move for Candy's benefit.

He handed his soul mate the glass. She accepted it without a word and sat. Starc joined her on the couch. Solfa sat on the other side of his soul mate. Alex's cousin took Shirl's hand and held it. They comforted each other, as Shirl continued to sip the alcohol he had given her.

"I will start cooking one of Alex's favorite dishes." Tolfer shared with the group. "She will probably be starving when she gets home." People all have different ways of dealing with stress. Tolfer was a nurturer, cooking for Alex was his way of coping with her absence. However, in a crisis situation, Tolfer was invaluable. When Tarsea had been stabbed, Tolfer had made sure that he did not bleed out until medical attention arrived. He saved his brother's life that night.

Probably twenty minutes had passed since they arrived, when he heard the front door open. Footsteps followed once the door closed and then Alex appeared weighed down with packages. Everyone just stared at her.

"What?" Alex said. She actually seemed taken aback by everyone's presence and the looks on their faces.

"Where have you been?" Tarsea yelled. Starc figured his worry had instantly changed to anger. They had been all scared to death that something had happened to Alex and she had been shopping. He imagined he would be acting the same manner if it had been Shirl.

"You have a birthday coming up," Alex explained. "I met up with Sondra and Jessalyn since they knew the best stores to find gifts that I hope you will love. I left you a note in the bedroom. Since I had both the girls with me, I felt I was safe from that worthless piece of shit."

Tarsea stalked out of the room and returned moments later with a piece of paper in his hand. "Fine! You left a note I did not find. Why in the world did you not respond to me through the soul mate or the warrior channel?"

Starc noted the confusion on Alex's face. "You did not send me any communication. Even the warrior's channel was unusually quiet."

"Alex, there was a lot of chatter in the warrior channel," Shirl responded to her friend. "Chartail was discovered and arrested. Starc and I were detained in The Palace for several hours. Tarsea was also coordinating efforts to find you through that channel. I even tried contacting you through the channel you and I now share with Chartail."

Leenea Childers rose and approached Alex. She hugged her son's soul mate. "I am fine, Leenea, thanks for asking."

"Wait! Alex you heard my mother ask you how you were?" Tarsea asked.

"Yes. Why are you asking such an asinine question?" Alex was starting to get testy from all the questions thrown at her. Starc always got a kick out of the snarky Alex. Leenea helped Alex place the various packages on the wet bar's counter.

"I do not understand what is going on," Tarsea said. "You cannot hear anything through the soul mate or warrior channel, but you can hear the communication through our familial channel. It should take months before you can access that pathway."

"The little one has moved things along," Tarsea's mother replied.

"What little one?" Alex inquired.

"This little one," Leenea said as she patted Alex's abdomen. "You are pregnant. Your body for the time being will interrupt access to all external channels except the familial one. When the baby is farther along a temporary channel will open between you and the child until it is born. Once that has occurred, you should be able to access the other channels you had access to before."

Alex looked shocked and a little pale. "I have to sit down." Shirl immediately rose and brought her friend to a vacant couch. "It has been two weeks max. Maybe at this point I should have a fertilized egg. I mean, based on what I've read, there is not even an embryo until the third week."

"Sweetheart," Leenea said, "your body is preparing for the baby. As soon as I conceived, the same thing happened to me related to the soul mate channel I shared with Zane. Remember, soul mate and warrior channels are stories based on myths. Troyk medicine does not have information concerning how the pregnancy is going to impact the variety of channels you possess. The communal channels and the familial channel you share with Norri, Solfa and Pattrice will remain unaffected."

"Tarsea," Alex cried, "we are going to have a baby! I am not prepared to be a mother."

"You will be a great mother, my little pixie," Tarsea said as he kissed his soul mate. Starc could see that Tarsea was still shell shocked by his mother's revelation.

"Shirl, we have to get Candy over here, I can't get married without her." Alex shifted and came into her friend's arms.

"I've got that covered," Shirl responded. "When I met with Jeryl Jarlyn this afternoon, I told him about Candy. He thinks I know nothing about Benko and that Candy will know less than I do. She won't have to hide who she is, like you have to."

Alex just stared at her friend, visibly paling. "You told that monster about Candy? What were you thinking?" Alex must have played back part of the conversation that occurred since she returned home. "Oh my God! What about Chartail?"

"Chartail will be sent to the penal colony, Alex," Shirl answered. "There was nothing I could do about that. At least I got Jeryl to agree to have Chartail's father see her before she leaves. Darden will accompany them to assure she is being sent there. I was still not comfortable he wouldn't send her back to the Nightshade universe. For some reason the man was extremely accommodating to me. He was almost foaming at the mouth at the prospect of what a female crystal telepath can do. I saw an opportunity to get Candy here with little drama and I took it."

Darden and Koel arrived as Tolfer announced dinner would be ready in ten minutes. Both men hugged Alex, relieved she was all right. "Wait," Alex said, "I am now eating for two. How cool is that? Tolfer, did you make enough food?" Starc could not help but laugh.

Shirl watched in wonder as Alex chowed down. Her own appetite still had not returned. She did not know if she was still feeling the effects of the fever or if something else was wrong. Butterflies invaded her stomach when Alex voiced concern about Shirl having told Jeryl Jarlyn about Candy. Self-doubt consumed her.

"Tolfer is going to take it personally if you do not eat more of his food," Starc communicated to her through the soul mate channel. She knew he was concerned about her not eating. He had made several comments during lunch. Part of her was touched that he cared about her well-being. Another part of her did not appreciate big brother watching over everything she did. She was used to men

looking at her, but not to the point they noticed what she was doing at any given point.

"Shirl," Alex said, "I am sorry if I overreacted to your news about Candy. Now that I think about what you said, it makes good sense. It will be so much easier for her not to have to live a cover story." Although she did not say anything about how little Shirl had eaten, Alex smiled after she took another bite of her meal. Shirl never had much of an appetite. Now it was non-existent.

"Darden is scheduled to go the Ginkgo Terra the day after tomorrow," Shirl said. "I figure that Candy is in Sedona looking for us. We have to come up with a story not only explaining your disappearance, but mine as well. I was supposed to have had dinner with the police commander I was working with the night I came across. Like everyone else, he was concerned I was not eating."

"I will come along. They can close the file on both our disappearances that way." Alex stared at her soul mate, almost daring him to object to her plans. Shirl thought the next nine months would be very entertaining, watching the tug of war between those two.

Tarsea had the good sense not to challenge Alex. "I will join you. Benko Jarlyn should have made it back from Chicago. It is time we start talking about the Troyk universe and the role he needs to play."

"Zane and Leenea," Shirl said, "would it be acceptable for Candy to join us here? Jeryl Jarlyn actually suggested it, but I wanted to make sure it was all right with the two of you."

"Shirl," Leenea replied, "we would love to have Candy here. Between everything you and Alex told us about her, we feel like she is part of the family already. I think she could be a trailblazer and be the first female CT Guard. Alex told us about the self-defense classes that Candy taught. It seems she would be a natural." Shirl thought that would be a great idea. Candy already having a role to play in this world would make her adjustment that much easier.

"Speaking about CT Guards, my brother just communicated to me. Starc and I have another assignment tomorrow with him. Jarlyn is sending us to Terra Nova. Am I being sent to another hell hole?" She was almost afraid of the answer, but she had to know. Her last two trips had been disasters.

"Terra Nova is an iron age world. They are relatively peaceful. Every now and then there is an uprising where one warlord hopes to get territory from another." Darden answered the question, although she was not sure what he meant.

Alex giggled. Her friend was probably grateful the attention had shifted away from her. "Shirl was not much into history. In our world, it was the point in time when man started to use iron, rather than bronze. Basically an agrarian world and weapons were swords. Picture guys with big biceps. Those swords must have been heavy."

"If you will all excuse us," Tarsea said. "I am going to take my pregnant, soon to be wife, to our bedroom. We need to have a discussion about men with big swords." Shirl could not help smiling at the wicked grin that crossed Tarsea's face. They could be amorous in public without losing control. It still bothered Shirl, how different her relationship with Starc was from Alex and Tarsea's.

She watched as the two left the room. There were still questions she had about Terra Nova. "Have either of you two been there before?"

"Once," Darden answered, "there was a rare crystal that Jarlyn wanted. I still do not know what he trades in place of all the crystals we pick up. After the Nightshade universe, I am almost afraid of finding out the answer. He has personal gatherers who deal with that."

"Do you go in armed?" Shirl asked.

"We will arm ourselves as we do with most missions," Starc answered Shirl. "Your safety is always my primary concern. That would have been the case even if we had not been soul mates. Now it is even more paramount that I return you safe to our world."

Something had been bothering her about her brother from almost day one. "Is Cianan one of Jarlyn's personal gatherers?" she asked, although she already knew the answer.

"Yes," Darden replied. "Some missions he goes alone, while others he almost has a CT Guard army with him. The good news is that Jarlyn treasures you too much to send you on any real dangerous missions."

"Really? I have been attacked by a vampire and bitten by a snake. If those were safe missions, I cringe to think what a dangerous mission would encompass."

Shirl pushed her plate away as she pondered what Jarlyn was really after and if she could trust her brother. She hoped Terra Nova was the first world she would visit where her life was not in danger. For some reason, she doubted it.

Chapter 21

～

The cold cut Shirl to the bone. Having lived in Phoenix her whole life, the moderate temperature of Terra Nova was like being on a frozen tundra. The lightweight jacket she had been given to wear on the mission did little to shelter her body from the elements. Even her shins ached from the cold. Starc and Cianan seemed unaffected by the chill.

"Where are the damned crystals?" Shirl asked, "Let's get them before I freeze to death." She was too frickin' cold to sense where the crystals could be found. Starc seemed startled by her comment. He momentarily stared at her and then proceeded to remove his jacket. Her soul mate wrapped his jacket around her. Warmth spread through her body. The lining had been warmed by his body heat. His scent consumed her, bringing about a different kind of heat rushing through her.

"We need to head south." Her brother's comment broke through her lust-saturated brain. "The inhabitants of this world are extremely territorial. I want to be long gone before they are aware of our presence. They are relentless trackers. Women are a scarce commodity in this world. If they get their hands on Shirl, not even a king's ransom will get her released."

Cianan's words confused her. Jeryl Jarlyn continued to tell her how rare and precious she was, yet he kept sending her to these hostile worlds. Was every universe going to present some type of risk to her life? No wonder the Troyk people, who did not support the mind control telepathic government, did not leave until they were forced to. Had it not been for the atmosphere on Earth, her former home was The Garden of Eden, compared to what she had witnessed thus far.

"Why is this the first time I am hearing I could be targeted on this planet because I am a woman?" Shirl asked. She was sick and tired of having things happen to her. Shirl needed to become the mistress of her own destiny.

Her soul mate looked at her sheepishly. "We did not want you to worry. Strong emotions after recovering from a fever could cause a relapse." She had never heard such nonsense.

She swore under her breath. Shirl had heard Tarsea do the same in response to something Alex did or said. It actually made her feel better. "Full disclosure in the future," she ordered. "I need to know what I may be up against before I enter the portal. It may be your responsibility to guard me, but I need to know what I may find when I step into another universe."

Starc nodded his acceptance at Shirl's decree. "We better get going." He led the way, followed by her, and then her brother. They left the meadow where the natural portal existed and entered the woods. The fallen dried leaves that littered the trail made it impossible to travel without making noise.

Anyone close by would know of their existence. As they made their way along the trail, her nose was assaulted by the smell of decomposition. It was nature's way of dealing with forest debris. She started to pray for wind. A steady breeze would drown out the sound of dried debris shuffling, as they made their way to the crystals.

She could not help but notice the number of times Starc looked into the woods. Shirl was tempted to ask him if he sensed anything, but she wanted to keep their telepathic channels clear. It was essential they could hear the approach of any party scouring the forest. A feeling of impending doom germinated within her stomach. No crystal was worth the danger the Prime Ruler's missions placed them in. If she survived, she was going to have to gather the courage to confront Jeryl Jarlyn. The man was up to something and she was tired of playing the role of an ignorant pawn.

Shirl heard the approaching party before Starc signaled for them to stop. Both men placed themselves between her and the four barbarians who emerged from the trees. The men seemed ready to fight, until they noticed her. She saw them shifting as they stood, trying to get a better look at her.

"We are from the Troyk universe," her brother stated. Obviously they were aware of the portal and the visitors who entered their world through it. "Our only purpose is to pick up rocks that hold no value to you."

"Everything holds value to us, if it holds value to you." This world must have fractured from Earth, since these men spoke English. Although Shirl had read articles on string theory, it was Alex who explained why numerous parallel worlds spoke English and other languages that possibly originated on Earth. Drake had explained the people of the Nightshade world had learned English centuries earlier as they sometimes portaled to Earth. "You are free to take whatever you can carry," their spokesman continued. "However, the woman stays here."

"Now would be a good time to open a temporary portal, Shirl," her soul mate communicated through the soul mate channel. She could not agree with him more.

Shirl concentrated on the frequency within her head and worked to increase the volume. She had practiced several times to get the frequency to a high enough decibel to open a portal once she returned from Terra Flora. Practice would make it second nature when a real emergency arose.

It had frustrated her she had not been able to open a portal in that world. She prayed performance anxiety would not prevent her now that they were in danger again.

Once again, something was blocking her ability to generate a portal. She could not understand why she had been able to open portals in the Troyk and Nightshade universes, but not here.

"I cannot open a portal. The same issue is preventing me from isolating the frequency as it did on Terra Flora. It is not an abundance of crystals nearby after all. We are going to have to fight Conan, The Barbarian. Maybe if we stun them, we can then make it back to the natural portal before they regain their senses," Shirl answered. She felt like a failure not being able to open an escape route.

Starc pulled a weapon. It was the same type of device she saw discharged on Terra Flora. The weapon produced energy blasts, powered by the crystal lodged within its base. Her brother stood between her soul mate and the men carrying large broad swords. She had read somewhere that Scottish Claymore's only weighed about five and a half pounds, but these weapons looked massive.

"You wear Allaway's colors," her brother said. Her brother was trying the diplomatic approach, rather than fighting. "He is an ally of our Prime Ruler's. We should be able to work this out without bloodshed." Cianan did not bother to communicate any covert plans for escape through either the communal or familial channels. Her brother was buying them time, assuming these men were willing to escort them to their leader. She would keep trying to break through the interference and open a temporary portal.

"I do not shy away from a fight, but it is best to know who you are fighting." The man kept his eye on the weapon Starc had drawn. He obviously did not want to fight any more than they did, especially against more advanced weaponry. His words allowed him to save face. "My name is Aifric Clacher. I will take you to Ervin Allaway. I will be asking for your agreement to act as comrades." Shirl assumed he warned them not to try and get away while they made their way to the village, or wherever they called home. For some reason, Aifric did not seem as big and threatening as he did before.

"You have our word," Cianan replied. He motioned for Starc to stand down. Her soul mate did not immediately comply, but ultimately lowered his weapon. The men who surrounded them did not seem eager to take Starc's weapon from him. "No one touches my sister or I cannot guarantee her mate's frenzied reaction." Shirl watched as the men sized up Starc. He was as tall as the men before them and just as muscular. For an instant she could picture him wearing animal skins and brandishing a sword. Heat once again spread through her body. She was going to have to remember that image for a less life threatening time.

Aifric and another of his men led their way along the wooded path, while the remaining men brought up the rear. They appeared to be as weary walking through the woods as her party had been. Darden had mentioned there were occasional hostilities between clans in this world.

"What do you have planned?" Starc asked her brother through a communal channel. They had made sure that Shirl would be able to link to that particular channel before they left on their first mission. Although Shirl had been able to link into additional Troyk communal channels, they continued to use this one during missions.

"I am trying to maintain the truce Jarlyn established with this clan years ago," her brother answered. *"We should be able to leave with the crystals and Shirl."* Shirl questioned whether or not her brother would have sold her to these men for a handful of crystals had Starc not been present. This was the third mission with her brother and she still did not know if he could be trusted. His behavior was so inconsistent where she was concerned, she did not know how to read him.

They had been walking for twenty minutes and there seemed to be no end in sight. The dense foliage allowed little sun to come through and Shirl could barely feel her fingers anymore. Starc's jacket had given her some relief, but she was freezing. The pace they set should have generated enough energy to warm her body. She did not want to appear weak to these men by asking her soul mate to wrap his arm around her. Terra Flora did not seem like a bad place all of a sudden, even with the Giant Larma beasts.

After another ten minutes they came upon a clearing. There were various stone structures scattered in the meadow. Aifric stopped in front of the second building they came to. "The woman can wait here while we meet with Allaway. There be food and a hearth within. Go warm yourself before your shivering wears down your teeth."

Shirl figured this was a male dominated world and now was not the time to strike out for women's liberation. The warmth of a fire was too inviting. Even though she had eaten what Tolfer had prepared, she was starting to get hungry.

"I will be fine," she shared with Starc through their link. *"Negotiate us out of here, but don't trust Cianan. Keep me advised of how things are going and when I should be ready to make a move. I will let you know if I am successful in opening a temporary portal."* She entered the building, as Starc continued with the men, to meet with Ervin Allaway.

As promised, there was a blazing fire to her right as she entered. She immediately walked to the hearth and warmed her hands. There was a chair not far from the fire she sat in, once her hands were warm. Shirl examined the room about her, trying to identify anything she could use as a weapon. The room was sparse. There was a small bed, a table with two chairs, and a couple of chests. She came from a world of abundance, it was strange to see a people who lived so frugally. Shirl wondered if the Troyk had a prime directive, like the Federation had on *Star Trek*.

The warmth from the hearth was lulling her to sleep. She found the cracking of the wood as it burned soothing. Shirl was startled awake by someone entering the structure. An old woman carried an arm full of clothing. She placed them on Shirl's lap and then left before Shirl had an opportunity to thank her.

Shirl barely had the opportunity to examine the garments when an old man came in with what she assumed was a tray of food. He too left his offerings and exited. Curiosity and an empty stomach got the best of her. She rose and went to examine what her nose had already communicated was hearty food.

There was a bowl of what she assumed was mutton stew. The aroma told her there was cinnamon, garlic, and clove seasoning. She took a bite and flavor exploded in her mouth. It would have been perfect with a little salt. Shirl noted that in the future, they could barter salt for crystals. If this place was similar to Earth's evolution, salt would have been a commodity used only by the very rich. Shirl remembered reading that in one of her historical romance novels. She quickly finished the stew and used the bread that accompanied the meal to sop up the remaining gravy.

Shirl directed her attention to the clothing she had been given earlier. There was a gown made of the softest suede she had ever felt. The garment was dyed a rich green. She could not resist the temptation of having the soft, warm material against her skin.

There was a privacy screen on the far side of the room, not far from the bed. She quickly made her way behind it and changed into the dress. It fit like it had been made specifically for her. The lightweight leather, felt sinful against her skin.

Under normal circumstances, she would have been thrilled with such a prize. There was a shawl, a similar color to the dress, she placed over her shoulders. There was a large silver brooch she leveraged to clasp the shawl. Shirl felt she was going to a costume party and was waiting for her date to pick her up.

But she was not on her way to a party. They were in a dangerous parallel universe and she had not heard from Starc. She had asked him to keep her apprised of their negotiations. That did not bode well for their chances of leaving this world in one piece. Shirl concentrated once again to open a temporary portal. She grew so frustrated, she threw the bowl across the room.

Starc finished his second bowl of stew, waiting for their negotiations to start. Cianan seemed to understand the customs of these people, so Starc followed his lead. He had not been happy about leaving Shirl behind as they entered the village.

The fact she had not called out for help through the soul mate channel eased his conscience. Since they had not started discussions yet, he had nothing to report back to her. He imagined she had dined and was now warm. Starc had been so focused on the threats present in the woods, he had not noticed his soul mate's discomfort. It irked him that Aifric had reacted to how cold Shirl was. He just assumed giving her his jacket took care of her chill. Starc had not thought of following up regarding her comfort.

He eyed the man at the head of the table. Ervin Allaway was not what he had been expecting. Allaway was a relatively young man and would turn any woman's head. He was powerfully built, no doubt he had fought his way to being leader of this clan. Unlike his men, Allaway was clean shaven. Starc could understand how such a man would want a woman like Shirl. Ervin would want a woman that gave him stature, as well as strong children. He had his work cut out for himself if he was going to leave with Shirl. Something told him that her wishes were not paramount, related to her fate in this universe.

A round of alcohol was served. After he downed the shot, his patience had worn thin. *"Start the negotiations already,"* he instructed Cianan. His soul mate's brother did not seem in any hurry. Shirl's words about not trusting him continued to play in his head.

Starc was not a smooth talker. He was a soldier, a follower. His brother Darden had always been the one who would communicate some grandiose plan when they were growing up. Starc excelled at executing that plan, a talent he brought into adulthood. Being a Crystal Telepath Guard was the ideal occupation for him. A follower.

"Ervin," Cianan started, "we have had a mutual, beneficial relationship for many decades. Jarlyn first came to terms with your father when they were both young men. You have many enemies that would gladly take everything you have built over the years. The Troyk have provided you supplies to help wage the wars with men who would take what is yours." Starc could not fault how Cianan started discussions with Allaway.

"Everything you say is true," Ervin replied. "However, you have never come here with a female. I hear she is very beautiful and would give me many healthy children." Starc had to hold himself back from the words Ervin voiced. He would keep silent until Cianan failed in his attempts to free his sister.

"The woman you mention is my sister. She is a crystal telepath, like I am. Jarlyn has had her accompany me on my trips to other worlds, in order for her to learn to navigate the portal properly. It would be a shame to destroy a relationship both our people have cherished for two generations over a woman. Let me make myself perfectly clear. Any action taken against my sister will negate any agreements our two worlds have entered into." Starc was impressed with Cianan's words and forcefulness.

The leader of this village seemed to be considering his options. Women were scarce; however, the trade relationship his people had with the Troyk universe had to be the difference between maintaining their edge against their enemies and losing everything they had. Ervin Allaway's eyes surveyed the room and fell on Starc.

"What does the woman mean to you," Ervin directed the question to Starc.

"I am a Crystal Telepath Guard assigned to protect Shirlyn Thork. The woman is also my soul mate and I will not give her up." Starc decided to lay all his cards on the table. Allaway seemed taken aback when Starc mentioned that he was mated to Shirl. He hoped the man recognized the truth when he heard it. There should not be a doubt in the other man's mind about what lengths Starc would take to leave this world with Shirl.

"There are tales about the power a mated female crystal telepath possesses. I grew up hearing such legends. My father would tell me about them every night when I was growing up. What can she do?"

Starc should have spent more time with Darden learning all the legendary tales about crystal telepathic women. Hearing legends seemed a waste of time when he had the real thing in his arms. He needed to answer this question very carefully, make it seem that the power came from the mated couple. Otherwise, he would never get off this world with Shirl.

"We have not been mated long," Starc confessed. "What we have discovered is that her additional telepathic abilities only comes about when she has physical contact with me. She is strongest after we have made love." Course, but true. He hoped he was convincing that Shirl had no additional powers without his presence.

"That would make sense," Ervin replied. "Such a woman would be worthless to me as a lover, but valuable as a friend to my people." Starc let out the breath he had been holding. He had hoped it had not been too obvious.

Ervin Allaway snapped his fingers and one of his guards came to do his bidding. The leader whispered into the guard's ear and then he proceeded to leave the building. "I have called for the woman we have been discussing to join us. We can finish our negotiations with her present." Ervin had another shot and started to talk to the man on his left. They were almost home free. Shirl's stature in this community changed once they knew what she was.

Only moments elapsed before Shirl joined them. She had changed out of her tunic, leggings, and overcoats. His soul mate was in a long flowing green dress with a shawl providing additional warmth. Troyk women in their revealing evening wear did not hold a candle to his soul mate before him. She was feminine, soft, and absolutely beautiful. Every man in the room was struck dumb by her presence.

The men's captivated silence was cut short by the banging of metal outside in the village. "We are under attack," someone cried.

Shirl felt uncomfortable with all the men in the room staring at her. Her whole life she wanted to be judged on who she was, not how she looked. The green dress molded to her every curve and she had brushed out her hair. She knew she had captivated every man in this room. It was not a stretch to imagine that anything she said would be discounted. She also wondered if her appearance would also add to the challenges to them leaving this world.

Havoc arose when a man yelled from outside that they were under attack. Every man in the room rose, drew their swords and screamed a battle cry, as they ran to face their enemy. Shirl dodged men exiting as she went to Starc's side. He pulled out his weapon, drawing her behind him.

A tall, broad shouldered man with dark auburn hair approached. "We will hold back the scourge. Be prepared for battle in case any of them make it through our defenses." He came up to Shirl and took her hand. "My name is Ervin Allaway. It will be my pleasure to get to know you better, if I am triumphant on this day." He kissed her hand and ran to join the men fighting outside.

"Shirl," Cianan stood before her, "take this crystal. If we are threatened, open a gateway and direct your anger at any approaching men who threaten you."

Shirl had no idea what her brother was talking about. She had not been able to open a portal in this world. Plus, she was not sure what directing her anger at anyone would do. Shirl looked at the crystal her brother had given her. It was one he picked up in Terra Flora. She was unaware of the qualities the crystal possessed. "I don't understand what you are talking about," she complained to her brother.

"Just do it," her brother replied. "Starc, when she opens the portal, make sure Shirl is between you and the gateway." Her soul mate merely nodded, too absorbed in preparing for anyone entering the room from the chaos outside.

She noticed a number of swords lying against the far wall. Shirl ventured over and picked up a number of the swords until she discovered the lightest. Looking the lady of the manor was one thing, self-preservation was quite another. She had no idea how she would fare against an experience swordsman, but she was not going to have any man take her out of this village. Starc came to her side. He took the sword and gave her his weapon. It was almost weightless in her hand compared to the sword.

"Simply point and shoot," Starc explained. "Easy. The weapon has a storage capacity of three energy blasts." Shirl merely nodded her head. She prayed she would not have to use the weapon.

A man breached the sanctity of their room. He wore different colors than the men they had met in the woods. She assumed he was the enemy. She raised her weapon and fired it as he approached. Her shot was left of the target and demolished a chair. Fortunately, Cianan fired a second shot that brought down the man.

Shirl had seen enough movies to grab the sword that fell at her feet. If the man was not mortally wounded, she did not want him having access to his weapon. She returned the weapon to Starc, feeling he had a better chance of stopping an oncoming lunatic than she had. One chair to her credit was going to be her crowning glory. Worst case scenario, she would use the sword to protect herself.

As she prepared for more men to breach Allaway's perimeter, she realized she had tried to kill a man and felt nothing. The horrors of the Nightshade universe must have desensitized her against violence. It was all about self-preservation at this point.

A few more men entered, battling each other. Two additional men not engaged with one of Allaway's men came directly at Starc and Cianan. Starc shot one and prepared to fend off a third man who entered. Her soul mate had only one energy shot left. Cianan aimed his weapon at his assailant and attempted to fire. Something in the firing mechanism failed. The man raised his sword toward her brother.

Without thought, Shirl grabbed a sword and placed it between the falling sword and her brother. She held on with two hands, knowing there would be a lot of kickback she was going to be deflecting. The force of metal on metal brought Shirl to her knees, but she still held the sword. Her opponent took a look at her and stopped dead in his tracks. His distraction gave Cianan enough time to grab a free sword and finish him off.

More men entered the room, a number heading toward her. Her brother and Starc held off as many men as they could. Her soul mate had used his last energy blast and now held a sword in his hand. She stood behind them, doing her best to channel Errol Flynn. The movie star's sword fight with Basil Rathbone in *Robin Hood* was legendary. She had watched that movie dozens of times. That was one of the reasons why she had tried on the dress. Growing up, she had wanted to be Olivia de Havilland's Maid Marion.

One of the men skirted Starc and came at her. She raised her sword in a deflected move. At least she had hoped it was a defensive move. She deflected two short thrusts before Starc took over, having finished off his opponent. It was not long before two more men made their way to Starc. Shirl was going to help him when another man came at her with an axe.

There was no way she was going to be able to hold off an axe with the sword in her hand. She backed up, looking for some type of shield. The man kept moving forward. Shirl dropped her sword. She doubted he would harm an unarmed woman, especially with women being as sparse as they were in this world.

The warrior grabbed her arm and started to drag her in the direction of the door. Although she was not going to put up a fight with a sword, she certainly was not going to go willingly with the man. She let her feet fall from underneath her. Let him deal with her dead weight! One of Allaway's men, free from the man he had been fighting, drove his sword into her capturer's side. He immediately released her and she started to crawl back to Starc. Another pair of hands captured her and brought her up against him. He was a man of short stature and slight of build. Shirl was able to take a step back and kneed him in the groin. Her assailant fell to his knees.

She temporarily admired her work, not immediately assessing her situation. Before she knew it, another man grabbed her. Unlike the other men, this one hit her in the face and threw her over his shoulder. Her assailant took only a few steps before someone hit the man in the back. She felt him fall forward, taking her with him. The man who slugged her cushioned her fall. She got up as quickly as she could, noting he was in the process of getting up as well.

Groaning, the fallen man reached out and grabbed her arm. She was helpless against his strength, as he pulled her toward him. "You will be mine," he told her as be brought her underneath him. She was momentarily overwhelmed by his weight and the stench coming from him. Shirl snapped back to her senses, as he roughly started to lift her beautiful dress.

Outrage consumed her. She could not believe this animal was attempting to rape her as men were battling around them. Frantically she looked around for some type of weapon. She would not be able to fend him off with her own non-existent strength.

Shirl saw a dagger that lay next to a downed man. Her assailant was so preoccupied with the clothing that hindered his plans, he was unaware of Shirl reaching for the knife. She stretched as far as she could, successfully grabbing the weapon. Her hand gripped the base of the dagger and drove it into his side with every bit of energy she had. The man did not move again after the weapon pierced his side. He was bleeding out, the crimson liquid saturating her dress.

He was a bear of a man, weighed over two hundred and fifty pounds. Shirl did her best to roll the dead man off her. A part of her thought about waiting out the battle hidden underneath the man, hoping the villagers were triumphant. However, she could never live with herself if anything happened to Starc.

They would live or die together, as soul mates were destined to do. She was not sure that was true, but it sounded impressive. She wiggled out from under the man she stabbed. In the process, she was kicked and stepped on, as men continued to fight around her. She needed to get back on her feet before she got trampled.

Shirl made her way back to Starc and her brother. She circumnavigated men fighting to their death. On her way, she grabbed a sword that had belonged to a fallen warrior. Starc was involved taking on another man. Shirl took her sword and swung it in the direction of his opponent's side. She made contact, taking the man down. Shirl ran into Starc's arms. Cianan had just finished off the man he had been fighting. The three came together, exhausted.

They watched in horror as more warriors from the rival village entered the structure. Ervin Allaway and a number of his men were still standing, but losing their battle. Fresh reinforcements to continue waging war and aid their wearied friends did not look promising. Starc and her brother could barely stand at this point.

"You have to open a portal now, Shirl," Cianan said. He wiped blood away from his mouth.

"I have tried," Shirl cried. "There is some kind of interference preventing me." The fight had physically weakened her. She did not think she had the energy to open a temporary portal, even if she had been successful earlier. What little strength she had left was better served holding back the next assault that was moments away from occurring.

"Shit," her brother said. He grabbed one of the crystals he wore, placed it on the floor, and crushed the crystal with his foot. "Try it now. Direct your anger toward the men fighting our allies."

She stared at the crushed crystal at her brother's feet. What had Cianan done? Starc shouted through the soul mate channel, *"Try it, Shirl!"*

She concentrated on increasing the volume of the natural frequency in her head. This time she was successful. A portal opened and Starc followed Cianan's earlier direction, he got on the other side of her. She turned and looked at the men fighting for their lives. Shirl thought of how well she had been treated by the people who lived in this village, of the brutality these raiders presented, and her sore jaw. She tasted her own blood in her mouth. Beside her, the air became unstable.

"Allaway's men, fall to your knees," Cianan shouted. To Shirl's surprise, the men went down.

The displaced air turned into the largest portal she had yet witnessed. The event horizon shimmered and then an energy burst blasted out. Shirl watched in horror as the men standing were incinerated. She collapsed to her knees, overwhelmed by what she had just initiated.

Chapter 22

Starc handed his soul mate a mug of tea, with a bit of alcohol in it. She had not uttered a word since the energy blast that eradicated the men who were before the portal. By some miracle, only one of Allaway's men was caught in the decimation.

Cianan kept his distance. The man had a lot of explaining to do. He knew what Shirl was about to unleash when he handed her the crystal. There was not a doubt in his mind that it was all orchestrated by Jeryl Jarlyn.

Ervin Allaway entered, carrying soup with him. "You have to eat," he said as he handed her the bowl. "Old Peigi made it herself. Her hands are crippled with age, but she wanted to do this just for you. Her grandson was one of the men you saved this day." Shirl looked at Ervin. She picked up her utensil and started eating the soup. Starc knew his soul mate well enough to know Ervin's words about the old woman slaving over the meal had caused her to eat.

Starc did not know what to say to his soul mate. Shirl had a haunted look in her eyes. She had no idea what she would unleashed before she did it. He did not understand why she felt so guilty.

Allaway kissed her hand and left. Starc sat next to his soul mate. "Talk to me, Shirl," Starc implored. He needed her to voice what was on her mind. She was used to talking, so he asked her orally, rather than through the soul mate channel. Telepathic communication could be too impersonal to her.

Shirl considered him for several moments. "I want to talk to Cianan." She then turned off once again. Shirl simply sipped her tea, shutting him out.

It did not take long for Starc to find Cianan. He seemed resolved that he had to talk to his sister. He could no longer postpone the inevitable. Cianan walked beside Starc, as if walking to his own execution. Considering how shell-shocked Shirl was, he was glad he was not in Cianan's shoes. There was so much Starc wanted to say and do to Cianan, but it was Shirl's right to act first.

Shirl looked up as they entered the structure she had temporarily been assigned. She had been unofficially adopted by the village. No one reacted to her in fear, only extreme gratitude. His soul mate was their legendary avenger. It did not matter the legend came from another dimension. She had bestowed her blessing and power in their defense. Had it not been for Shirl, every surviving man and male child would have been killed. What few women they had would have been taken forcefully by the victors, sentenced to a life of slavery, serving their capturer's depraved needs.

"You owe me an explanation," Shirl addressed Cianan. She spoke barely above a whisper. Sheer exhaustion reflected in her voice. "How did you know about the energy blast and why were you blocking my ability to open a portal at will?" Starc could hear Shirl holding back the anger in her voice. She must have felt betrayed by her own brother. Their relationship was strained from the beginning, but Starc could not imagine why Cianan did what he did.

Cianan sat next to his sister, taking her hand. Starc was surprised she did not forcibly remove her hand from his. "I do not know how to apologize to you. My whole life I was mad at you. You were the reason why my mother, our mother, left me. Jeryl Jarlyn used that anger to pit me against you. He played me as much as he did you."

"I don't understand," Shirl responded. "When our mother went through the portal, I was a year old. Why would you blame me?" Disbelief reflected in her tone.

"I overheard an argument between our parents on the eve of her leaving with you. Jeryl Jarlyn knew all the fables associated with crystal telepathic mated females. Although the idea of soul mates was legendary, Jeryl believed it wholeheartedly.

"When you were born, our Prime Ruler became obsessed with you. He wanted to adopt you so he could control you and find your soul mate. The power that you would have once mated, became his obsession. By the time you were born, our parents' marriage was over.

"She viewed Benko Jarlyn as her salvation. When he left our world, she followed with you. Mom told me she was leaving me with dad because she did not want to leave him alone. I begged her to take me with her, but she left. Our father disappeared that night. I assumed he followed to protect you. It was all about you."

Shirl stared at her brother. Starc knew she was digesting everything Cianan told her. They all assumed that Jenka Thork had gone with Benko strictly as his follower and the crystal telepath they needed to navigate the portal. It must have been overwhelming to his soul mate to learn everything her mother did to save Shirl from Jeryl Jarlyn.

"If she had taken you with us," Shirl replied, "you would be dead. She died terribly of a brain embolism. You would never have seen your twenty-fifth birthday. When did you become Jarlyn's puppet?" There was so much venom in Shirl's voice, even Starc was taken aback.

Cianan could not look directly at his sister. "Jarlyn called me to his office when you first arrived. He asked me to mentor you on how to navigate the portal. When we returned from the Nightshade universe, I was brought back before him to be debriefed. I told him what happened between you and Starc. In addition, I told him about you opening a temporary portal with little effort. It was not a leap of logic that you were now a mated female crystal telepath."

"You son of a bitch," Starc said. He had to hold back from giving Cianan the beating of his life. Shirl deserved answers. "Let me guess, he did not even have to use his mind control. You just volunteered the information."

"I was so angry with Shirlyn," Cianan replied. Starc saw Shirl cringe at her brother using her full name.

"Grow up, you bastard," Starc growled. "Take some responsibility for your actions. Blaming a year old baby for all the things wrong with your life is pathetic."

Shirl took Starc's arm and shook her head. She redirected her attention back to her brother. "Go on," was all she said.

"He gave me a crystal that would interfere with your ability to open a temporary portal. Jarlyn sent us to Terra Flora for me to get the rare crystals that would allow you to use the portal as a weapon. The stones you picked up were just a smoke screen. I was to release the portal block when you were desperate enough to harness the power of the gateway. He said there would be an energy blast, but I had no idea the extent of that blast."

"When we return to the Aster Province, what are you going to tell Jarlyn about what happened here?" Shirl asked, she sounded weary.

"I am going to have to work that out. It will be half-truths. His mind control telepathic abilities can only identify lies. There is no way I am going to communicate the magnitude of the energy blast. We will also have to talk with Ervin and his people about what to communicate, when gatherers from our world visit this village."

Shirl sighed. Starc figured whatever her brother confessed and was going to do going forward, would not be easy for Shirl to hear. He wrapped his arm around her shoulder. Rather than shake him off, she nestled into his body.

"I fantasized my whole life about traveling," Shirl confessed to her brother. "Fellow orphans dreamed about finding a family, while all I wanted was to escape. When the portal in Sedona first opened, it was a dream come true. You have turned it into a nightmare. We will head out to the portal to return to the Troyk universe in an hour. That trip will be my last through the portal, ever."

Chapter 23

"All right, there has been enough moping. You need to talk to me and get out of this mood of yours." Shirl looked up as Hurricane Alexandra entered her room. Alex had one of those determined looks on her face. She did not want to deal with her friend right now. Shirl was still dealing with everything she learned and had done in the Terra Nova universe. Alex joined her on the bed, undeterred by her desire to be left alone.

They lay in silence for several minutes. It felt good having Alex close. Maybe it would be a good idea to get some of her feelings off her chest. She knew that Alex would be there for her, regardless of what she shared. Besides, Alex had not witnessed the extent of what Shirl had unleashed.

"You would not understand, Alex" Shirl said. "I feel like a pariah. No one should have the power I exhibited on Terra Nova. I killed several men with weapons in self-defense. That, I can live with. The blast of energy killed everything in its path. I was like an atomic bomb."

"Get a grip, Shirl," Alex said. "You are not a pariah. Turns out you are a mated crystal telepath with a shit load of power. Men on Ginkgo Terra have the power to decimate a city with just pushing a button. The issue is not about having the power, but showing the strength not to use it. There are times you are going to have to reach deep inside and figure out what you are not willing to lose, before you draw that power forward again. That is what being a grown up and taking responsibility is all about."

Shirl knew her friend was right. She just did not know if she could live with the death of all those men on her conscience. "I incinerated dozens of people, Alex. How am I going to be able to sleep at night?"

"First, you did not know you had the power that resulted in those men's deaths. Had you been told about this power, you could have learned to regulate the energy blast. Jeryl Jarlyn has a lot to answer for. Secondly, would you have been willing to lose your brother and Starc if you had to do it all over again?"

Shirl did not have to consider the question, but answered immediately. "I would have done it all over again. That makes me a monster."

"A monster would be able to sleep at night. The fact that you are struggling with what you did clears you of being a psychotic fiend. Would you have killed those men to save Cianan and Starc if you had a semi-automatic rifle?" Shirl nodded, although she had never even picked one up. "The difference is that one is an external weapon, while the other is internal to your genetics. You have a gift, Shirl."

"Alex, all that was left of those men was ash. It is frightening, the power I am able to harness." Shirl shuttered, thinking about it. The scene played in her brain countless times since her return to Aster Province. She did not discount Alex's recommendation of trying to harness the power. Bringing about another portal to practice controlling that power scared her to death.

"Those men would have killed every man in that village and then done God knows what to you", Alex said. "They got what they deserved. The only difference is that the villagers will not have to bury shot up bodies."

Shirl looked at Alex in disbelief. "That's not funny, Alex!"

"I don't mean to be glib," her friend replied. "If I had that power and you were threatened, I would not hesitate to use it. I gave up Chartail to the Troyk Government, in order to reduce patrols around the portal. My primary concern was bringing you here, regardless of what I had to do. That, I can live with. You have to figure out, what you can live with."

Shirl's brain was wrapping itself around everything that Alex shared. Somehow Robert Oppenheimer, father of the atomic bomb, was able to live with what he unleashed. She was going to have to find a way to do the same.

"When did you get so deep?" Shirl said, needing to lighten things up a bit.

"A lot has happened since I arrived in the Troyk universe. Sometimes the things I have done scares the shit out of me. When things get too heavy or I question what I am doing, Tarsea and I have a conversation. We really open up to each other. I don't know if it's the whole soul mate thing or I just choose to be brutally honest. After we finish one of our discussions, I no longer feel dirty. It kind of cleanses my soul."

Once again Shirl wished she had that close relationship with Starc. He was her protector and they had frighteningly great sex. She knew she wanted more, she was just not sure how to take the next step.

"Starc and I are not like you and Tarsea. He does not feel the same way about me as your soul mate feels about you. It's all physical and about responsibility." There, how was that for opening herself up!

"How do you know? From what I understand, the two of you let off some steam and then parted ways. True intimacy happens after the orgasm. You have to lay your soul out there for him and vice versa. Starc is taciturn. You are going to have to work to open him up. Take the risk, Shirl. It's frightening, but the benefits are worth the discomfort in the beginning."

"Starc wouldn't want that, Alex," Shirl admitted to her friend.

"I love you, Shirl," Alex said. "But you have to stop playing the victim. Your whole life you complained about people not taking you seriously, only reacting to how you look. I've seen you drive forward since you arrived, only to take a step back. You need the mental fortitude to keep driving to what you want. Starc wants a deeper relationship with you, I guarantee it."

"Then why isn't he here instead of you?" Shirl answered in anger.

Alex did not seem taken aback by her friend's violent response. "Frankly, I think he is scared to death he'll lose you if he confronts you with his feelings. I see the way he looks at me and Tarsea. There is longing in his gaze. He wants the same type of relationship that Tarsea and I have."

Shirl could not help it, she grunted at Alex's comments. She wished what she was saying was true.

"You are soul mates," Alex continued. "The physical part of the relationship is violently activated as soon as you first touch. That is the easy part. I think under normal circumstances we would have gotten to know our soul mates a little better before things turned sexual. In that period, our two souls would have gotten to know each other and been prepared for the next evolutionary stage, once we made love. I think we just jump-started things a little early. Besides, you said Drake manipulated the soul mate connection. It's time to play catch-up and get to know Starc. He is a wonderful man. I would not have been able to select a better soul mate for you if I tried."

"You exhaust me, Alex." Her friend seemed to suck the air out of the room, as she threw one thought after another in Shirl's direction. Their relationship had changed. Alex was not going to fix this for her, she was just showing her the way to do it on her own.

Her friend laughed. "Yes, I know. You have a lot to think about. Just prove to Starc you are not going to fall to pieces or break if you start having frank conversations. The trials that Jeryl Jarlyn has put you through would break anyone's spirit, but you persevered. Starc never left your side, when you returned with the snake bite. Prove to him you have the mental strength as well to tackle what life throws at you."

Alex rose from the bed and kissed Shirl on the forehead. "I'm starving!" Alex advised her. "I am going to see what Tolfer has cooking and see if I can talk him into giving his niece or nephew a small portion before everyone sits down to eat." She left the room, leaving Shirl to her thoughts.

Shirl did not want anything more, than she wanted to get closer to Starc. She did not know if she could handle him turning away from her. They had not talked about the energy blast that she generated in Terra Nova. It scared her to death that he would now look at her through different eyes.

Starc looked up from the drink, he held in his hand as Alex pranced into the kitchen. She immediately went to Tolfer and started chatting with him. He heard Tarsea groan next to him.

"If Alex had to choose between me and one of my brother's keen dishes, I think I would come in second." Tarsea kept his eyes on his soul mate as Tolfer dished out a small bowl of food for her. She joined them at the table. "How is Shirl? She must be better or you are really hungry."

"Both," Alex said, as she winked at Starc. "What happened on Terra Nova has really shaken her. She has always thought people judged her on how she looked and now she is afraid this new power is going to define her. I can talk until I am blue in the face, but there is only one person's acceptance she really needs." As Alex took another fork full of food, she directly looked at Starc.

"Me?" Starc asked, bewildered. Shirl had been avoiding him like the plague since they returned, barricading herself in her room. He was afraid to approach her. "I wanted to give her space."

Alex gave him a knowing look. "The last thing Shirl needs is space. She will wallow in self-doubt until every ounce of her self-esteem is gone. Her greatest fear is losing you because of the power she can wield. She won't admit it to you, so you need to address it with her directly."

Shirl was not the only one battling with self-doubt, Starc thought as he left the kitchen. He should not have left Shirl alone for so long. It should have been him who went to talk to her, not Alex. Once again, he failed his soul mate. These festering issues between him and Shirl had to stop. He needed to man up and talk to the woman he could not breathe without. She was now a part of him and he had to fix their failing relationship.

He stood in front of Shirl's bedroom door. Taking a deep breath, he knocked. She immediately bid him to enter. Starc walked into the room and found Shirl lying in bed, still wearing the clothes she had on in Terra Nova when they left. She had not even bothered to change. Part of him wanted to continue to let her be, to gather her strength.

The part of him that knew he needed to confront his soul mate won out. "How are you feeling? You look a little pale." Not exactly the words that led to the discussion he wanted to have with her. Her wan complexion took him aback. The discoloration of her jaw also alarmed him. It was swollen, and yellow had joined the black and blue from earlier.

"I am just a little tired. My brain just won't shut up and let me rest," Shirl replied.

"What are you thinking or worrying about," Starc said, "maybe I can help." He hoped this was the opening he longed for to start a dialog. Alex had encouraged him to ask her directly. Starc just did not know what to say to Shirl. He did not want to disturb her any more than she already was.

"Starc, I am scared to death, I will not be able to control my powers and end up hurting innocent people. I feel like I am a disaster waiting to happen. Plus, my brother sold me out to Jeryl Jarlyn. That man scares the shit out of me. Part of me wants to leave this universe, but what I've seen of other worlds, there is no place to go."

He removed his shoes and joined his soul mate on the bed. Rather than just lying next to her, he decided to take her into his arms. Nothing was more important than comforting Shirl and not letting their sexual attraction derail the discussion they needed to have.

"You saved my life," Starc shared with her. "I am supposed to protect you, yet it was you who saved the day. There was a big part of me that berated myself for putting you in the position where you had to discover your new power. But then I realized what a partnership was all about. Saving each other's butts when one of us has the opportunity."

She looked at him in wonder. He did not think he had strung more than a dozen words together when talking to her. His soul mate did not seem ready to continue the discussion. It was up to him to relieve the guilt she felt, or at least share it.

"Shirl, you had no idea what would happen when your brother directed you on how to manipulate the energy of the portal. You just knew that I was in danger and would have died had you not taken action."

He brought her fully into his body. His left arm wrapped around her shoulder, while he massaged the small of her back with the other. There was nothing sexual about what he was doing, yet his body generated heat. It was a healing warmth that his soul mate soaked into her body. She sighed with contentment.

Shirl lifted her head and looked into his eyes. "I was chilled to the bone and you warm my soul, Starc. Alex asked if I was willing to lose you and not use my power to save you. I told her I would have done the same thing again. That scares me to death."

"What scares you? How you feel about me or the ability to generate an energy blast?" He held his breath, as he awaited her answer.

"That I would be willing to kill for you, Starc," Shirl answered. "The thought that I could have lost you on Terra Nova makes me physically sick. I feel like I barely know you, but you are interwoven in my being. It was that feeling that powered the portal. I don't know how to better explain it. My feelings for you generated that blast."

There it was. The unexplainable bond between soul mates that scared them both. Alex and Tarsea reveled in it, while Starc and Shirl shrank from it. Those heart wrenching words gave him hope their relationship could develop into a true soul mate bonding.

"You are an amazing woman, Shirl," Starc answered. "I am truly humbled by your words and feelings for me. Our feelings for each other can generate the specter of death. That is a burden that we must carry together. Shirl, you are not alone."

Shirl let out a short burst of breath, a sort of half laugh. "I dreamed of traveling my whole life. It never dawned on me that it was not the journey that was so critical, but who I traveled with. I spoke in haste when I told Cianan I was never going through the portal again. I just wish we were not Jeryl Jarlyn's puppets. He purposely put us in danger to test my powers."

"We can add that to the ever growing list of why we need Benko Jarlyn to come home and challenge his father. Nothing would make me happier than exploring wondrous parallel worlds with you. In the meantime, we need to be wary of where Jeryl sends us. Based on the challenges we have had, I think I can negotiate more protection as we enter hostile worlds. The less danger either of us is in reduces the chance of a lethal energy blast being generated. But if we need it as a weapon, it can be a strategic tool in our arsenal. Like anything else, we need to learn how to control it. I doubt it always has to be such an incendiary blast. Let us try to bring it down to something that will just stun. Together we can make that happen."

Shirl nuzzled Starc's neck. "Thank you, Starc. I do not think I ever felt so alone in my life. In the orphanage I had Alex and Candy. But this power, it isolates me from everyone."

"You are never going to be alone again, love," Starc said before he took possession of her mouth. In a matter of moments he deepened the kiss. He could not get enough of her taste.

Shirl felt renewed, as well as totally turned on. His kiss consumed her. She lifted her hands and grabbed locks of his hair. For such a powerful man, he had baby fine hair. This time she was willing to stay on the bottom. She liked the feel of his strength, his weight on her body. Shirl wanted to be dominated by this man and then meet it with her own need for dominance.

She grabbed at his tunic, pulling it up his torso. He broke their kiss in order to get the garment out of the way. His chest rubbed against the soiled tunic she wore. She wished she had showered and changed.

"Too many clothes," she managed to communicate between kisses. She was so absorbed in what he was doing to her, Shirl forgot she could have shared those thoughts in their private channel. He pulled her tunic off with little effort and then started to remove her leggings. It was not long before she was naked beneath his body. His hands urgently explored her, staying at no part of her body for long. There was a restlessness about his need.

Finally, his eager fingers found the entrance to her sex. First one and then a second finger parted her folds and entered her. He moved his fingers in such a way that he brought about immense pleasure for her with little effort. She wondered what he was saving his energy for. Shirl did not have to wait long to get the answer.

Starc entered her with one powerful thrust. She pulled back her head and called out his name. He drove in and out of her at a frenzied rate. By some miracle she was able to keep up with this pace. Her breathing quickened and she started to see stars. As before, they climaxed together.

Starc rolled over on his side, taking her with him. "I am sorry, love, it was over so quickly. The urgency I was feeling in worrying about you took over my control."

Shirl closed her eyes and took an assessment of how she was feeling, both physically and mentally. She was exhausted, Starc had set an Olympic gold worthy pace. The amazing thing was, she was content mentally. After all the doubt and self-loathing she went through this afternoon, peace had finally come over her.

"We needed to release energy and this was far more enjoyable and less lethal." It amazed Shirl that she could joke about what had been haunting her since she unleashed the power of the portal, although Alex would have found wittier words.

"Give me a couple of minutes and we can release more energy. This time slower and more methodical."

"Methodical?" Shirl questioned him. "That does not sound too promising." It sounded too cerebral.

"I want to explore every inch of you and see what responses I can get out of you as I worship your body." Starc caressed her ear as he spoke. "When I am done with my exploration, it is only fair I give you the opportunity."

Starc was true to his word.

Chapter 24

Shirl dragged herself into the kitchen. She needed coffee. Once she had gotten over the initial symptoms of portal sickness, she exchanged drinking the herbal mixture for coffee. Once she finished her first cup, she would be able to do an assessment of all the aches and pains assaulting her body. She was sore in places she did not know could get sore.

Alex was already in the kitchen, sipping her herbal beverage. She looked up as Shirl entered the room and merely raised her index finger to acknowledge Shirl's presence. Neither Alex nor Shirl were morning people. They normally dragged themselves into the kitchen when they visited each other, not saying a word until each had at least one dose of caffeine. Candy was the morning person. Shirl was going to leave for Ginkgo Terra later this morning and bring her friend here. Candy was going to take over the room Shirl had been using and Shirl was going to move in with Starc. After last night she wondered if she had enough energy to live with him. She took another sip of coffee and did some mental replays of their erotic activities.

Shirl glanced once again at Alex and noticed she appeared as exhausted as she was. "Late night?" she asked her friend.

"That man is insatiable. I don't know whether to complain or thank my lucky stars," Alex replied. "Starc and Tarsea are in the common room. They are probably high fiving each other's performance. The walls are just too thin. When I saw Leenea this morning she just smiled and returned to her own bedroom. Amazing!"

"Is everyone here?" Shirl was too exhausted to get up and check out who was in the common room. The fact that Alex was not eating anything led her to believe that Tolfer had not yet shown up. Only Starc, Tarsea, and Darden were going with her to get Candy. They all felt that Alex's presence would draw too many questions on both sides of the portal. Shirl was concerned that her own story of where she had been would not fly, if she ran into any of the Sedona police.

"Darden arrived twenty minutes ago," Alex replied. "He knows he is going to see Cassie, so he is anxious to head out. He said he would tell us about Candy's family in this universe once she is here. I would have liked to have met with them and prepared them for Candy's arrival." Shirl imagined Alex did not want a repeat of what happened between Cianan and herself. Alex was once again trying to fix everything. Although Shirl did wonder if Alex had talked to Cianan beforehand- if it would have made any difference.

There was a knock on the door. Both women looked at each other and broke into laughter. Neither bothered to get up and answer the door. Odds were the visitor was not there to see them, unless it was a member of Alex's family. She heard voices in the hallway, but could not make them out. The morning fog still had its grubby claws on her.

She was surprised to see Cianan following Tarsea into the kitchen. Tarsea did not bother to announce her brother. He merely walked over to Alex and kissed her. Men were so funny. Tarsea was staking a claim to a woman who almost had a neon sign announcing to the world she was his.

Shirl did not feel the need to be diplomatic. She could blame it on morning grogginess later. "What do you want?"

"I came to apologize," her brother answered, "and tell you what I reported to Jeryl Jarlyn." That certainly woke Shirl up. Her heart started racing. She got up and poured herself more coffee. It would not slow down her heart, but she would certainly feel better. Shirl had not bothered to offer her brother any.

"Let us go into the common room," Tarsea suggested. "I know everyone here would like to hear what you have to say." He took Alex's arm and walked alongside her. Tarsea let her and Cianan walk in front of them, under his watchful eye.

Cianan did not appear to be thrilled he was going to have an audience. What happened when Cianan first met Shirl was not a distant memory for Starc or Darden. She now had a posse to protect her. Shirl immediately sat next to Starc, not even considering taking any of the other open spaces in the room.

"Go on," Shirl said. "Tell us what you reported back to Jarlyn." The other men in the room sat up a little straighter, after Shirl mentioned why Cianan was present. Yet again, it had not dawned on her to forewarn the men using the warrior channel. This telepathic world was going to take some getting used to.

"I told him you were able to generate a bright beam of light from the portal, nothing more. Legends just mention an energy blast and light is energy. He seemed disappointed, but did not question me further. He told me he was going to conduct an inventory of his crystals and would contact me in the next couple of days regarding where he was going to send us next. Jarlyn mentioned you were bringing over a friend from Gingko Terra today, possibly another surviving relative. I think he is secretly hoping she is his granddaughter."

"What is the significance of having a granddaughter to him?" Shirl inquired. She knew that Candy was not his granddaughter, but Cassie was. She looked at all the men, so when she looked at Darden, it would not be obvious that she wanted to see his reaction. He shielded any particular interest in Cianan's answer well.

"I do not know," Cianan said. "Both Jarlyn and Benko are mind control telepaths. There is a strong possibility that any offspring that Benko had would be a mind control telepath, as well. I am unaware of any Troyk legends that would set Jarlyn off, like those about mated crystal telepathic females." Her brother cast his eyes down while he said the last sentence. At least he was now uncomfortable with his duplicity.

"We need to be leaving soon. Is there anything you need?" Shirl asked her brother. She did not know why, but her brother's presence made her anxious. He reminded her of conceit, loss, and betrayal. She had to prepare herself mentally for her trip to bring Candy to the Troyk universe. Her brother was in the way.

"What can I do to make you trust me, Shirl?" Her brother looked sincere. She just did not want to deal with this now.

"There is only one way. I cannot tell you what it involves," she replied. "It is something that can only be earned, not bought." She hoped what she said had been vague enough. She knew that only his ability to link within the warrior channel would truly mean she could trust him. Until that point, she could only assume he was still in Jeryl Jarlyn's pocket.

Her brother looked at her and nodded. "I do not want you to think I am buying your trust, but this belongs to you. It belonged to our mother." Her brother handed her a package.

Shirl took the box and opened it. A copper familial bracelet lay in the box. When she had looked at Alex's bracelet, she had almost convinced herself that it did not matter that she did not have her mother's copper cuff. Shirl had been wearing Chartail's bracelet just to fit in. Now placing her mother's bracelet around her wrist, she knew she had been fooling herself. She felt tears falling down her cheek. Without a word, she stood and hugged her brother. Shirl felt her brother's arms tighten around her.

"Thank you," she cried. "It really means a lot." She did not say anything more, merely walked out of the room.

She headed to her bedroom and grabbed a tissue. Sitting on the bed, she let loose the flood of tears she had been holding back.

This time Starc did not delay checking on her. He entered the room, without knocking. He sat down on the bed and embraced her. "Welcome home, Shirlyn."

For the first time since she had entered the Troyk universe, she did not mind hearing her true name. She *was* finally home- purple sky and all.

The End

Can't Wait to Read Candy's Story?
Enjoy the 1st Chapter of 'The Warrior Woman'
Worlds Apart Series: Book One

Chapter 1

⁓

Gingko Terra/Earth

Candy Phillips was going to kill her two best friends. She wasn't sure how, but proficient in self-defense, she could inflict serious damage to the human body. Whatever method, it was going to have to be slow and deliberate. They were going to suffer as she had suffered the last two weeks. Her friends had vanished and she had been frantic. The Sedona police department was clueless related to what had happened.

She had just purchased her third box of facial tissue since arriving in Sedona, when Shirl called. Shirley Tomlinson, Shirl, disappeared while searching for their mutual friend Alexandra Mann.

All three women had grown up together in a Phoenix orphanage and were closer than most biological sisters Candy knew. It hurt that Shirl had not even informed her of Alex's disappearance. Candy had returned home from taking her high school volleyball team to a tournament, to find they were both missing. Candy had been crying non-stop since she arrived.

She never cried.

A feeling of abandonment she had not experienced since she was a little girl, overwhelmed her. Last night she tossed and turned, unable to sleep. Her mind kept running horrible scenarios over and over again about what could have happened to her friends. Now, out of nowhere, Shirl called to request she meet her at a nearby restaurant. And that she not contact the local authorities. What kind of trouble had they gotten into?

Candy pulled into the restaurant's parking lot. At three o'clock in the afternoon, plenty of spots were open. She stopped in a space on the far side of the building. Candy needed to cool down before she saw Shirl.

Tears were once again flowing. She reached for the next box of tissues, pulled off the cardboard cover, and grabbed a couple to blow her nose. She wasn't sure if she was crying because she was furious or so relieved that she could fall apart now. Either way, the fountain of tears kept flowing.

Candy had purchased a chocolate bar at the drug store as well. She tore off the wrapper and broke off a couple squares. If chocolate couldn't make her feel better, nothing would. She popped a few pieces of the creamy, dark goodness into her mouth. Leaning her head against the headrest, she closed her eyes for a moment. After collecting herself, she was ready to confront her friend.

There was not a doubt in her mind, she looked a mess. Her eyes were probably swollen and her nose red from continual blowing. She needed to clean herself up before she met up with Shirl.

She pulled the elastic from what was left of her ragged ponytail. Her hair was her one vanity. With all the sports she played, it would have been so much easier if she had cut it short. Instead, she let it grow past the small of her back. Maneuvering around the steering wheel, she quickly braided it, then was as ready as she ever would be to re-unite with her friend.

Slamming the car door had released some of her pent-up aggravation. It shouldn't have felt so good to abuse her poor car. As she made her way to the entrance, she took several deep, cleansing breaths. The wooden door was heavier than it looked. She put more of her weight's strength into opening it, one of the few advantages of being a big girl. The extra energy she expended further reduced her annoyance with Shirl.

As she entered, her eyes were immediately drawn to a middle-aged man. He was very attractive with his sable-colored hair and light brown eyes. The gray wisps around his temples gave him a look of sophistication. She wasn't normally attracted to older men, but this man was noteworthy.

Her eyes basked in the sight of him; unfortunately her body did not respond in kind. In her twenty-two years, she had never reacted physically to another person. The man held her gaze for an instant and then directed his attention back to his drink. Candy felt a loss, once the man looked away. It was a very weird reaction she had to a complete stranger.

She needed to focus on the task at hand. Candy continued further into the restaurant looking for Shirl. She saw her at the rear of the room. A man she had never seen before was seated next to her. He had strawberry-blond curly hair and his body reflected someone who worked out regularly. The man fit with her friend, as no one had before. She'd had one outrageous thought after another, since entering this establishment. What was wrong with her? Once again, she chided herself. She needed to focus!

Shirl looked up as Candy approached their table. A huge smile crossed her face. Shirl looked absolutely stunning. Her blond hair was pulled back from her face and her light brown eyes sparkled. Candy couldn't remember a time her friend looked happier. Shirl stood and the two friends embraced. Candy felt an overwhelming sense of relief, knowing Shirl was all right. She hadn't realized how lost she was not knowing where Shirl and Alex were.

"Where the hell have you been?" Candy asked. Obviously, she wasn't ready to let go of all her anger. She felt Shirl loosening her hold before returning to her seat and grabbing the hand of the man next to her.

"There is so much I need to tell you," Shirl replied. "This is Starc. He is my soul mate." Candy would have laughed if anyone else had uttered those words. Shirl was not a starry-eyed princess who believed in fairy tales. She had said those words with a certainty Candy had never heard in Shirl's voice. For the time being, she would go along with whatever Shirl said. When they were alone, she would cross-examine her friend.

"It is nice to meet you, Candy. Shirl has told me all about you." Starc had a baritone timbre to his tone. He had no discernible accent to place where he was from. But the man was gorgeous, that was for sure.

"We should be going," Shirl said as she stood. She came around the table ready to take Candy to God only knew where. Shirl wore a tunic with leggings and a copper bracelet Candy had never seen. At first glance, it appeared to have multiple etchings on it.

"What in the world are you wearing?" Candy blurted out. A number of responses played in Candy's mind. None of them were good. She examined her friend's face and body, trying to identify any camouflaged bruises. Shirl was always self-conscious about her looks, unlike Alex, who never worried about physical attributes.

She had been so focused on Shirl, she had momentarily forgotten about her other missing friend. "Where is Alex?"

"Do you trust me, Candy?" Shirl asked. Her friend was dancing around answering her question. It only fueled the suspicions growing in Candy's mind. An uneasiness once again started to consume her.

"Of course, I trust you," Candy said in frustration. By some miracle, she was able to hold back her temper. "But you are beginning to scare me. I want to know where Alex is!"

Shirl paled before her eyes. "I am sure Alex is fine. I need to show you something that will explain everything. Please trust me for the time being."

A pleading look shone in Shirl's eyes. Shirl had never knowingly harmed a soul, as far as Candy knew. When they were children, Shirl played the mother hen where she and Alex were concerned. Never in a million years would Shirl do anything to harm either of them. She'd put her faith in her friend.

"This better be good," she said under her breath. Candy did not like playing mental games. As with sports, she liked to see what was coming at her. *Never take your eye off the ball,* was her mantra. Reluctantly she followed Shirl and Starc.

Candy was steps away from the exit when she heard "*good luck.*" The words had not been uttered, she was sure of that. They came from within her mind, as if telepathically transmitted. She turned and the man she had seen when she first entered the restaurant was staring at her. He raised his glass, downed the contents, picked up his paper, and started to read. Before she had a chance to question what had just occurred, she was being herded into the back seat of an SUV. Two more strangers were in the front seat. Had she just been kidnapped by some kind of cult?

Candy didn't know if she should call for help or just play along. Shirl reached for her hand and held it for reassurance. That gesture calmed her nerves a bit. No one in the vehicle said a word. There was some nodding and a chuckle, almost as if the occupants were engaged in a conversation. Candy needed to relax and prepare herself for any eventuality. Shirl tightened her grip on her hand.

The men in the front were wearing the same type of outfits Shirl and Starc wore, based on what little she could see. The blond driver had the same type of cuff bracelet Shirl wore. Candy glanced at Starc's wrist. He too had on the same copper jewelry. Everyone wearing identical clothes and bracelets only confirmed Candy's worst fears.

If they were a cult, she decided to wait to make a move until she was with Alex. Alexandra was level headed, although she had once thought the same thing about Shirl. She and Alex would find a way to escape and head straight for the authorities. The fact Alex was not with them, told Candy that Alex had not fallen for any of the malarkey Shirl had obviously swallowed.

She felt the SUV slow just before it turned into one of the Boynton Canyon's parking lots leading to the hiking trails. The same spot where Alex had disappeared, according to the police report she had read. Candy barely swallowed past the lump in her throat. Blood rushed through her veins as her pulse rate skyrocketed.

Shirl bounded out of the SUV. She waved for her to follow. Fear momentarily paralyzed Candy. *"Let's go,"* she thought she heard Shirl say, although her lips had not moved.

She was in the middle of a nightmare. That was why she was hearing things not being spoken. Candy would wake up shortly and find herself in her hotel room. This was just another scenario juggling in her mind.

"We mean you no harm, Candy," the man with short black hair and lovely greenish-brown eyes said. He stood just outside the vehicle door, Starc had exited. "Some things have to be witnessed to be believed. If I told you who we are and where we are from, you would not believe me. Have you ever seen Shirl look so healthy?" Candy was not sure how to take his reassuring words.

Candy shifted in the back seat and looked at Shirl with a critical eye. Her friend had been suffering debilitating headaches and looked terrible the last time she had seen her. Today Shirl was the poster child for health.

She slid across the seat and exited the SUV. Candy stood next to her friend to get a better look. There were no circles under her eyes or stress lines across her forehead. Her eyes were clear and bright. "How are you feeling, Shirl?" Candy asked suspiciously.

"I have not had a headache since I left," Shirl said. She had not clarified where she had been since she had vanished off the face of the Earth. Once again, she decided to take her friend at her word and follow them to wherever they were holding Alex.

The tall, slender man with sun-bleached hair who had been driving the car approached. "My name is Darden. It is a pleasure to finally meet you. The man who addressed you earlier is Tarsea. Walk alongside me, as we make our way up the trail."

He stepped to the side and extended his arm, indicating for her to join him. Taking one last look around, she realized no other hikers were visible. Candy reluctantly edged closer to Darden. Starc and Shirl led the way, while Tarsea brought up the rear. There was nothing threatening in how they moved or behaved. But Candy pulled on her self-defense training and mentally prepared herself for any aggressive move on their part.

The canyon was absolutely beautiful, but she was too uptight to enjoy her surroundings. Sedona was one of the loveliest places on Earth and it was all lost on her.

They had walked for twenty minutes when Shirl and Starc stopped. Her friend turned and Candy noticed Shirl's amethyst was glowing. Candy reached out and touched the crystal, bringing a huge smile to Shirl's face. Then Candy noted that Darden and Starc had gems around their necks, also glowing.

"I am a crystal telepath, Candy," Shirl explained. She took Candy's hand and walked with her to a spot on the trail where the air shimmered. "Our late parents came from another universe, parallel to the one that exists in our reality. My mother was the crystal telepath who navigated the portal to bring our parents here. Unfortunately the pollution caused by burning fossil fuels destroyed their telepathic brains before they could escape this world. The headaches I was experiencing would have eventually killed me. I have no headaches in the Troyk universe. Let me take you to your true home, Candy."

At first Candy did not know what to make of the incredible story Shirl had spun. The words rang true, but how that was possible was beyond her comprehension.

Candy stood before the portal, dumbstruck. Shirl's healthy demeanor and the air displacement in front of her were not figments of her imagination. Her friend had read everything she could on string theory and alternate universes, but Candy never believed that crap. Now, the evidence was right in front of her and she had problems wrapping her brain around the fact it was all true. Or maybe she was right all along and she was dreaming. This could not be reality.

"What about Alex?" Candy inquired. Even with the overwhelming evidence before her eyes about the existence of multiple dimensions, Candy could not let go of her concern for their absent friend. Could Alex have been pulled into one of these event horizons and ended up God knows where? Had she literally vanished off the face of the Earth?

"I am sure Alex is fine where she is," Shirl answered. Candy did not like the vagueness of her friend's reply. "Your headaches will start soon, if they have not already. You are two years younger than I am and my headaches started about the age you are now. This world is a death sentence for us if we stay. Our life expectancy here is twenty-five years, if we are lucky." Shirl took Candy's hand and squeezed it. The little girl she once was, knew she needed to follow Shirl wherever she led. "We can walk through the portal together."

Candy was still absorbing the existence of the portal and parallel universes. It was true, she was starting to get headaches. If in fact she was dreaming, what harm would it do to go through the portal? She tightened her grasp on her friend's hand indicating her consent.

The men entered the portal first. Candy took a deep breath, closed her eyes, and stepped in alongside her friend.

After Candy's Story
Make sure you read
'Nightshade'
Nightshade Saga Series: Book One

Did you miss Alex's Story?
Enjoy the 1st Chapter of
'The Chameleon Soul Mate'
Worlds Apart Series: Book One

Chapter 1

~

Arizona

Alexandra Mann, 'Alex' to friends and foes, disconnected from the call center system and let out a long, painful sigh. People never called to comment on how great things were, just to complain.

But she had the ability to stay calm under pressure and deal with any situation. Didn't matter if it was a customer yelling or her two best friends coming to her with their latest crisis. Alex took whatever life threw at her and made lemon drop cocktails.

Finally, Friday was here and Alex was going up to Sedona with three friends. They had been planning this trip for five months, and the countdown was finally over. This weekend was a double celebration: her twenty-first birthday and her best friend Shirl's twenty-third.

She had actually taken a half day of vacation so she and Shirl could get a jump on the traffic that headed north every Friday afternoon. Two of her co-workers were joining them, but had to work all day and would drive up later.

She grabbed her purse and pulled out her phone. The display showed that Shirley Tomlinson called. Shirl, as she liked to be called, had grown up with Alex at a local Phoenix orphanage. Although Alex was younger than Shirl, they were best friends and as close as sisters. Shirl and Candy, who also grew up with them at the orphanage, were Alex's only family. The three were connected, at times it felt like they could read each other's minds.

Alex had given up on the dream of a real family long before the orphanage stopped parading her in front of perspective parents. Years of couples talking and playing with her, only to have them walk away, had taken their toll. The disappointment she felt at the continual rejection caused her to cry herself to sleep on many occasions. She would find herself blending into the shadows in order not to be passed over again.

To this day, she had a tendency to blend into the background. Her best friends were always in the spotlight, where Alex tended to be invisible in their presence. Shirl was tall, blond, and stop traffic gorgeous. Candy, on the other hand, had a self-confidence that made her radiant. When they were together, both men and women would flock to Candy.

Having left her cubical, Alex took the opportunity to listen to Shirl's voice mail message. "Alex, it's Shirl. I've got a killer migraine and I can't make it to Sedona this weekend."

If anyone else had canceled on her, she would have been angry. However, she knew Shirl got terrible migraines that would down a small elephant. It seemed as though the headaches were growing in frequency and she was concerned about her friend. Alex recently started having migraines herself. She and Shirl were so close, she felt they were probably sympathy headaches.

When Alex reached the call center's lobby, she called Shirl before she walked out into the Arizona heat.

"What?" Shirl growled as the call connected.

"How are you feeling? Do you need anything?" Alex asked.

"Can you get me a new brain?"

"Doubtful, but I'll look into it. I am so sorry you won't make it to Sedona with us."

"I know, Alex," Shirl's voice began to fade. "Candy will stop by before she takes her class on this weekend's field trip. Don't worry, I will be fine."

Shirl hung up before Alex could say anything more. Alex placed her phone in her purse and walked toward her car in the stifling Arizona heat. The car was all packed and ready to go for the trip up to Sedona. Since she was not picking up Shirl, she immediately got on I-17 and headed north.

Alex loved Sedona and started thinking about what types of adventures she'd have this weekend. Something unusual always happened when she was there. It was odd, she was never able to put into words what she experienced. Some invisible force always seemed to draw her.

Alex made good time. Leaving Phoenix early afternoon was the trick, beating the hordes of commuters heading home after work. She headed straight to her hotel.

It would be some time before her call center friends would join her. In the meantime, Alex had time to hike in Boynton Canyon. She opened her suitcase, pulled out a T-shirt and shorts.

The Boynton Canyon Vortex was one of the four vortexes that contributed to the energy felt throughout Sedona. Alex generally hiked Boynton Canyon because she felt the best energy there and enjoyed the trails. A lot was written about Sedona's vortexes, including the belief the energy was the result of inter-dimensional gateways. She did not believe all that nonsense, but her friend Shirl certainly did. With that thought, Alex felt the loss of Shirl not being there. She could almost visualize her friend standing next to her, clutching her crystal necklaces.

She walked to her car and made the short trip between the hotel and Boynton Canyon. The parking lot closest to the trail was packed. Fortunately, she had the world's smallest car and found a spot where someone had parked badly, leaving only three quarters of a space. She easily fit into the spot and patted the dashboard of her beloved car. It was fire engine red, with a white racing stripe down the side. She loved zipping around town in it.

Alex changed from her sneakers into her hiking boots, locked the car and made her way to the trail head. She loved the sound her boots made against the gravel trail. Alex had just purchased a new pair of hiking boots as a birthday present to herself. The boots almost came up a quarter of her leg and were kind of clunky. She was not going to take any chances if she came across a snake along the trail.

Although the lot had been full, she didn't see anyone on the trail. A flash of light caught her eye. It was the reflection coming off a bracelet worn by someone suddenly ahead of her. Her eyes left the cuff bracelet to the man who wore it. He was tall with blond hair, and she couldn't help but admire his body. The man was oddly dressed for hiking. It appeared he was wearing a tunic and leggings. He had broad shoulders underneath the blue tunic and the leggings were molded to his powerful legs. She could see the muscle definition of his legs even from this distance. He must have decided to take a little hike before performing in a Shakespearean play. Sedona was known for supporting all art forms.

Alex admired his body, but unfortunately her body was not reacting to his. It never did, regardless how attractive she found the man. Oddly, Shirl and Candy had the same problem. She dated, because girls her age dated. She had not been with a man in over six months. Every relationship was disappointing when it became physical. The guys she dated didn't want to sustain a relation-ship if they had to deal with an ice queen in bed.

As she continued on the path, she kept an eye on the man, closing the gap between them. He was carrying a number of sacks that seemed to slow him down. Another oddity about the man. Who carried sacks on a day hike, rather than a backpack?

He was in her sight one minute and the next he vanished. Where did he go? Alex ran forward, thinking the man had fallen and needed help. She arrived at the spot where she had last seen him and there was no sign of him.

An invisible force pulled her forward off her feet. She screamed, as the motion continued and her vision went black. Her lungs seized and she fell into what she could only think was an endless void.

About the Author

W hen Evelyn Lederman retired from her career as an insurance execu-
tive, she cheerfully anticipated the freedom to finally spend as much
time reading as she'd always wanted. The twist in her story came when as-yet
unwritten characters started cropping up in her thoughts, asking her to tell
their stories. Now, she spends her days in Florida on the beach… with her
laptop.

'The Chameleon Soul Mate' and 'The Crystal Telepath' are the first two books in her paranormal romance series, Worlds Apart.

Contact her at evelynlauthor@gmail.com and visit her website at http://www.evelynlederman.com